# The Pleasure Seeker

**ROBYN MICHAELS**

The Pleasure Seeker

Printed in the United States of America
ISBN 979-8-218-24169-8
Cover and Interiors by Teknigram Graphics • Teknigram.com

This book is dedicated to the

global Sikh community,

and to people who have been trafficked

or forced to give up their homes.

# Table of Contents

# CHAPTER 1

B ecause we were starting the tour, we had to do publicity. My friend Jimmy asked me to be on his TV show while we were in L.A.

When you see people on talk shows, it may seem that the conversation is random, but it isn't. Jimmy said he'd ask me about my new teaching position, and about *MagicScore*, but we really didn't have time to actually rehearse. I had to rehearse the song I chose to highlight with his orchestra, and we got a little off track.

I performed "Sabre Dance," hooking up *MagicScore* to the piano. The display of notes as I played always got a great reaction.

"That's amazing! How did you do that?" Jimmy asked, as the applause died down.

"Hours and hours of hard work, and magic," I responded, winking.

Jimmy laughed, as did the audience.

"Actually, calculus," I added.

"So, you're moving to America, teaching at Northwestern, a Wildcat."

"It's a great academic fit and the love of my life… ."

"You've been in Switzerland since 1986. How did you meet a woman who lived in Chicago?"

"Oh, I've always known her. She's the granddaughter of the man who bought my father."

There was a collective gasp from the audience.

"Bought? Seriously?" Jimmy responded, giggling.

"My parents were trafficked. I thought you knew."

It was as though I had sucked all the air out of the room. Deafening hush. Jimmy was looking at me with his mouth open. There were a few twitters in the audience. His director looked like he was having a heart attack. He motioned Jimmy to move things along.

"I had no idea. What year was this?" Jimmy enquired.

"Well, it doesn't often come up in conversation. Sometime after the end of World War II, the late 1940s, my father thought. When he was about 14, he got snatched off the street in Mumbai, and transported to Africa. He was purchased by a German Jewish businessman, Glazer, in Tanzania. Mara is his granddaughter. Both my parents were street children."

"I didn't know," Jimmy remarked, looking surprised.

"You see, Europeans didn't want black Africans as servants because the African men would only take so much disrespect. The men wanted wages, partly because of the hut tax. The European missionaries had this genius idea of ending the slave trade and making Africans pay cash to live in their own homes. They were no longer chained, they became wage slaves…"

There was laughter from the audience.

"Seriously," I said, looking into the audience. "This was how it was. They'd go back to their homes when they'd had enough cash. The wazungu, white people, who could afford a servant, wanted Indian workers because they couldn't run off. Where were they going to go? Back across the ocean? To what? Most were orphans or petty criminals. After they paid off their contracts, their employers gave them the opportunity to open or partner in businesses.

"Mara's father was born in Arusha, but went to school in the USA. He found a community of South African Jews in Chicago, and he met Mara's mother. They returned every few years to Arusha. Mara knew me before I had a beard."

"Really," Jimmy replied, looking surprised, shaking his head.

"When I became a teenager and Mara's family came to visit, I decided I wanted her and took advantage of an opportunity," I said, raising my eyebrows and smiling.

The audience started laughing again, and Jimmy chuckled.

"I so loved her," I went on, "but she told me our parents would not allow it."

"Because of the difference in race, or what?" Jimmy asked.

"So many reasons. My parents wanted me to marry a Sikh woman. Mara also told me I had to stay in school as long as I could; she would not marry a school dropout. She went back to America. I got a scholarship and met my bandmates, the other Pleasure Seekers, and we were very lucky as a music group."

There was applause from the audience.

"My father met Sita's father... ."

"Your first wife," Jimmy explained.

"Yes. I liked her immediately, and it lasted ten years. Both of us were unhappy, so we divorced."

The audience buzzed.

Jimmy paused, and asked, "So... in Africa, is there still slavery?"

I chuckled. "You know, you Americans think at the end of your civil war, that was the end of slavery. In Deuteronomy, the law says a servant must be freed after six years. Your Christian Bible has Saint Paul telling slaves to obey their masters. There's slavery all over. Some people are born slaves. Humans are trafficked from so many countries. People are lied to, told they'll get good wages. Their passports are taken away, if they ever had real passports. Some are brought in by diplomats or other elites, slaves disguised as relatives."

Jimmy looked shocked. I rambled on.

"Really, you guys, you allow your politicians to give aid to countries that ignore human rights." The audience grew quiet, but I hardly noticed.

"You're the greatest country in the world. This really gets me. You give aid to Tanzania, my country, an economy that can't absorb us. We have to leave and become economic refugees. It's why I'm working here. Where does it end up? Private autos for elites, not for improving schools or access to medical care."

There was a slight twitter again from the audience. Jimmy hesitated and asked, "What can Americans do?"

"We're in the modern world now. Email your politicians and tell them to quit taking money from lobbyists and public relations people who tell them what to put into foreign aid appropriations budgets. Take care of Americans first… ."

I got huge applause. I went on: "Tie aid to respect for human rights and rule of law, improved social indicators. Women don't have access to education or family planning services. You build infrastructure to take our resources and destroy our environments. You all think you are giving humanitarian aid, but mostly you give military aid, and the corrupt leaders use it to terrorize their own people. Let me tell you, missionaries are no help."

There was a collective gasp from the audience. Jimmy was nodding his head. I was on a roll. I went on, after taking a breath, "You've elected leaders who are ripping you off! They tell you that you can't have single-payer health services, your 'Medicare for all' but they take that money and give weapons to dictators. Then *you* Americans get involved, on the wrong side, and you wonder why there are so many refugees." I shook my head.

There was laughter in the audience and a bit of applause. Jimmy continued laughing and nodding.

"Peace Corps is the best foreign aid you can send. Were it not for them, I would be a servant, not an engineer."

We went to a commercial, which gave us a little time to recover. "Are you sorry you asked?"

"Social indicators," Jimmy responded. "I really had no idea."

During the break I hooked up the computer to Jimmy's trumpet and his orchestra's bass player. I had tweaked the program so *MagicScore* would change color, depending on how low or high our notes were. We played the Queen song, "Let me Into Your Heart Again."

I apologized to the audience, and told them, "This is the perfect size room to hear music. You're hearing performers, not sound system."

The next day, I got an email from Levine, asking, "What did you do? I'm getting messages from all over."

I've never known a time I didn't know the Glazers. My father managed their business for them, in Arusha, which is just a few miles west of Mount Kilimanjaro. Mara described Arusha as a "wild west" town out of 1930s America. Only two streets were paved back in the 1980s, and where the pavement ended, the savannah began. There were three main streets in town, and none of them had names.

My parents' home, which was burned brick and had a tin roof that made so much noise when it rained, had belonged to the Glazers, and was at the end of one of those streets. It was really an unremarkable crossroads, and didn't get to be a *place* until foreigners started coming from around the world to go on safari to see the animals. We had the Colgate-Palmolive plant, which manufactured soaps and toothpaste, and the Philips plant, which made electrical household appliances and generators. Those were the first international companies to manufacture in East Africa. Arusha is a big city now, but back in then, everyone knew everyone.

In the 1970s, when I was a very young child, giraffes and gazelle grazed meters away from Maasai cows just outside our windows when school was in session, and skittered off when we were let out. The golden-shaded savannah rolled on to the horizon north and west of us, meeting a rich blue sky dotted with flat topped acacias. Every day was a nice day, even during the rainy season. I didn't realize this, of course, until I moved to the northern hemisphere, with "weather."

All the boys had to wear white button down shirts with blue trousers, and shoes. I stood out, though. I was lighter skinned, with long hair in a bun (in a patka—sort of a scarf on my head) and kohl around my eyes. They all had shaved heads. Most Europeans and Asians living in Africa sent their children abroad. Everyone called me *Mhindi*, meaning *Asian*. There were no white children—*wazungu*.

Someone had given my school an old, upright piano, but it could not be played as most of the wires and hammers were broken. It just fascinated me. A teacher was always calling out, "Wewe! Mhindi! Singh! Unafanya nini? Ondoka kwenye piano hiyo. Kaa chini!" (You! Singh! What are you doing? Get away from the piano and sit down!).

I was a good student because of my brothers. By the time I

was around five, my brothers were in boarding school in Moshi, a town south of Kili. Avi was ten years older than I was, and Sodhi eight years. I didn't understand why they had to go away, although we had talked about it for weeks. The first days they were gone, I couldn't eat I was so upset. It wasn't until they returned at the end of the week that I started to understand, because Baba took me in the truck to fetch them. It was too far to return every night without a vehicle.

I lived for the weekends they returned. By teaching me, they reinforced what they learned. Then, they went to Singapore when I turned seven, and were gone for months. It was exciting getting their letters and postcards every month. Their first visit home from Singapore, they brought books, which were still a luxury. They brought my mother a Hindi copy of the Adi Granth, our scripture. She was overjoyed and couldn't wait to learn to read it. We also read the Christian Bible as literature. Back then, there was no media. Story telling was our entertainment.

In Arusha, it didn't matter that we were Sikhi. The Europeans were minorities. The few left were Greek, German Jews, some dual-citizen English, and Portuguese. There were Arabs, Indians, lots of mixed race people, and black Africans of many tribes. Our races and skin colors didn't matter. We were all Swahili: People of the coast.

Mara's father, Ira, visited Arusha every year in the 1970s, to work with Baba, but he felt without telephones, it would be too difficult to grow the import/export business in Tanzania. It was easier to develop a business in the USA. Also, after independence in the middle 1960s, African life changed.

With wages to buy things, more people had radios. More Africans could speak, read, and write European languages, and they didn't want to be second-class citizens. The Asians and the Jews were stuck in the middle. They really could not go back to where they came from, and they were vital to the economies of all the African countries. They were *others*: not Black Africans, but part of the collateral damage that the Christian Europeans had brought about. In East Africa, they were part of Swahili culture.

My parents, who had been servants, moved from servants' quarters into the brick house when the older Glazers moved to Nairobi. They had a water pump on the property they lived in; they had city electricity, rudimentary as it was, for lights. They had a vehicle at their disposal. They owned a radio (which only really worked at dawn and dusk), and they could afford a houseboy and pay local school fees for their sons.

My brothers had taught me so much. In a class of over 40 students, the teachers had to teach to the beginners, so I was bored much of the time, staring out the window at animals or just daydreaming. I was doing statistics when my schoolmates were learning to add and subtract.

The Peace Corps Volunteers, their teachers, suggested to Avi and Sodhi that they apply for scholarships to boarding schools abroad. Then, they'd be able to continue to college. The Peace Corps people helped them fill out applications for both European and Malaysian schools. My brothers got prompt replies from Singapore, where schools were secular. They would be taught in English and not have to learn another language. Once they got to Singapore, my brothers were encouraged to concentrate on learning applied physics and engineering.

In reading the applications, they found that although they'd get room, board and tuition, they had to come up with the funds for transportation, either by plane or ship.

They went to the hotels in Arusha to see about being waiters, but the Europeans who were in charge preferred to hire adults. What the hoteliers suggested, as it would be easy for us boys to do, was negotiate with the Maasai for honey, milk, yogurt, and their beaded jewelry to sell in the gift shops. The Maasai usually avoided Wazungu because they didn't want to be proselytized to as they already believed in one God.

In the early 1980s, I also negotiated with the tailors to make shirts, skirts and bags to sell. Sometimes I could get my Chagga schoolmates to carve little animals, bracelets, and bowls, and sell those. They'd hunt, and I could sell skins until that became illegal. Later, as I was pretty well known around town, I could get Tanzanite, malachite, and sometimes dia-monds brought up from South Africa to resell in Singapore.

My brothers got part-time work when school was out, as interpreters for the Hadzabe men who were hired as game scouts by the tour companies. Some of these African guys spoke enough English to get by, but so many white tourists didn't feel comfortable with just Africans, and my brothers' English was so elegant. Also, both my brothers could drive. They got great tips in hard currency. When not on the safari lorries, they were smoking ganja with the Morani: teenaged Maasai boys who had just been circumcised, or with the Peace Corps Volunteers, teaching them Swahili in exchange for books and American things we didn't have access to.

In 1081, when I was about 11-years-old, Ira first brought his daughters and wife on his visit to Arusha. We were waiting at the airport when they arrived. Baba and I were shocked to see, as they walked out of the plane, that they were wearing miniskirts. We had seen photos of this fashion in magazines that my brothers had brought back from Singapore. However, miniskirts would not be permitted in Tanzania. We never, *ever* saw women's legs. To explain, we saw bare breasted women, not in town so much, but on their bomas: women who were nursing, and widows, mostly. Rarely did you see a woman's legs above the ankle. We explained this to them all on the ride back into town, that they would have to wear kangas, pieces of cloth, to cover their legs. These were long legged women, too. Mara was Sodhi's age, and Shayla was a three years younger. Anya was younger than I was.

I wondered if Ira really had to spend a month with Baba. The work really started at harvest time several months later. From just listening to them talk, I learned it gave them a chance to talk with farmers, address fuel costs, and contracts with the logistics firms. They also had to find places to store commodities until it was time to ship. I learned a bit about futures trading, and that helped me when I began trading as an adult.

If you're not on safari, there's not much to do in town. The girls were disappointed the first time they came that there were no lions or elephants in town, and the small monkeys stayed in the trees unless they wanted to steal our things. I taught the girls to juggle fruit, which all the African kids did, and how to spell their names in Hindi and helped them learn Swahili.

They brought books, a record player (which we had to wire to the house as their electricity was different), records, and board games like Scrabble and Monopoly, and *Mad* magazines. Who doesn't love *Mad*? Those *Mad* magazines made me very popular at school. At first, one of the British ex-pat teachers called me into the headmaster's office. They wanted to chastise

me for reading junk, but the Peace Corps Volunteers came
to my defense, explaining that *Mad* magazine was real American English.

Mara wrote a lot of letters to friends and to her husband.
She had been with the guy since she was fifteen, and now she
was 19. I asked her, "Why didn't your father bring him?"

"He didn't have a passport. My father told him to apply, but
I don't think he wanted to get a yellow fever shot, and he has to
work to pay for school anyway."

"My brothers buy jewelry and dairy from the Maasai and
resell it to make money," I told her.

"There are laws regarding trade in food, and people who
make jewelry sell it themselves. Dan's working as a janitor,
cleaning office buildings overnight. It doesn't pay well, but
that's why he's going to college. When I go back to the USA, I'll
get a job grooming dogs, washing them and cutting their hair,
to pay for school."

She showed me photos, and some of those dogs looked like
small sheep. I could not imagine having so much money that
you could spare it to pay for someone to cut your dog's hair.

When tourist season was over, everyone left. I didn't realize
how much they all meant to me until they were gone. I felt
lonely, but I had things to do. School was starting. I had to pick
up my brothers' provisions business because we all needed the
money for our transportation costs and incidental expenses, as
well as clothes and shoes. By the time I was 12, I could ride the
motorcycle, so I could get around.

Mr. Curtis, my main customer, ran the largest hotel in
Arusha and also rented out cottages, where the Glazers stayed.

Bwana Curtis was always busy. He was a wiry Greek mzungu who changed his name because he said it had too many letters. In his hotel gift shop, he sold the clothes I had the tailor make, Maasai jewelry, Makonde carvings, and the pillow slips my mother embroidered. He also got a lot of *mambo ya wazungu*: things expatriate wazungu left.

One day, when I brought him jewelry, he said to me, "Singh, I want to show you something." He beckoned me to follow him into his big dining room, and I saw this thing as big as a small elephant. It was a grand piano. I had only seen photos of them. It was like a beam of light came from the heavens, like a spotlight on it, making the dark wood glow. The angels started vocalizing. I was immediately mesmerized.

"These ex-pats are moving to Hong Kong, and they decided it made more sense to sell it than pay to have it shipped. You can probably make good money selling this. I have a piano and don't need *kitu hivi* (this thing). I told the wazungu I'd try to sell it. I bet with all the people you know you can sell it and make a good commission."

I went over to it, lifted the door cover to the keys, struck one, then another. I struck all the keys, and they all worked. I felt the sound in my body, an interesting feeling. Now, I'd describe it as frisson. I lifted the cover to look at the wires and hammers. I couldn't think, I was so awestruck. Selling it would be difficult. It was a big thing. I couldn't imagine anyone in town having a place for it or knowing how to play it. The churches? I considered the commission, but I was interested in both music and this machine. I couldn't articulate it to myself at the time, but I recognized that music was patterns of notes, and had something to do with mathematics. This was an opportunity.

"How much do they want for it?" I asked.

Bwana C told me what it was in shillings, and I rolled my eyes. It was something like four hundred dollars. That was impossible. I had a little more than that saved up, but I needed to have saved at least the equivalent of a thousand dollars by Christmas, three months away, to stay on track. My brothers needed the money, and I would, too, by the next year.

"Tell them I can pay" … It was the equivalent of two hundred dollars. I don't remember the exchange rate, the TZ shilling fluctuated so much. I could only do so much on the black market. We always feared a currency change, which meant we'd lose money. Bwana C told me they wanted the money in pounds sterling, so that meant a conversion fee, but I knew he wouldn't rip me off.

I ran home and yelled to Ama as soon as I could catch my breath, "Amaji! Curtis bwana has a piano. I want to buy it and I could, but I need to save for our expenses."

"What's a piano?" Ama asked, as she was chopping vegetables for dinner.

"It's a machine that plays music."

"You have a machine that plays music." She meant the phonograph the Glazers had brought.

"This is a different machine. Not electric. I have to learn to play it."

She tried to talk sense to me. "*Mtoto*, you'll be going away to school soon!"

"But I will come back. Don't you want me to come back and play the piano for you?"

"I don't even know what it is!" she responded. She actually did, she just didn't know it was called a piano.

I wanted to learn to play it not just to make music, but because I was interested in how it worked. I hadn't thought about what I'd do in school.

I didn't know it at the time, but Ama was saving for a generator so she could have a refrigerator. We boys never asked for anything, so she knew it was important to me. I brought her to see it and she laughed and asked where we'd put it.

She told me she'd make up the shortfall somehow if I couldn't by the time I needed the money, but I'd have to diligently learn to play. It would be another four years before she could get the generator and fridge, but I did learn. We moved furniture around to make room for this wonderful thing. My school teacher found another Peace Corps Volunteer, Jim, and he taught me how to play in exchange for practicing Kiswahili with my parents. Once a week, he came and gave me a lesson and stayed for dinner, and I practiced about four hours a day. I must have driven my parents crazy, but they never told me to stop. In fact, one afternoon Baba invited Mr. Curtis for tea while I was practicing. I was just learning, and let's say the sound was dissonant. You can imagine. Mr. C started to get up to leave after he finished a cup of tea, and Baba asked him to stay for another cup, and appreciate that I was learning, thanks to him. I'm sure Mr. C *got it*.

I really enjoyed playing. It made me so happy. It was very difficult the first three or so months, but it got easier, and Jim was a good teacher. He taught me chords, started me on Mozart and Bach, and taught me to read music. I could hear the notes in my head as I saw them on the paper score. I particularly liked *Rondo Alla Turca* by Mozart.

After school, I'd make the rounds of people I'd have to see to sell what I got from the Maasai, take orders for what the hotels wanted, and play piano until dinner, and before bedtime.

In 1983, I started to mature physically. I grew about six inches in six months, and my hands and feet got larger as well. My mother stopped making me wear a patka and bought cloth for a pagri/turban. I had to wear my brothers' old clothes. I developed a downy beard, and body hair. My voice? I never knew what was going to come out of my mouth. I started sweating. Worse, suddenly I was getting erections. I was a mess, and for some reason, all I could think about was Mara. I'd be reading, get tired, my mind would wander, and I'd get hard. I tried to keep busy, and playing the piano really helped because while I was learning, I had to really concentrate on that.

By this time, there was a good market for Maasai jewelry and carved animal trinkets among tourists. The trouble was that our currency kept losing value, and I had to convert it quickly to hard currency. We had a currency change in 1984, which was a huge nightmare. I remember people crowding into the bank to convert old shillings to new. People paid us *watoto* to wait in the bank queues for them, because you could only convert a limited amount at a time. Thankfully, my father had an international account and I didn't have to explain where I got so much hard currency. The hotels were pretty good about this: Everyone knew I was saving for school. In a way, they were overcharging me when converting shillings, but it evened out because the hard currency didn't lose value. I told my brothers in a letter that when and if they could afford it, to buy gold. The point was to not lose money on the money we made.

The year I turned fourteen, I joined my brothers in Singapore for the next school year. We traveled by steamer, which would have been boring without books and magazines. There was not much to see on the open ocean. We couldn't get off at the ports of call lest we be snatched.

For me, it was like moving to another planet: Indoor plumbing (my first experience with flush toilets) and electricity that worked all the time, telephones. I learned to use a washing machine and dryer. I had to learn to cross the street in traffic. I think what I felt was called future shock.

Avi was doing energy-related engineering, and Sodhi was doing telecommunications. They were moving north to Kuala Lumpur at the end of the year, several hours north of Singapore, to work.

The first week in Singapore, I was late twice for morning homeroom, and Dr. Schultz asked me to stay after class. "Mr. Singh, class starts promptly at eight. Why are you late to class? This is not Africa. What time do you go to bed?"

I found his question odd, and a bit personal, but I really didn't know how prompt I needed to be.

At home, in Africa, it got dark around 18:00. I was usually in bed by 20:00, because our electricity either went out, or our 40 watt bulb wasn't enough to read by. Then, we were up at 5:30 when the muezzin called prayers.

In Sing, the electricity didn't go out, and our lighting was good. I was falling asleep reading. I had to buy an alarm clock, and a watch. They were so cheap!

Grocery stores with freezer sections, stores that sold clothes, stores that sold records and televisions. We never bought cereal or packaged food in Africa. Not only because of the expense, but because it took so long for things to come up from South Africa. Then, as likely as not, there were weevils in it. I got to try lots of different foods including ice cream and chocolate, and I made myself sick. The second time they came to take me to dinner, after I had been in school two months, Sodhi said, upon seeing me, "Kiboko!" KiSwahili for "hippopotamus."

"Wapi?" (*where*)? I responded.

Both my brothers laughed at me.

"Look at you! You've gained at least a stone and your skin looks awful. You're eating snacks, mzima kabisa," Avi admonished me. They took me to the gurdwara, the local Sikh temple, for the langar, the free evening meal, by public bus. "When we first came to Sing we were also tempted, but you should eat here at the gurdwara's langar at least once a week and quit eating snacks," Avi directed me. The food was more what I was used to as well, always a vegetarian meal with dal, potatoes, or rice with a green vegetable. Some of my schoolmates went with me.

My classes were, first, homeroom for announcements, then physical education every morning for an hour. I learned about stretching, body building, tennis, football rules, and how to swim in a pool. After that, calculus for an hour, then physics, each twice a week. After lunch, I had world history, geography or biology. They just glossed over African history. It seemed they thought we had nothing of importance until the continent was divided in 1885 among all the Europeans and King Leopold. I knew this wasn't true.

I learned to type 60 words a minute, which was a useful class. It helped so much when I started to do coding. Two nights a week I had art history. The other two nights and Friday afternoon, I interned with an engineering company.

My track was physics, of course, and quickly I moved to applied physics, then mechanical engineering. I kept taking tests, and they kept trying to challenge me. I learned to program main frame computers with FORTRAN. It was like a game. At one place, I got a job debugging programs in UNIX for some side money, and they had electronic piano keyboards. You could make so many different sounds, and I was able to keep up what I had learned.

My brothers were still in touch with Dr. Schultz. He told them that I would be better at a school in Switzerland because I could start college courses there, and get research assistantships, and better contacts. I would also learn another European language. I started learning French.

Both my brothers intended to stay in Asia because of the opportunities. Avi had met Siri, another Sikh, and planned to marry. Her parents lived in Singapore. Avi and Sodhi invited me out to dinner towards the end of the school year. I was shocked that they had cut their hair, and weren't wearing pagri, or what the English call turbans. They still had beards, very much trimmed, but were also dressed western, not in shalwar khameez.

Sodhi said, "Never mind our hair, it will grow back by the time we go home and we'll have turbans on, anyways. We want to tell you Dr. Schultz wants you to transfer to this Swiss school after the break. He taught us both and we trust him. He will make sure you are given a scholarship. You need something more challenging."

"We'll miss seeing you, but the way Dr. Schultz put it to us is that you have a lot of talent, and you'll benefit," Avi added.

Avi wrote to my parents that he planned to marry Siri. There was excitement about Siri. Being modern people, her parents were happy that Siri had met such a well-educated Sikh boy. Unfortunately, when the time came, my parents could not attend the wedding. Travel was too expensive for them, and Avi didn't make that much money at that time.

My brothers and I, with Siri, returned for the summer. I was happy to be back at my piano, but at first, I was concerned that we wouldn't make enough money from all our activities to pay for our transport back to school. My brothers reminded me that they both had jobs to return to, and to just worry about myself. Being gone the whole school year, I had missed opportunities. I explained to my parents, "I am going to have Alfred come over. He's Chagga. He carves, and so does his father. Take what he brings and deal with the hotels and gift shops and give him a commission. Half would be fair. I was able to sell all the things I had in a few hours a week, after school, so it's worth the time. Also bring cloth to Ngoma, the tailor, to make shirts and skirts." My father had plenty of time, so he agreed.

I explained to all my contacts how it would be, and thanked them all for helping me so much. All the business people were impressed that I was going to school in Europe. ✪

# CHAPTER 2

I was forever adjusting to something. I was still growing taller. My beard got coarser. I had to get totally different clothes for school in Europe. I needed to buy white dress shirts and dress trousers that zipped. I actually had to buy briefs. Our traditional clothes didn't have zippers. We never wore underwear. It was too expensive, and the *kachera* (Sikh underwear), like an apron, were a pain in the neck. Getting used to wearing western-style European clothes, having to button shirts, I never got comfortable. I had to buy shoes, boots, gloves, and a winter coat in Switzerland. I was surprised that these things cost so much. I wondered if my savings would hold out for the year.

My first plane trip, ever, was to Zurich. I was scared and fascinated at the same time. It took about 12 hours, and I don't remember how much I slept. The food was... interesting. I had never had cheese or wine, and didn't like the tastes.

It was autumn in Switzerland, the cold and wind were a big shock, and I was told it would get much colder. Also, *wazungu:* I had never seen so many white people in my life.

The Swiss speak an odd German, but in school, depending on who was teaching, classes were either in German, French or English. All the teachers spoke English. Since most of my classes were in mathematics or engineering, if I could see a concept on the board, there wasn't much of a language barrier for me. It was physically stressful, and the weather didn't help. I had what I thought were pangs of loneliness, or depression, but the part of my soul that was intrigued by how things worked and how to make them was being satisfied.

My minor courses were in European history, chemistry, and, because I wanted to continue to play the piano, music. It was a great stress reliever for me. To study music in college, you have to audition. I made an appointment with the department chair, Madame Chabon, a tiny French woman. I decided I'd play the Rimsky-Korsakov song, "Flight of the Bumblebee." I practiced for about a week. It was the fastest music I had ever played at that time, a good showcase for my talent.

I was a bit nervous, because Madame was so serious. When I finished, she was silent and I could feel my heart beating.

Without emotion, she said, "You're very good, Singh. I'd like you to join the school orchestra. We practice together once a week, Thursday evenings, and you can book studio time. We give a concert at the end of every semester. For two weeks before the concert, we practice every day. You'll need a tuxedo."

"How much will a tuxedo cost?" I asked.

"I don't know, as much as a suit. Why?"

"I'm on scholarship, and money is tight."

She seemed to think for a few seconds, and then said, "Let me see what I can do." She then recorded me playing several classical pieces, which she sent to some sound engineers in Montreux.

I practiced every chance I got. That was how I met Peter and Adam. They heard me in the studio and stopped to listen, and surprised me when I opened the door of the studio. I just about bashed into them in my rush to my next class.

"You're new here, aren't you?" Peter asked me in French. He was slightly taller than me, very thin, had long blondish hair and a wispy moustache.

"Yes, I arrived three days ago." At least that's what I thought I said in French. Both guys laughed. I actually said, "I will arrive in three days."

The other guy, Adam, asked, "You're more comfortable in English? Where are you from?"

"Tanzania," I responded.

"Where's that?"

"In Africa, on the Indian Ocean. Ernest Hemingway wrote *Snows of Kilimanjaro* about hunting there, when we were called Tanganyika."

"You don't look African," Adam replied, looking me up and down. He was my height, clean shaven, with styled brown hair. He had a beautiful smile, like out of a toothpaste ad.

"How do Africans look?"

"You know. Darker, wooly hair…"

I grinned. "Not all Africans are black. I'm Asian. My people were originally from India. There are lots of Asians in Africa."

"You don't look Asian, either. Anyways, your piano playing is astounding," Peter said, interrupting. "We never heard anyone play that fast and not screw up!"

Peter van Heusen told me he was from Holland and studied political science. He played the guitar, bass, and, he said, some piano. His parents were wealthy enough that he didn't get a scholarship. "My parents sent me here because I tend to not study seriously at home."

"I'm studying anthropology and music. I'm from Nice, in France. My parents thought the music program here was excellent and affordable, though money was never a problem. I play the bassoon in orchestra, but brass, woodwinds and piano as well," Adam Boulanger told me

We walked along to my next class, in the engineering building. "You're religious?" Adam asked.

Ah, the pagri… turban. "Me? No. but my hair is very long. It's tradition to keep it wrapped. The original gurus, our leaders, noticed at the time that only elites wrapped their hair, and since they wanted everyone to be equal, they started the trend."

"Do you believe in God?" Peter asked.

"Yes."

"You're Moslem or Hindu?" Adam asked.

"No. I'm Sikh…"

"You mean ill? That's why you wear a turban? To keep your head warm?" Peter asked.

I had to laugh. "No, I'm not ill. It might seem confusing, because we use many Hindu holidays as our own. But we believe in one God. We don't worship deities, we don't have saints except for our original gurus, and we believe in reincarnation. Not heaven. Also, we don't have a caste system."

"What's caste?" Peter asked.

"I can't really explain, but we don't have social rules about who people can interact with, or who is better based on genetic background. Sikhi don't believe your genetics are important. We're all human."

"You don't believe in Jesus, our savior?" Peter asked.

I chuckled. "We don't doubt he existed, but we're like Jews that way. We don't need an intermediary to talk to God. We believe three things: Naam, which is mindful awareness of divine presence. God is all over. When I meditate, I use scripture, the Adi Granth, to remind me. We believe Daan, which is altruism and giving back to our community, which makes us all feel part of the community, and Ishnaam, which means doing good deeds that cleanse the body and mind."

"That's it?" Adam asked.

"Yes. The virtues we strive for are truth, patience, contentment, humility, self-control, love, wisdom, and courage. Simple, easy to understand."

Peter smiled and asked, "So, if you sin, you don't ask anyone for forgiveness?"

"Just the wronged party, I guess. I don't think I've sinned yet. Our sins are pride, anger, lust, greed, and attachment to worldly things."

"We've all sinned! We're born sinners!" Peter exclaimed.

I smiled, but trying to take him seriously, responded, "Wow, that must be rough. To not even know what you did and feel guilty. Is it because you were ashamed of being naked?"

Adam started laughing.

With a surprised expression on his face, Peter responded, "The sin is knowing…"

"Knowing what? That they were naked or had sex?"

Peter gasped.

"You're pretty funny," Adam said. "We're going to get along great."

Peter was some sort of Protestant, and Adam was Catholic. I could not understand the nuances, the whole idea of Jesus being a son of God and God (how can you be your own father?), but for the most part it didn't matter. I was asked my religion every day by other students. I started getting a better idea of what I really believed, and what they believed.

I had no social life other than Peter and Adam, so I was eager to go to Montreux where I had been invited to audition. School was outside Zurich, so I had a long train ride through the beautiful countryside. Those mountains, right out of a storybook: deep green and blue, mostly snowcapped, dotted with chalets and cows.

I dressed in a suit and tie, as this was a job interview. I was surprised that they were all dressed in T-shirts and jeans.

One guy came over and greeted me. "Swami, we've been expecting you. Have a seat at the piano."

Swami? That was a surprise, but I was to be greeted that way more and more. "Please, call me Singh. I'm Sikh," I responded.

"You mean ill?"

"No, my religion is called Sikh."

"Sorry. Everyone's welcome here if they can play. My name's Walt, by the way. Take a seat at the piano, put on headphones, and we'll cue you."

There was another guy at the soundboard in the booth. I had never seen one, and it captivated me. All those knobs and levers. "Do you mind if I take a look and can you explain how you do this?" I asked.

"This guy here is Paul, and we'll show you how to do everything," Walt told me.

I met eight other guys that weekend. Two were on guitars, one had a saxophone, one had a trumpet, and there was another keyboardist, a percussionist, a drummer, and a violinist.

Walt gave me scores. We were recording radio commercial jingles, so everything was short. Paul told me he'd mix in vocals during the week.

After I spent a day with them, they immediately offered part time work, and told me they'd pay for the train and give me a place to stay for the weekends I could play. They told me to dress comfortably. They'd call a few days ahead (I had them call the music department as I didn't have a telephone) to give me a heads up on what classical music to practice. They offered what was the equivalent of $10 an hour, which was a fortune. I started meeting many well-known European musicians. I played all sorts of music, from classical to jazz, and got to practice on organs and a vibraphone. It's how I met Oscar Martinez, our drummer.

Getting that gig for two weekends a month helped me so much. When I got my first paycheck, I could hardly believe it. I opened a bank account and then went to a florist and had them send Madame Chabon a bouquet of roses.

I was very busy, which took my mind off being unsettled. Adam and Peter, the only people I could consider friends, were older than I by a couple of years, but I don't know if they ever thought about our age difference. I liked them because we had music in common, and they didn't laugh at my questions about life in Europe. They asked me if I wanted to rent an apartment with them the next school year. My board was paid for by my scholarship, and I didn't think I could use board money to pay for a place of my choice. I could not pay for it on my own because I needed the money to get back to Arusha.

"It might be fun to live together, but I'll have to ask Dr. Schultz. I'm on scholarship. You guys know I'm playing in Montreux for extra money," I told them.

Dr. Schultz was very kind. "Think about this, Singh. They are studying softer, more artsy subjects. I don't want you to get distracted."

I understood what he was saying. "I think I'll be ok. I'm a very focused student."

"Your room and board is about $150 a month. Let's try it, but I want you to work as a teaching assistant next year in calculus and statistics."

When I next saw Peter and Adam, I told them, "You guys. I'm doing a lot of complicated math problems and can't have distractions. I can't party like you. In fact, next year I have to teach. If I get off track, or if Dr. Schultz thinks I am, I'd have to move. Come visit me for a few weeks in Arusha if you guys can afford to at summer break. See where I come from."

"He wants you to teach? You're not even at college level yet, are you?" Adam asked.

"I guess he thinks I have something to offer."

They did accompany me to Arusha. I took them to see the Maasai and my friends who lived outside of town, and we went on a few safari runs.

My mates got a good taste of what real life was like for me. I pointed out to them that my family was middle class, living in town, and my parents still didn't own a refrigerator, or a stove, but we needed the truck and the motorcycle so we could use the appropriate vehicle for errands and not waste petrol.

They asked how long my family had been in Africa.

"My father came after World War II. A Jewish businessman happened to be seeing an export container off, in Dar, and needed a houseboy and saw my father working on the dock with other teenagers. When he earned back what Glazer paid, he was free,"

"Wow. Did he even know where he was?" Adam asked.

"Wait. You mean your parents were slaves?" Peter asked, astounded.

"Yes. They were trafficked. That's what I said. The next time Glazer went to Dar, he took Baba and he picked out my mother. They lived in servants' quarters. Now, Hassan, their assistant, lives there."

"Is that guy, Hassan, a slave?"

I chuckled. "No, he helps my parents and pays no rent. I think he might be hiding from his wives. He's Somali.

"The Glazers taught my father how to do household tasks, like washing clothes, polishing furniture and the floors, ironing, and cooking. Baba could barely read Hindi, which would have been his mother tongue. My brothers helped him and my mother learn to read English and do math. Glazer started teaching him bookkeeping. Baba learned the business and exports sunflower oil, tea, coffee, pyrethrums, and, until it became illegal, animal skins and ivory. He imports dry goods from South Africa and India that we can't get locally, like safety pins, screws, and chewing gum."

"I've never met a Jew," Adam remarked.

"Yes you have. That girl Susan Horwitz, who plays the viola, and that guy Josh who plays the French horn are Jews. You didn't know they were Jewish? Anyways, many Jews left to go to Israel or South Africa. Although they had a working relationship with the Lutherans, they were not part of that culture. The Jews were *others*, as were the Indians. Many of the Parsi men who came over as indentured servants bought out their contracts and opened their own little stores, or dukas, mostly in Zanzibar. They were harassed and mostly went to England or Australia.

The guys stayed with me in our house for the first week, but then decided they wanted to try to climb Kili, so they signed up with a group and did that in the few days before they left. ✪

# CHAPTER 3

My brothers and Siri came for just two weeks because they had to get back to their jobs in Malaysia, and there was a two day overlap when the Glazers came at the very end of June. The Glazers were again staying in a cottage on the grounds of the Curtis Hotel.

I didn't feel the girls had changed, but they all remarked about how much I'd grown. Also, they made a big fuss over how long my eyelashes were.

Shayla told me straight away that Mara was now divorced. I had a lot of questions, but I knew it would be impolite to ask. I had a more serious problem. I could not do anything without Mara popping into my thoughts. I was besotted with her. The first time she smiled at me, when she said "Habari yako!" I almost exploded. She had me crazy. I don't think she knew it, but Shayla did.

I had no idea what was happening to me. It was an automatic physical reaction of lust. I felt sick. At first, I couldn't eat, and Ama could tell something was wrong with me, but of course I couldn't tell her. I spent a lot of time in the choo, jerking off. That helped some. But it was always Mara or Shayla, usually with Anya in tow, coming by after breakfast to fetch me: "Dayal, can we go up to see the Maasai? Can you take us on a game drive? Will you go with us to the market so they don't take advantage of us *wazungu*? Will you help us with our Swahili?"

My emotions were so mixed. I wanted to smell Mara and to touch her breasts, and all I could do was take furtive glances. I wanted to be with them and I didn't.

I played the piano most afternoons, and Mara usually would come in and recline on the chaise to read. "Your piano playing is so beautiful, and you have lovely hands," she told me.

I was dying. I had to stop, go jerk off, and come back.

After dinner, the girls would come by and we often did a jigsaw puzzle, or played some board game. At least our bottom halves were under the table, but they'd go home, and I'd go to bed… and jerk off.

Mara wanted to go to Mombasa but her parents didn't want her to be squeezed into a matatu (a truck outfitted with three seats to be used like a bus), nor would they borrow our truck because there were too many drunk drivers on the roads. They told her that if she could find a Peace Corps Volunteer to go with her, she could go, but they couldn't be away from their sites for more than three days.

The Glazers were visiting one night, and Ira was joking about Mara's obsession with going to Mombasa. "She won't give it a rest," he chuckled to my parents.

I didn't understand why she didn't just go. She was in her 20s. She could take care of herself. But I also knew that if she went against their will, her parents would be frantic.

Her mother said, "I'm afraid the Morani would molest her in a matatu."

"Kidada (sister), they're harmless, really. Very shy boys," Ama responded.

"It's too bad Sodhi had to go back to work, or I would have told him to escort her," Baba added.

I smirked to myself when I heard him say that. They—my brothers—would have refused. But… why not me? Here was my chance to be alone with Mara. I brought a plate of biscuits to them and I said, "I'll escort Mara. I don't think I can handle all three girls, but I can keep her company."

Ira looked at me. I could tell he was sort of bemused, but he didn't laugh. I might have been a gangly teenager, but I was now big.

"Ndugu (brother), Dayal is very responsible, and well behaved. He always has been," Baba remarked.

So both sets of parents agreed that they would allow me to escort Mara to Mombasa and Malindi for a week. The Glazers would give us money for the train. Mara would pay for everything else. They would tell her in the morning. Our trip was two weeks off.

I could maintain my composure, but I was thrilled. The next morning, Mara came in shouting, "Dayal! Ndugu! Thank you so much!" and she ran over as I was sitting at the table eating breakfast, and she hugged me and kissed me on the cheek. Such an American reaction. I was hard at "Dayal!" And again, trapped for a few minutes, but I did not disengage from her embrace. I smiled at her and lowered my eyes.

Shayla came in moments later, saw us and said, "You know, you guys have the same exact smile and facial expressions. You both have dimples."

Both Mara and I giggled, and Shayla said, "You're mirror images of each other."

Of course, I started fantasizing, but we kept to our normal routines. Thankfully, Mara's parents kept her busy sending telegrams or packing.

A few days before we left, my parents had the generator and small refrigerator delivered. My brothers had gone to the Philips office to make sure the electricity was right, paid for it, and had showed me, with an instruction map, how to wire the generator to the house. We were all excited over this. Hassan, our houseboy, was excited over the boxes the parts came in, because he wanted to resell them to people who wanted them as chicken coops. By rights, the boxes were mine, but I made him a deal: he got the boxes if he took me to the prescription chemist to buy condoms. With him doing the buying, there wouldn't be gossip to my parents about *me* buying condoms. They already thought Hassan was a rascal. At least Hassan was discreet. His attitude was if he didn't ask questions, he wouldn't know anything if asked.

Ama asked my father, "What should we put in there?" He looked at her, sort of puzzled, and said, "Water." She was still confused. It was funny, to me. I said to Ama, "It will be ice in a few hours. Then, let's mash up some mangoes with sugar. And we can get some cream and sugar..." My father started laughing and said, "You have big plans, don't you?"

Saturday morning I walked to the cottage to fetch Mara about 5:30, and she was ready. I had a small bag I had brought from Europe. Mara had a small bag as well, and her purse. We walked to the market and I went around seeing which matatu was going to Namanga. I figured we'd have to get out at Namanga, cross the border, and then catch another matatu to Kajiado, then on to Nairobi.

The matatus don't leave until they are full. Mara was pretty nervous about that. I explained to her that the train didn't leave until about 18:00, and we had plenty of time. At least the weather wasn't too warm, because we were going to be stuffed into the matatus.

The matatu left Arusha just before eight. The other passengers smashed in with us were four Maasai women who each had a child, three adult men with two more children, and several chickens. We got to Namanga just after ten. When we got out, Mara said, "That was intimate. It's like being in a clown car." I had no idea what she meant at the time.

The border guards made a big deal about Mara's American passport and slowed us down a bit. They were subtly trying to get a bribe: "Eh, kwanini dada ana pasipoti ya Merikani na wewe pasipoti ya Tanzania?" They asked what we planned to do in Kenya.

I told them, in English, "We are taking the train to Mombasa because we both liked the train." Finally they let us through with just paying the ten-dollar visa fees, which Mara had to pay in American dollars.

It took almost two hours to get to Kajiado. We saw small herds of Thompson Gazelle close to the road. Such beautiful animals, so striking in their coloring.

When we got to Kajiado, the matatu driver said he didn't know if he'd go north to Nairobi or south back to the border. We didn't have any choice but to wait, and finally left about 13:00, and got to the Nairobi train station around 15:00. I sorted out the tickets and Mara bought snacks from the vendors, and then we had to wait until 17:00 to board the train.

The weather was warmer in Nairobi than it had been in Arusha. I wondered if it was because there were no trees. We wandered around the market for a while. Mara said she wanted to just sit and read in the station, so I went to the used clothing market.

I had never been on an overnight train, so this added to my excitement. Finally, they let us board. We had gotten second-class tickets because they weren't that much more expensive than third-class. We found our car and settled in. Mara said she wanted to read until the train started moving. I was nervous with anticipation and had all this energy, so I decided to explore the train.

Just after 18:00, the train started, and I could not believe our good fortune. We had the roomette, designed to sleep six, to ourselves. Maybe our bunkmates were wandering around the train, but wouldn't they have brought their luggage to the car?

Mara was looking out the window at the scenery. I decided to try to make small talk with her. "Are you going to return to school when you get back to Chicago?"

"Probably. I just need a couple of courses for my degree. I'm thinking of grad school for ethology. I want to do more with animal behavior, but I don't want to experiment with animals. I don't know what I can do with anthropology. What about you?"

"I'm taking a few music and computer courses. I'm going to be a teaching assistant for calculus and statistics this coming year."

"They must think you're a math wiz," she responded. "I bet you have Asperger's. All engineers are probably on the spectrum."

"Asperger's?"

"It's neurological, a way of processing information. A teacher told me she thought I had Asperger's because of my dog obsession. We think differently than most people, and aren't as aware of social cues. We're obsessed with ideas and details others don't see," she added.

"That's definitely me."

We sat in silence for a while, then she said, "Thanks for accompanying me. I had a big argument with my folks over just coming up here. They said unless I went with someone, it was too dangerous for a mzungu girl."

"Oh, it's my pleasure," I responded. I was so nervous.

I saw she was yawning. I mulled over how to frame my question, but couldn't think of an elegant way to tell her I wanted to kiss her. I decided it was as good a time as any, so I asked her, "Mara, do you miss your husband?"

She smiled. "Sometimes I miss the sex, but there were so many issues. Why do you ask?"

I hesitated, but I had to go for it. "You've been very kind to me and I like you. I want you to teach me about sex."

I had been sitting across from her and went to sit next to her. I put my arm around her and took her chin in my hand and kissed her. Oh! The feeling! Like a jolt of electricity. I put my face into her cleavage. She was so soft!

She looked surprised and like she was trying to suppress a laugh. We were holding hands, and she smiled and said, "Ndu-gu, you're too young."

I took her hand and put it on my erection so she could feel I was hard and whispered, "I don't think so."

She gasped, shrieked slightly, and giggled. I stood up and took my turban off, shook out my hair and unlocked the bed on the other side of the roomette. I reached for her hand and said, "Njoo hapa *(Come here)*."

She came and sat next to me and put her hand on my shoulder and we kissed for a few minutes. I cupped her breast and realized I felt very hot all over.

"You're a really good kisser." Then she asked, "How long have you been hard?"

What a question. I broke the kiss and responded, "Since this morning."

She smirked and said, "No, really."

I wanted her and I wanted her to know it. I was scared but excited. "Since we got on the train. What does it matter?

Whenever you're around, I'm always hard. Sometimes I've had to leave the room I get so excited when I see you."

She looked embarrassed. I got her to lie down and took her hand again so she would feel me. She started caressing my penis, and I thought that if I didn't come I would faint. I groaned.

"Are you OK?" she asked.

"That feels so good." I put my hands on her breasts and exhaled. I was in heaven. She had to recognize how brave I was.

"Let's get undressed. You need to know where all the parts are."

The parts? What was she talking about? I responded in a whisper, "Let me undress you." I kissed her and lifted her tunic over her head and untied her pants. She was wearing lacy underwear, and I just sat before her and admired her for a few seconds.

"You will be at an advantage if you can unhook a bra with one hand," she said. I was looking at the bra. "In the back."

So I held her shoulder and mumbled, "I have no idea what I'm doing," and fumbled a little, but I did it, and slipped it off. There I was, face to face with her naked breasts. I was in ecstasy. I put a hand on each one and just felt them, squeezing slightly. I felt euphoric. I put my face into her cleavage again and said, "Mmmm." I probably had a goofy expression on my face.

She said, "Keep going. You're not there yet."

I slipped my hands down and removed her panties, which were wet. I was beside her and was just staring at her crotch. I didn't expect there to be hair. I looked into her eyes.

"Touch me." She took my right hand and put it between her legs. She was really wet. I was almost in a trance as I started feeling her.

"Very nice. Now, stick your middle finger into my vulva. This is what we call 'pussy.'"

I looked into her eyes again. I had no idea what I was doing. She was smiling and said, "Don't be afraid. Just start feeling and put your middle finger in. It will slide in."

It took me a second, but I did it. She was warm and squishy. I felt like I was dreaming.

She sighed and said, "Oh! Now, you probably can't feel this with your fingers, but when you put your penis in me, *uume mgume*, right? You will feel it is at an angle. But if you want to give pleasure and want a woman to want you, take your fingers out and I want to show you this," and she spread what I would learn was her labia, with her hands.

This was happening! I didn't know anything about female anatomy. I was to learn I didn't know that much about my own. I didn't know there were so many names for so many body parts. I learned a lot of American slang: "to do someone," "pussy," "fuck," "dick," "hard-on," "cum," "cock," "eat," "blow job," "69," "foreplay."

"Look. This small part up here, so many inches away from the vulva, is the clitoris. Like the head of your penis, it is very sensitive. You can lightly touch it with your fingers, but it is better, for me, for you to lick it lightly, with your tongue. Do you understand? We call it 'eating,' and if you do it gently and right, and take some time, in a few minutes, I will have an orgasm and come. Do you understand?"

I nodded, but of course, I didn't. I was so excited. She said, when I went to lick her, "Do you want me to do you at the same time?"

"No. I want to concentrate on what I'm doing." Eating her took my mind off myself. All those folds of skin, but she guided me and told me where my tongue felt the best. I knew I had to be smelling her, but it was so subtle. She tasted very bland. The sounds that came out of her mouth were very arousing. Her breathing quickened, and she was moaning and saying. "More! That's so good!" By this time my balls hurt a lot, I had been hard for so long without relief. When she came, she shouted, "Oh wow! Dayal!" and took my face in her hands, and I could feel how wet my beard was. "You're wonderful!" She kissed me passionately as I lay on her and I felt her breasts, like pillows, against my chest. I will never forget that feeling. I loved it then and I still love it. Then she said, "Lie on your back and I'll do you."

What she did was kiss me under my ear, and she used her tongue and tasted me. The sensation! She worked her way down my body, kissing me that way, as she stroked my dick. She stopped at my nipples and kissed each, then kissed her way down my chest and belly to my penis. She put her lips on it and her tongue just under the head. She could not put all of me in her mouth, I was too long, but she fondled my balls and I gasped.

She stopped for a second and said, "You're really hot, and I have to tell you, I've never been with an uncircumcised man."

I didn't know what to do with my hands, so I put them in her hair and I came immediately. She took her mouth off me and I spurted on to her breasts. I was breathing hard and shaking. To me, it was totally different than jerking off.

When I got my breath back, I raised myself up and kissed her, and got her lying down next to me. I said, "Thank you so much, Mpendwa. That was wonderful."

I called her Mpendwa because that's what she was to me: my dearest love. I enfolded her, and it was wonderful having her in my arms. Oh! The warmth of her body next to mine.

The train was moving very slowly, but it was nice. Towards morning, I woke up and I wanted her again. She said to me, "Are you sure this isn't a piss hard on?"

I had no idea what she was talking about and I said, "Sena tena?" which means "Repeat what you said.'

She hesitated and then said, "A piss hard on. You have to urinate so you're hard. You don't really want sex."

I giggled and replied, "Oh, I want sex!"

"OK, we'll see. She turned her back to me and said, "Put your dick between my legs. You're not going to enter me without a condom."

"I have them."

"You do?" she responded, surprised. "How did you get condoms?"

"I went with Hassan to the prescription chemist and had him buy them for me."

"Why?"

"I wanted you and I wanted to be prepared, and nobody would say anything if Hassan bought them, but if it was me, it would get back to my parents, and, you know…"

"You devil! Well, this time, we'll do it this way," she said, giggling. "When we get to the room, it'll be different. I feel you. Put your hands on my hips and thrust."

I started with my hands on her hips, but I moved one hand to her breasts and the other to her tummy. She just put her hands over mine, and vocalized, "Mmmm." It felt great, and I ejaculated quickly. I didn't even think about whether she came, but she seemed to not really care. I hugged her and she said, "I guess it didn't matter."

"What didn't matter?"

"Whether it was a piss hard on or not. I wonder if they're serving breakfast yet," she said as she kissed me and moved to get up.

I realized I was also very hungry. "Well, I have to urinate now, so let's get dressed, stop at the loo, and go to the dining car."

The train didn't actually get in until after 9:00. We had a great breakfast—white table cloth, silver, goblets for water, china plates. They served toast, butter, fried eggs, tomatoes, bacon and cheese, a real treat. I had tasted cheese in Switzerland, and learned there were many kinds. They also gave us a choice of juices and coffee or tea. I had never had coffee. Mara told me to put in several tablespoons of cream and two of sugar. I thought it was like liquid dessert. Also, as you ride into Mombasa the scenery changes drastically, from the dry, gold savannah to the rich blue greens of the coast. You start to smell the spices. It was like entering paradise.

We got into our room at Mombasa Palm Tree at about 10:00. It was quite a walk from the train, and the air was humid and scented with spice, but there was a breeze.

The hotel was an old mansion. Everything is old in Mombasa, or at least it was in the 1980s. This place really had the charm of the pre-colonial era. The rooms were around a courtyard. Every bedroom had a bath, but the old kind, where the shower's over the toilet and sink and when you use it the whole room gets wet. Mara flopped onto the bed. She might have been ready for a nap, but I wasn't. I was ready to "do her" for real this time. I took off my turban, shook out my hair, laid down next to her, loosened the string on her trousers, reached in and started stroking her pussy. Her eyes had been closed, but she opened them, and said, "Really?"

I smiled and said, "Yes, of course." The expression on her face, I could just tell she was ready to play.

"Put the condoms under the pillow so we have them." She loosened my pants and I took them off. I gave her a condom packet, and I was straddling her and she was caressing my dick. "You are so hot! I can't believe how hot you are. You're burning," she remarked.

She put the condom on me. I slid into her and came immediately. She gasped. "That didn't take long. You'll have to learn to get control of your dick. Let's take a shower and go out."

"That wasn't good?" I asked her, surprised.

"No, it wasn't."

"Oh. I'll be ready again in a few hours."

"I don't know," she said. "Four times in less than 24 hours is a bit much."

"No. Since you've been in Arusha, three or four times a day has been normal for me." I took her hand and led her to the shower. I was all wired up still. I turned it on and got under the water first. It got warm quickly and I beckoned her. She took the soap and started washing me, starting at my chest and down to my legs. I was hard again; I knew I would not come, but I was so aroused looking at her. She had a smile on her face. She stroked my dick and said, "Impossible," shook her head and giggled.

I took the soap and started washing her breasts. Then I dropped the soap, put my hands on her rear and lifted her up slightly so I could put my dick inside her. I was hardly thinking, I just wanted to be as close as possible to her. I leaned her against the wall and moved slowly, in and out. "Is this how it should be?" I whispered to her. Water was pouring over us. She moaned and hugged me, and I was enraptured. As I moved, I guess I was vocalizing, "Mmmm," and I could feel her. She inhaled sharply, and I could feel her arch her back, press closer to me, and come. She exhaled and said, "Oooooh! mmmm," and held me tighter.

"I can feel you, Mpendwa. Oh, nakupenda sana. I love you so much," I whispered to her. I felt so happy, so attached to her, and I never wanted the feeling to end. I just hugged her to me and kissed her neck. I held her there until she broke her embrace. She looked up at me and she looked like she had tears in her eyes.

She put her hand up to her eyes and said, "I'm so sorry. I'm just overcome with emotion. You have, I think, *joto ya ngono.*" That means "sexual heat." I felt so proud when she said that.

She grabbed a towel and sat on the edge of the bed. She didn't look happy. She looked overwhelmed. "You're not happy?" I asked her.

"No, I am. It's just that I wasn't expecting…"

I was enjoying being with her so much.

"Let's get dressed and go out and sightsee," she said. We walked all over. We found Biashara Street and looked at old khanga, our traditional Swahili cloth. I was surprised at how many people asked if she was my sister.

We talked as we strolled. She said, "You know, for all the time we've spent together, I really don't know you that well. I know you guys are Sikhs. What do Sikhs believe? Is God an old man in your mind, or what? All I know is that you don't cut your hair."

"We say 'Sikhi.' Our scripture is a long poem, not at all like your Bible. We don't think specific incidents are controlled by God, *Ik Onkar*, but everything is. Does that make sense? I think of a force, a power. Sikhi believe God is all around us, and inside us. We believe that it's important to respect others, because nobody is more worthy than any other. We don't cut our hair because we believe God made us perfect as we are. Also, our scripture, the Adi Granth, addresses lust, but never says anything about what sex is ok or what isn't. How about you?"

"You know, we're not that religious. My family is more culturally Jewish. That's how it is in the US. We're told America is not a Christian country, but it is. I think the Old Testament is scary. It seems that we were constantly fighting wars to worship one God. Like the part in Joshua, where God tells him to start wars and take over towns because the people were evil. I always wondered how a just God could think that was fair. I think your idea is very close to mine, but the Bible says God is to be feared. The Bible actually tells us to not cut our hair, but you know, the Christians came up with the New Testament, and so many things that were forbidden in the Old got to be OK in the New. Because the disciples said things changed? Who told them? Or you pray to be forgiven for doing things that you know are dishonest or hurtful? The Christians believe you can petition God with prayer. The Bible doesn't condemn slavery or prostitution. We wonder why the holocaust happened if we're God's chosen people."

I smiled and nodded. "My father told me about the holocaust, and how fearful your grandparents were. Your Bible is a bit fantastical."

Mara looked up, smiled at me, and responded, "Isn't it, though! I'll have to find a copy of your Adi Granth."

We returned to the room about 16.00 and took a nap, but by about 18:00 I was ready for another go at her. I kissed her to awaken her, like Sleeping Beauty, and she smiled at me. I said, "Let's make love again!"

She smiled and said, "Oh my God, you're crazy!"

"Crazy in love with you, Mpendwa. I want to feel you around me."

"You're not in love. You have to learn the difference between love and sex. You have to learn to control your dick, and you have to learn about foreplay."

"Foreplay?"

"Yes. It will be the rare woman who wants to jump your bones without foreplay. You need to romance us. You have to make it so a woman trusts you. Think! She is allowing you into her body."

"Do you trust me?"

"Yes, but I know that you never had intercourse. You're going to meet women who don't know anything about you. You will have to learn to say charming things and how to touch a woman. Don't just ask, 'Are you ready for me?' because that's crude. First, you have to kiss. You have to hug and caress. Don't just go for the breasts. Take your time. Then, gently, slowly, get your fingers down to her pussy and stroke her. I mean me. Tell me what you like."

"I need to learn words."

She kissed me and continued to kiss me down to my nipples and sucked slightly. "Does my body hair bother you?" I asked her.

"No. It's masculine. I like it. Some women will and some won't. Shall I caress your dick?"

"I'm afraid I'll come too fast."

"Well, this is what we're dealing with now, so if you think you're going to come, tell me and I'll stop."

We kissed some more and I tried to be gentle. She said, "You should get a copy of the Kama Sutra. Remember, this isn't a race. Ask a woman what she likes and go slowly. She always comes first if you want to see her a second time."

So, we kissed and caressed each other for a while, but I had been ready, so I begged, "Mpendwa, please…"

She stopped touching my dick, took a condom, unrolled it on me, and as I was about to enter her, she said, "Now pay attention. You can't be thinking about your dick right now. I want you to slowly enter me, say the Latin alphabet backwards, and not move."

I looked at her and said, "Sema tena?"

"Z, y, x… Come on. Enter me and let's hear it."

Well, as soon as I entered her, I could feel her heat and how tight she was. Mara saw the expression on my face and she said, "Pull out," and she pushed me.

"I'm so sorry," I said, "but…"

Mara got a very serious expression on her face. "Do you think I'm joking? I'm not. If you don't get control of your dick, I will hurt you."

I was shocked. "You'd hurt me?"

"Yes. I will pinch you in a sensitive place. As soon as you enter me, I want to hear you say 'Zed,' then y, then x, got it? And quit looking at my tits. Look at my eyes. You want to learn to make love? Listen, or we won't be making love. I'm serious."

I really hadn't thought what this would be like. So, I tried again. I put my hands on her rear end, entered her, and I had to ignore the feeling, and said, "Zed, y, x, w…"—and I then really had to think what came next— "v… uh, u…"—so I wasn't thinking about my dick, and I was trying to ignore how hot she felt and how excited I was.

I looked over her head and I asked, "Can I move now?"

"I don't know. Can you? I'd like you to, but I'd like to hear the entire alphabet!"

I pulled out again and said, "This isn't fun. I'm starting to hurt. That can't be right." I was feeling frustrated and discouraged. I was still hard and I wanted her, but my balls hurt.

We lay there for a few seconds. I was breathing hard. Mara sighed and said, "Let's start over. Sema tena, zed, and keep saying…"

She guided me in and I said, "Zed," and I took a breath, then I said, "Y," and I could not look at her. I so wanted to look at her. She was like a dream woman to me.

She said, "You're really really hot!!"

I kept saying letters. I moved slowly. I felt like my erection was expanding, and I felt hot all over. I heard her saying, "Oh, oh my God, oh wow." I could feel her, her hands were on my hips, and they moved to my butt. I tried to ignore her, but I could feel her coming. I got to M and shouted, "M! mmmm…" and I just exploded into her, and yelled, "Oh wow! Oh! Oh, Mara, I love you so much!" It was a very strong orgasm. I felt like she turned me inside out and I collapsed onto her, loving the feeling of her breasts. She was hugging me, and we laid together for a while.

"When you pull out, make sure the rubber doesn't come off." So I held onto it.

"Was that OK?" I asked, thinking it was wonderful.

She smiled and said, "Very good for a start, but I want to get you to at least *h*. After that, it's diminishing returns. Let's rinse off and go find dinner. I'm hungry."

We went and found some wonderful grilled fish. She started talking about her husband.

"I'm so glad we got to come here. This is such a magical part of the world. The last year with my husband was a nightmare. I wondered how he changed so much. I was shocked that I really didn't know him at all. Not like I thought. He was really into kink. He wanted me to wear a garter belt and stockings and to tie me up and spank me. Other stuff, too."

I was shocked. "Where did he get ideas like that?"

"From pornography? From his friends? I don't know. They say the heart wants what the heart wants, but clearly, the dick wants what it wants. Once he gave me chlamydia." Mara scowled, shook her head and rolled her eyes.

"What's that?"

"It's venereal. I knew then he had to be cheating on me."

I had seen pornography because Peter had it. I was more grossed out than aroused.

She changed the subject. "It turned out that our ideas about money were very different. He had no savings. You don't have to think about this now because you don't have any money, but start planning for you future."

She told me she had dreamed of owning a kennel and taking care of dogs, because she had worked in kennels and liked it. She had been saving money to buy property, and it would take more than love to make a marriage, that you should have something in common with a partner, more than sexual attraction.

"My parents didn't object to us marrying so young because they thought he had a bright future, and that they wouldn't have to pay for my college education. He was a Christian, but not religious, and I think they also thought that he'd come to Judaism. We don't proselytize, but when *goyim* marry Jewish women, lots of times they convert because we don't live the gobblygook."

"Do you think Christians really believe everything in their Bible?"

Mara smirked. "They have no idea what the Bible says. When you tell them you believe in God and we're all God's children, their response is that we'll rot in hell if we don't ask Jesus to forgive us. They teach their children to call us Christ Killers."

The next morning, we seemed to stir at the same time. I kissed her and I immediately put my finger in her pussy. She yawned and said, "What are you doing?"

"What do you think I'm doing? I want to make love to you and I want to know you're ready."

"This is not the way to go about it, Ndugu. More hugging and kissing, then you take her hand and put it on your dick like you did. If she doesn't kiss you back, then you have to retreat a bit. But no matter, let's do 69. We'll do each other."

She turned around and stroked me, and I put my hand back between her legs, and started licking her. She admonished me and said, "Gently." But she immediately put me in her mouth and gently sucked and licked me as she stroked my balls. I didn't think I could get any harder, but she stopped after a bit and said, "You are the hottest guy."

I could feel how hot she was. She continued licking me and caressing my balls, and I could feel I was coming and I shouted, "Mara Mpendwa!" and she could feel me and then she had me come in her cleavage. She gave me so much joy. I shouted, "I love you so much!"

She looked serious, and then she said, "We have to talk. Let's shower and go for breakfast." Of course, we showered together. I wanted to spend more time in the shower touching her, but she said, "I'm hungry," and turned away from me.

We got down to the restaurant and ordered. Then she said to me, "Listen. This is serious. You can't be shouting out 'I love you' when you come. You don't love me. This is sex. You have to get real about that. For your own mental health, you have to get some perspective."

I was listening to her, and I was hearing that *she* didn't love *me*. I didn't know what to say. It was as though she had slapped me. She went on, "I've done a terrible thing. You are too young. In fact, in the US, they could put me in jail."

I was shocked. "How can that be? For what?"

"You're confusing sex and love. In many places it's not legal until you're eighteen."

I thought for sure she was teasing me. "You've done nothing wrong," I said. "It was *me* who seduced *you*. Mtu hufanya upendo na mwanamke amependezwa na upendo."

"Yes, I know: in Swahili the man makes love and the woman has love made to her, but in the US the Christians make the rules and it's illegal in many places to have sex outside of marriage. It's fornicating. It's especially illegal for an adult to be with a child, even a teenager. It's to protect the children who haven't gone through puberty, and also, to protect you from thinking you're in love."

I felt she was rejecting me. I suddenly felt frightened and asked her, "Are you saying you don't love me?" I buried my face in my hands and started to weep.

"Dayal! Calm down. What's going through your mind? I leave the week after we get back. How did you think this would play out? That you would go back with me to the US?"

I hadn't thought beyond the next time I would have sex with her. I said, "Yes, I will come with you and get a job."

She could tell I just drew that out of the air and gave an incredulous laugh. "You'll do no such thing. I wouldn't have you if you did that. You will stay in school and maybe we can revisit this when you're eighteen. That's just two years, right? You must stay in school as long as someone will pay your scholarship. You absolutely must. They've asked you to teach! Clearly they have confidence in you. But you have to know, too, that when we get back to Arusha, when we get off the matatu, you will go to your house and I will go to the cottage, and we won't see each other after that. Unanifahamu?"

I could not believe what she was telling me. "Why?" I asked, anxiously.

She rolled her eyes and said, "They'll all have kittens."

"Have kittens? We don't have a cat."

She rolled her eyes again and sighed. "Because everyone will know and our fathers will kill us. My father will kill me for having corrupted a teenage boy. Your father will kill me for corrupting you if my father doesn't kill me first, and for giving both our mothers strokes. You are still your mother's mtoto. I can't imagine how hard it is for her to see you off to school. It's like she's lost all her children. She has gone without many things to make sure you boys could have a future, because you know it won't be in Africa. In fact, they will most likely find a wife for you. So, for your own mental health, rein in your enthusiasm. If you have a good time, tell me you are a 'very happy man,' and I will tell you I am a 'very happy woman.' I want to continue to make love to you, but I beg you to not get too emotional. I'm teaching you so you can please women and have choices."

"I don't want other women. I want you." I really did want her.

"Don't start that. Your parents would never permit it. Please. You're going back to school." She sounded angry. We ate our breakfast in silence. I took what she said to heart, about my own mental health. That was something I had never thought about before. She was an alter ego before I knew what one was. Obviously this was important stuff.

I knew there was sexual exploitation of children, but it was not an issue I understood at the time. Many of my Maasai friends, teenage Morani, had sex with older women. The younger ones had sex play with each other. It wasn't considered taboo or sordid. It was entertainment. I guess because life expectancy was so low, you got as much fun in as you could. This was our culture. I wasn't aware of any laws about sex.

That day, we took a matatu up to Malindi to the beach on the Indian Ocean. We stayed a couple of nights there in what was really a shack on the beach, and it was so peaceful. We plaited each other's hair and applied kohl to each other's eyes.

At breakfast one morning, we were sitting out on a patio. Nobody was around. They served us toast with honey. Mara took my hand, kissed it, and poured about a tablespoon of honey onto my palm. Then she licked it off, but as she did, she licked between my fingers. Then, she slowly licked the tips of my fingers. She was staring into my eyes. I understood what it was to be sensuous then. She really had me aroused. I lost all interest in eating and couldn't wait to get back to the room, and told her so. She laughed, but very slowly ate her breakfast, and whispered, "I want you to understand, sex is more than intercourse."

She taught me more about my anatomy, and more sex positions. We stroked each other with our hands, and made each other come. I had her on my lap, which wasn't particularly good, but we could hug and I could move her. She wanted oral sex if we were going to have sex more than once a day or she said she'd get sore. I asked her, "Do you really like having a penis in your mouth?"

"No, but I the expression of a man's pleasure at the sensation turns me on. I hope you will get that eating pussy, because most women think their sex organs are ugly and smelly, yet we get more sensation from tongue. Many women won't ask for what they want. You have to ask them what feels good. Remember that."

Just having her with me, to cuddle, to share ideas, was so great. I never ever imagined being with a woman would be so wonderful. She answered all my questions honestly. I asked her again, about being divorced.

"I should have never gotten married, but it didn't matter to Dan whether we were married or not and it enabled me to buy a house, because otherwise, as a single woman, I couldn't get credit. Even though I had a job and he didn't. In fact, in America, the banks don't lend to single women, black people, or Asians unless they already have the money they need." She hesitated and added, "The irony is, when we got divorced and I paid Dan off, I got title to the house with no problem."

She told me that her former husband wasn't bothered by debt, and when they got the bill for his student loan and he wasn't going to class regularly, she might have to be responsible for his debts.

That was interesting to me. I didn't know anything about mortgages or borrowing money. In fact, I didn't think any of the banks that lent in Africa gave mortgages. My father's business had a line of credit based on past history, and it was what they called a "float": the interest rate could fluctuate, but if it was paid off in the time frame in the contract, the interest didn't go up. Nobody got a loan to buy property, not unless they had a European partner.

"I could see the writing on the wall, Dayal. It was important for me to own property because of inflation, and to build equity."

She told me that the interest rates on mortgages are locked in and by law they can't fluctuate and for most people to build wealth in America, they have to own property and build equity. She told me she thought it was ironic that even though her husband was a student with no credit history, because he was a man, they could get credit. This seemed unfair to me, as in Sikhi, men and women are equal. I didn't really think of it then, but when I started making money, I appreciated that she gave me more of a financial education that I ever would get anywhere.

When we got back to Mombasa, I had more confidence in what I was doing. I thought I had control of my penis. I could tell when I was about to ejaculate. I wanted to feel her without a condom. I told her I would pull out.

"I'm only trusting you because I expect my period in a few days, and because I know you don't have a disease," she said.

I had no idea what she was talking about. "What's a period?" I asked.

She smiled and mumbled, "I'll tell you later. Come on…" and she gently guided me in. I had my hands on her butt. She put her hands first on my hips, then on my legs, just under my balls. She had a look of wonder on her face, and I could tell she was losing herself to me. I never felt it was "just sex" with her, ever, but I was not allowed to say that I loved her. I could feel her, and I knew that I would come and I pulled out and came on her.

She shouted, "Oh, wow! Mmmm!" and I lay on her and rolled her to my side and just held her and whispered, "You've made me a very happy man. I hope I've made you happy."

She whispered back, "Very happy."

"So, what's a period?"

She explained menstruation, and that it's supposed to happen every 28 days, and sometimes it does and sometimes it doesn't, and cramps, and what an inconvenience it was. This explained my friends' sisters sitting on mounds of sand away from their houses, and my mother staying in her room. I had known this, but didn't know it was called a "period."

She explained that in most cultures it was a taboo topic because men don't like to hear about blood, and they make women feel unclean for bleeding. She explained that the Orthodox Jews make women take a ritual bath after their periods. She also told me you could do birth control if you could figure out when a woman was going to ovulate. That was more information than I needed at the time.

The week I spent with Mara was the best week of my life for years and years. We were carefree and I tried to keep in mind what she said about perspective, but I could not help loving her and appreciating her.

We took the morning train back to Nairobi on Sunday, got a matatu to Kajiado and transferred again at Namanga, It must have been about 21:00 when we got to Arusha. Anya and Shayla were with Hassan at the market waiting. Mara's parents would not have let them out so late to the market, which was closed, without a male companion.

We got our bags off the top of the matatu, and hugged. I couldn't even kiss her. I hugged Anya and Shayla. We all walked to my house, and the girls continued on to the cottage. I fell into bed. ✪

# CHAPTER 4

The next morning, my automatic reaction upon waking was to reach for Mara. I had a brief moment of panic, but it was more, then, of wanting her, and having to remember what she told me. I put on trousers and stumbled to the choo, then back to the dining room. My mother served me tea and asked, "How was Kenya? Did you get to the ocean? Do you know I've only been to Nairobi twice?"

"Amaji, it was wonderful. We ate great Swahili food and the fish was excellent. Mara bought khanga and some small trinkets for her sisters. We went to the ocean in Malindi. Lots of wazungu tourists there."

Ama brought me a couple of fried eggs and toast. Then, she asked, "She wasn't too much trouble for you? I know she can be a handful."

I smiled and responded, "No, Amaji. She was very well behaved and good company. I enjoyed being with her." There was no need to elaborate.

Ama sent me to the market, and I happened to see Shayla and Anya also going, so we walked together. I didn't really know what to say to them, but I knew they'd start chattering soon enough.

"So how was Mombasa? Did you do everything you wanted to do?" Shayla asked, smiling, and winking.

I looked at her. So she was going to be like that, eh? I started laughing. "Yes," I said, "I believe we did everything... I mean *everything*, we both wanted to do."

Shayla started laughing, but it was over Anya's head. "Is it? Everything?" She phrased it as we translate it to English. We don't say, 'Really?' But 'Is it?' like, 'Is that so?'

"Kweli kabisa. We did things I didn't know I wanted to do!" She had me giggling.

"Like what?" Shayla asked, smirking. She raised her eyebrows. Anya was looking at both of us, confused.

"Ask Mara. I don't think I should say more and cause trouble. We both had a wonderful time together. Is she still asleep?"

"No, I don't think so, but she said something about getting her period and after so much excitement with you, she needed to rest."

"Is that what she said? Excitement?" I'm sure I was smiling like a fool.

"She said you had an exciting time and you were better company than she anticipated. My mother was listening, so that's all she said. Unanifahamu?" Shayla teased.

"Are you at the market for anything specific?"

"We want cherimoya. She said to look for starfruit, too."

"I don't think they'll have that inland." We walked around and spoke KiSwahili, so they were less likely to be overcharged. Shayla said, "I'll come over in the afternoon. Tutaonana *(We will see each other)*." So we parted.

I was restless. The Glazers would leave at the end of the week, but I would not leave for school for a month. I went to the tailor and ordered several shirts and some pairs of pants and both black and white tuxedos, because it was cheaper to have them made in Arusha than I could buy them, even ready-made, in Europe. Also, they'd fit better. Then I went to see some local school chums. They were happy with the business I had given them. Two of my friends, Albert and Wilfred, had bought their mothers ceramic-lined jikos (cookstoves, like braziers), which needed less fuel to cook than regular ones.

I practiced the piano in the afternoon, as I always did. I was hoping Mara would change her mind and come over, but she didn't. Shayla came by herself and sat next to me on the piano bench, something she had never done. That surprised me, and I smiled, but I kept on playing the Beatles' Song, "Ticket to Ride." Suddenly, she put her hand practically in my crotch and whispered, "Nataka tufanya upendo kwa kila mmoja." *I want us to make love to each other.*

I almost had a heart attack. "Lini?"

She laughed at the expression on my face and said, "As soon as possible."

We both started laughing. I got serious and asked her, "What makes you think…?"

She interrupted me and said, "Mara told me to ask if you have any messages."

I wanted to tell Shayla to tell Mara I missed her, but she'd think I wasn't keeping perspective. I said to Shayla, "If anyone asks, tell them you're going to look at the stars with me. We'll meet by the market, around 19:00, if that's ok. Bring a blanket, and I'll ask Hassan to get me a few. Also, could you bring me something of Mara's?"

She hugged me and said, "Sure. Now, keep playing."

I could only think that Mara sent her to me, but to make love? I didn't think too deeply about it. Although I wanted Mara, Shayla was fine, and maybe this was some of the perspective Mara wanted me to have. I told my parents I was taking the truck so the girls could see the stars outside of town. Shayla and I went towards Namanga, and I pulled off the road. There

was really too much moon to see stars, but of course, that
was just a pretense. It was really romantic, so quiet out in
nature, but if you took time to absorb it, you could hear the
nocturnal animals.

As we got out of the cab and climbed into the truck bed and
arranged the blankets, Shayla said, "Mara said you're very hot,
and to tell you to say the alphabet backwards."

I didn't know how to respond and smirked. Shayla put her
hand on my shoulder and leaned over to kiss me. As we kissed
and explored each other, she whispered, "Mara described you
accurately."

"How do you mean?" I whispered back.

"She said that you were a good kisser.'"

I laughed and kissed her again. I hugged her to me, then
straddled her and put my hands on her breasts.

She was feeling my chest, but she reached down and untied
my pants. "I love how your beard and chest hair feel, and here
you are, and you really are so hot…"

"Mmmm. I love your big cushiony breasts…" I responded
between kisses.

She laughed. "You're goofy. Cushiony breasts…"

"Goofy? What does that mean?"

"Funny… *chezi.*"

She started stroking me and asked, "Is this ok? Harder?
Foreskin up or down?"

I was relishing the feeling of her. All of her. The bed of the
truck wasn't ideal, but it didn't matter. We were making love
under the African sky. We stroked each other for a while, then I
asked her, "Are you ready?"

She kissed me, and whispered, "I'm going to try to roll this
on you, but I may need help."

In the dark, I think sensations are more intense. Shayla was very hot, and it felt like she was pulling cum out of me. She was moaning a little and I could feel her. "Wow, oh Dayal oh oh, you are so hot, I'm coming. Oh God!"

That was enough. I could feel her undulating. A few more thrusts from me and I felt like we had melted together.

After I withdrew, we lay there catching our breaths, and she said to me, "That never happens. Ever. God, you're good," and she kissed me passionately.

"What do you mean?" I asked as I pondered if it would be ok to toss a spent condom out into the bush.

"I've only had an orgasm from intercourse once. Oral sex is better."

"Mara told me for most women tongue was better."

This was Monday night, and we went out Tuesday night, too.

"Thy staff, it comforts me…" she said as we kissed.

I had to laugh. "I can't wait to feel your soft pussy around me, Shaylaji."

"Let's do 69," she said as she turned around and then put the tip of my dick in her mouth.

It felt so natural. "I love how you taste," I whispered to her. I really did. It was the taste of sex, and I was finding the taste aroused me, too.

Mara hadn't been as vocal, but I was really into Shayla talking. We Sikhi don't really have an expression for "talking dirty" as how can expressing admiration for your lover's physical form be dirty? It was years later that I realized how compelled I was by sound.

The experience of being with Shayla was fun. I felt comfortable with her, and she took my mind off Mara.

We went out Wednesday night, and she said, "Let me see if I can put a rubber on you with my mouth." I'll never forget that experience, either.

We went to the Curtis hotel for a moussaka dinner Thursday night, all of us except Mara. Shayla said she had a headache.

We needed both our truck and Curtis' truck to take them to the airport because they had so much stuff. Mara was pleasant, but reserved. We all hugged each other. Mara hugged me and whispered, "Stay in school. Write to me." If I had known it would be so long before I'd see her again, I would have never let her go.

When we got home, I went to the piano, but Baba beckoned me into his office. That never happened unless it was something very serious. I feared he was going to tell me either he or Ama were dying. He started out speaking to me in Hindi, asking me if I was prepared to return to school. Then he switched to English and said, "You know, the Glazers have been very good to me. Our lives would have been very different were it not for Mr. Glazer's father. I was considering offering to have you escort Mara, but then you offered on your own, and I did not send you to, ah... ngono ya kupendeza."

He said it in Swahili because he was too embarrassed to say it in English... or Hindi.

I almost fell off my chair. "How did you know?" I asked.

"Before you went on the safari, she was over here all the time. I knew something had to have happened for her to stop coming over."

"Shayla told me she, uh, it was her time of the month, you know, and wasn't feeling well. Does Ama know?" I sputtered.

"If she does, she isn't saying anything to me. You have made a big mistake by not waiting."

"Baba, Mara is a good person. She taught me a lot."

"I bet she did," he responded and got up and walked out of the room. He apparently didn't know I had been intimate with Shayla. It was a few years before I understood why he thought it was a 'big mistake.'

When I returned to school in September, I moved in with Peter and Adam. They could cook, for one thing, and that saved me from having to go to the cafeteria and dealing with a lot of food that didn't appeal to me. It was a modern building, and we were on the third floor. There were washers and dryers in the basement. We had linoleum flooring, like in the dorms, but we had rugs. Adam was a bit neater than Peter, but there were school books, magazines, and papers all over. Their furniture was modern, but definitely used. Adam told me students passed it on as they graduated.

They joked about me folding my clothes and keeping things just so, but when they needed a ruler, or a pen, or even a paperclip, they always came to me. They also joked about how I made a point to practice piano half an hour a day, alone. Having a routine kept my stress level down. Dealing with trying to understand French and German, and my studies left me fatigued at the end of every day.

My parents were not from vegetarian backgrounds, and we ate fish and sometimes chicken, never beef or goat at home. I had tasted pork in Sing. I could not get lentils or pulses, nor garun masala (a spice blend), anywhere in Switzerland. It was nice that Adam could steam vegetables and make sauces, and I learned about cooking from him, sort of.

They had friends over frequently, so I had more interactions with other students. Always the conversation started with why I wore a turban in public (at home, I kept my hair tied back), and what Sikh was.

Everyone I met thought all those who were born in Africa were black and that we all lived like the Maasai, in huts. I was questioned constantly. People didn't believe we had cities, or roads, or that we actually spoke languages and had literature. People think they are educated, and know so little of the world outside the country they live in. Mara had told me that when she was in primary school, she was taught that Africans had no languages or culture, and that whites civilized Africa. Also, the black slaves brought to America were lucky. When she told her teacher that Swahili culture was over a thousand years, old, the teacher rolled her eyes and laughed at her.

She told me, "I told my teacher that my parents were African, and she actually said, 'Mara, I've met your parents. They're white. I'm going to tell them what you said,' I wondered, then, what else they were teaching me was bullshit," she said.

I enjoyed Peter's and Adam's company, and playing music with them, but we came from different cultures and economic situations. I'd been hustling for income since I was seven-years-old. That's what I had to do. These guys never had to worry about money. I started taking them with me to Montreux to the recording studio, and they started thinking about the possibility of earning money from music. In exchange for working around the studio cleaning up and doing paperwork, the engineers taught us about recording. I took it seriously because of my engineering studies. Until I started playing at the studio,

I had never heard my playing played back. When you play an instrument, you hear, but not like when you sit back and listen. It's the difference between creating a painting and then seeing it on a wall in a frame. In some ways, I was better than I had thought, but in other areas I could hear I needed improvement. I hadn't thought about how talented either Peter or Adam were, but this playback helped them as well, and we got better in terms of technique, timing and harmonies. Peter, for all his goofiness, was very good.

Peter and Adam noticed that I was always in class, the studio, or the engineering lab, and asked if I was feeling ok. I had lost a lot of weight because I was busy all the time.

This was my academic life. My sexual life was nonexistent. The truth was, I was lovesick. So often, in the shower at night, I would start thinking of Mara, get hard, but find myself sobbing. She haunted my thoughts.

More often than not, I would awaken with an erection and expect Mara to be sleeping next to me for that brief second. I had her shirt and panties, so I was smelling her essence. Was this a blessing or a curse? There were lots of young girls around, but none particularly appealed to me because they'd always proselytize about Jesus and getting saved. I was still jerking off at least once a day. I started working out, running regularly, and doing yoga to deal with stress. I also read our Adi Granth as meditation, before bed. Adam taught me to ski and we often skied when we had four hours off. I was beginning to feel that Switzerland was home.

The next summer break I returned to Arusha. My brothers visited from Malaysia at the same time. I got to see my school chums and had clothes made, but I wanted to do more on the computer, which was impossible in Arusha. I so wanted to travel to America to see Mara, but the expense, even if I could get a visa, I couldn't afford. We had written to each other a few times, but Mara kept her letters very general. She'd ask how my studies were going. She was back at school and grooming dogs. Shayla was the one who gave me what would be gossip: whether she or Mara were seeing anybody.

I returned to school a few weeks early to get on the computer. Dr. Schultz told me that I could start my BSc. I had to teach calculus and trigonometry classes, but I never had more than 20 students.

The university had a Prodigy account, where you were charged by the minute. My brothers had accounts where they worked. What you'd do was compose a message, and then attach the modem to the computer, which would connect the computer with a phone line, and send the message. We were in touch this way about once a month, which was more than we had ever been. This still could not be done in Africa.

In January, Sodhi messaged me that my parent's friend had found him a wife. Her name was Anu. He had only seen photos of her at that point, but he planned to meet her in Singapore in a few weeks. My brothers were both now living in Kuala Lumpur, which was a very modern city.

I wrote to Shayla asking her why they didn't visit. Europe was not nearly as far as Africa. She responded quickly.

*Dear Ndugu Dayal:*

*Everything's gotten so expensive. Inflation is supposed to be down, but the price of gas (petrol) affects everything. Reagan is an idiot. I wonder if he knows how he sounds. Crack cocaine addiction is rampant. You know we're fighting a "secret" war in Nicaragua. Also, I'm getting married. I'm pregnant! I don't think I'm going to be going anywhere for a while!"*

That surprised me. I wondered how her father felt about this, and asked in my next letter to her, but she ignored it.

I thought I was doing ok, but Adam and Peter thought I'd be a little more chill if I had a girlfriend, but *not* a *girlfriend*. They thought it would be a good idea for me to visit prostitutes with them and experience more women. I did this several times, but I didn't enjoy the experiences as much as I hoped I would. For one thing, this was always a business transaction. The emotional feeling, for me, was terrible. I wanted affection, and all the talk and the touching. I wanted to take my time. These women wanted you in and out quickly. I wanted a blow job, and a woman wanted to charge me about thirty dollars more.

I learned that most of the women were trafficked from Poland and Bulgaria. I asked them why they were doing this, and they told me it paid more than being a housemaid, they could send money back home for the education of their children, and they got doctors exams once a month.

This wasn't how I wanted sex. I needed a *real* girlfriend. My mates tried to discourage me.

Adam said, "Dayal, you don't want to complicate your life. A permanent, regular girlfriend will have all sorts of expectations."

I couldn't imagine how my life could possibly be more complicated. I felt I would have less stress if I had a regular sexual partner. If you were over age 16, you were *of age*.

I was a *demisexual*. I wanted to have an emotional connection to my lover. What was complicated was finding the right girl. All around me were Christians white girls, who seemed to have fairy tale fantasies about dating and love.

In Africa, girls grow up quickly—emotionally, if not physically. Nobody dates. I mean, where are you going to go in the bush? Guys just try to fuck girls. I hate to be crude about it, but just listening to my brothers and their Morani friends joke about their antics, and what those guys had to say, it was definitely not about romance. They were going to get as much sexual experience with whomever they could convince until they could accumulate enough cattle to get a wife, which they knew might take years. It was normal to fuck widows. We really were coming from different cultures. I knew I would have to make compromises, but I suffered a lot of rejection. So many white girls would not have an Asian guy, not one as dark as I was or a guy who wore a turban and had a beard. Pete told me a lot of them thought I was a terrorist. He thought that was funny. They all wanted to know if I knew Jesus. The ones who wouldn't reject me on my looks or background, I'd take out for coffee and try to learn about them. They wanted to just hang around! Peter and Adam had tried to warn me. I refused to believe what they were telling me. I was determined to find a girlfriend and have both a sexual and emotional relationship with the same woman.

I became friendly with a French girl named Angela. She wasn't comfortable speaking English, so my French improved. She was studying art history, and was pretty in the way most teenage girls are pretty: long, shiny light brown hair, clear skin, slender. Angela and I went out a bunch of times, and we kissed (that was *making out* in English), and she didn't stop me from feeling her, at first. Once I got to the point that I was trying to get her clothes off, she would tell me I was too excited and stop me. After a few weeks, I decided to not call her. Dealing with her was too frustrating. She finally called and asked me if I was angry.

"I'm not angry, but I want a girlfriend who enjoyed my company and who wants to touch me," I told her.

"I do enjoy your company, but I don't want us to get too serious. I'm only sixteen and want to finish school."

"I don't understand what one thing had to do with the other. Serious about what? Marriage? I don't want to get married yet, either."

We agreed to have dinner the next Friday night. After dinner, I brought her back to the apartment. I knew both guys wouldn't return until after midnight, so I had plenty of time. We started kissing, and I started undressing her. She took off her blouse and let me unhook her bra. I took off my turban and my shirt.

"Wow! Your hair is longer than mine. I'm surprised."

"Does it matter?" I asked as I kissed and fondled her.

"I'm just saying you look really dramatic. You're really a sexy guy. Why don't you leave your hair loose?"

"My mother would have a heart attack."

She started giggling, but at the time, I didn't realize how ridiculous I sounded. But we Sikhi don't look on sex the way Christians do.

We kissed some more, and she whispered, "I'm not ready for intercourse. I'm too young."

"I don't want intercourse: I want a blow job (*fellation*, in French)," I told her. I did not want to risk getting a girl pregnant even by accident. "I am going to do something to you that I think will feel good, and if it doesn't, stop me." I went down on her. It didn't take as long as I expected. She started moaning, then after a few minutes, she arched her back and shouted, "Oui! Oui! Oh, Dayal!" and a jumble of French, and she came.

I sat up and looked at her. She looked surprised, but I could not tell if she was actually happy.

"Où est-ce que tu as appris à faire cela? *(Where did you learn to do that?)"* she asked.

What was I to say? "The Kama Sutra," I replied.

"What's that?"

"It's part of the Vedas. The Hindu bible," I said as I stroked myself.

"From a religion?"

"Yes. The part that addresses pleasure."

"I thought you said you weren't Hindu."

"I'm not. That doesn't mean I can't read their scripture. I've read *your* bible."

We looked at each other for a few seconds more. I said to her, "I want you to do me." I untied my pants and took them off. She gasped, but didn't say anything. I lay down next to her, and she moved towards me, and lightly touched my dick. I was wet and very excited. She had a serious look on her face, and said, "I've never done this before."

"There's a first time for everything," I said. "Did you ever have a guy eat you before?"

She shook her head. She was sitting at the edge of the bed, and barely stroked me.

"Had you ever had an orgasm before?" I asked her.

"I guess not. At least now I know what it is."

"Haven't you ever masturbated?" I asked her.

"No. I think only boys do that."

I sighed, then, I said, "You don't have to put the whole thing in your mouth, just the tip."

She got to almost putting her lips on the head of my cock, and then she sat up and said, "I can't do this. You're too big."

This was not going as planned. All I could think was, *Oh no...* I asked her, "Didn't I just bring you to the height of ecstasy?"

She nodded, smiled, and said, "Well..."

I was very frustrated. I put my hands to my face, groaned, and was trying to think. Headache stress with a throbbing dick.

"Are you Ok?" she asked.

"No. I'm not ok. I need some relief. Look at me."

Angela raised her eyebrows and replied, "There is no place in my body where that would fit. It's, uh, very impressive, but..."

"Have you ever seen a guy jerk off?"

She shook her head and said, "I don't even know what you're talking about. I've never heard the term. Masturbate?"

"Well, this might be a useful skill for you to have," I said, as I stroked myself.

"What do you mean?" she asked.

"I don't want to offend you, but you need to know that guys do this. A lot. The thing is, if you don't want to have inter-course, knowing how to jerk a guy off could be helpful. Lie down next to me."

"What do you want me to do?" she asked as she put her hand on my chest.

"Give me your hand. It won't take long." It didn't. I leaned over to kiss her and spurted on her and she gasped. I was lost in the sensation, but I moved to wipe her off. She had a sur-prised look on her face. "Sorry," I said. We just laid there for a few minutes more.

"Are you going to want to do this every time we get togeth-er?" she asked.

I sort of smirked and nodded.

She looked like she was trying to suppress a laugh. "You know, I like you. This was interesting. It did feel good, but I don't know, I have to think about it."

"Do you want to take a shower with me?"

She shook her head.

"If you wait, I'll walk you back to your dorm."

"That's ok. It's not that late. I'll make my own way and think about this."

About a week later, Angela called and wanted to get together. "I like you and want to spend time with you," she said, "but the sex thing…"

I said, "Look. We apparently want different things. I want a girlfriend who's ready for a sexual relationship with me. That doesn't mean intercourse, or even love forever, but someone who wants what I want. You don't, not right now. This is important to me, so it's best we see other people, OK?"

Suddenly, I was getting calls from other girls. Maybe she thought one of her friends would like me. Or try to save my soul? I had no idea. Peter and Adam thought it was beyond amusing. "Why are girls calling you all of a sudden?" Peter asked.

"I'm not sure, but I went down on Angela," I said, as I was transcribing some notes.

They both went nuts. "You ate her? Why would you do that?" Peter asked, excited.

"Because I wanted oral sex. Why do you think?"

Both guys started shouting at me at once and laughing. "So, now you have all these girls calling who want to be eaten but they don't expect to blow you. You know that, right?" Adam said.

Was I naïve? I realized this might be true, so I had to have a plan to deal with this.

I started calling girls back and asking why they called me. Of course, the response was that Angela had said I had done *something wonderful* and they wanted me to do that to them.

Astrid sat down at our lunch table one day. Astrid was gorgeous. She had wavy, strawberry blond hair, green eyes, and a willowy build. She looked like an angel you'd see on a greeting card. I went out with her once, so hopeful, and she immediately started talking about Jesus. She played violin in orchestra, and I tried steering the conversation over to music, but she kept asking me how I could live not being saved.

"Bonjour!" she said, smiling at me, as she sat down. Adam sat across from me, reading the newspaper and eating, but he looked up. I was pouring over a music score and humming to myself. I turned to her and smiled. She leaned over, put her tiny feminine hand on my shoulder, and whispered. "Angela says you're impressive."

I was taken by surprise, but I responded, *sotto voce*, looking into her eyes, "Yes, I have a one holed flute that sings arias," hesitated for a second, and added, "Would you like to learn to play it?"

She raised her eyebrows, blushed deeply, and smirked. Adam laughed but he choked on something he was eating and started coughing, so I got up to get him some water. The whole room turned to look at us.

I recognized some of the callers as girls who asked me if I knew Jesus, so I told them, "God gave me something I think is better than what he gave his only son." That ended those conversations.

I told one of those girls that white boys' dicks are smaller, and to practice on one of them. Peter heard me and confronted me after I got off the phone, "You really think white guys have smaller dicks?"

I had been at my desk calculating and was very aggravated by my situation. I pulled my tape measure out of the drawer and responded, "Do you really want to know? I bet with a degree of statistical certainty that mine is longer. I saw a lot of white boy dicks in showers in Singapore." I stood up and untied my trousers, but I felt the whole situation juvenile.

Peter hesitated, pulled his dick out, and said, "Give me a minute."

"Grow up. They're more concerned with your tongue than your dick."

Peter responded, "Most people do not have oral sex. It's perverse. It's in the Bible. Prostitution is not prohibited by God. Why don't you just do the easy thing? Your God hardly makes you do anything for salvation, so why not just pay for the sex you want?"

"There is nothing about oral sex in the Bible, and there is no salvation. When you die, that's it. Same God as yours and God tells us to do three things. I told you what they were when we met. I don't want to fornicate."

He responded with a laugh and said: "Well. God tells us to keep ten commandments and ask his son Lord Jesus to forgive our sins…"

I gasped. Trying to stifle a laugh, I said, "Actually, your scripture says God sent 613 commandments, not just ten, and you need a scholar to guide you through your religion. Then you pick and choose which commandments you will obey. We believe in the same God, but He hasn't given me more than I can handle. No religion should be that complicated."

Peter looked like I had opened a lid to his brain. He sputtered, "I can't believe in a God without a face."

I burst out laughing. "*You're* telling *me* that because our artists haven't rendered 'God' in paint, and yours have, you really believe that's how he looks? Caucasian? We believe in the same God, whom we all believe is everywhere, but you're saying what I believe is not real because our people haven't painted pictures of Him? You know something? God made the Jews his chosen people, iteration 1.0, then God started tinkering and the apostles got involved and 2.0 was obviously a total disaster, and we Sikhi are 3.0 Same God, he doesn't make it complicated. The things we have to do are enough."

The next semester a Japanese girl, Yuki, came to school. We met at the club I was jamming at with the guys. We were playing Don Fagen's "The Goodbye Look" which was great for keyboards. Everyone told me I was great. Yuki came up to me after our set while I was still sitting at the piano, and asked, in oddly accented French, "Can I buy you a drink?"

I looked at her and asked, in English, "How old are you?"

She looked younger than me! All the Japanese look way younger than they actually are. She looked to be twelve-years-old. I don't think she was even five feet tall.

"Seventeen."

"Can I see your passport?" I asked, skeptically.

She was very slender and had very smooth skin. She told me that she liked that I was hairy and was very comfortable with oral sex, that in Japan, this was common. She was intelligent, funny and pragmatic, but so tiny. I really liked her. I found her very exotic, and we were both outsiders. I remembered what Mara said. Don't take unnecessary risks. Don't confuse love and sex. Be appreciative. She comes first. ✪

# CHAPTER 5

One Saturday that Spring, I logged on to my computer account and I found a message from Sodhi. He went to meet Anu's family, and they would marry in about a year in Singapore, because she was still in school. He and Avi were working on getting my parents passports.

With both Avi and Sodhi married, I was afraid my parents would start looking for a bride for me. I felt when I had the money, I would ask Mara.

Peter, Adam, and I had been going to the studio in Montreux and recording ourselves, with Oscar, a fantastic drummer. Adam made a tape of us doing ten songs. They were mostly covers of other artists' songs, but a couple either he or Peter had written. He sent tapes to some radio stations in Europe. We won some sort of listener's poll, (with *Steve Winwood's* "Empty Pages") and one of the engineers sent a tape to a guy who managed bands. We were playing locally, but suddenly our cover of "Empty Pages," was being played on the radio and we were in the top 40 in Europe. I hardly listened to the radio except for morning or evening news. Classmates and teachers were coming up to us at school, congratulating us. Adam and Peter were ecstatic. I hadn't heard it.

The guy who managed bands, Alvin Levine, a very outgoing guy, was actually from London. He came to hear us at Montreux, and was very flattering. "You guys are phenomenal! I can't believe you produced and mixed the tape yourselves. I assume you don't have representation, and I hope you'll work with me." Then, he looked at me and asked, "Dayal? Are you wearing eye makeup?"

"It's kohl, cultural. It protects you from the evil eye." I never thought about it. I just put it on in the morning.

"Cultural?"

"I'm Asian, Sikh. It's why I wear a turban."

"It makes your eyes look very dark and mysterious." The others laughed but agreed. I hadn't really thought about how I looked.

"You're happy with the name of your band?" he asked.

I looked at Adam.

"I had to pick something, so I called us '*The Pleasure Seekers*,'" Adam explained.

Oscar didn't care, but Peter agreed. Levine encouraged us to keep working and to write our own songs. I had a few ideas, but I also knew we could be a fleeting success. I had my studies and work, which was still doing back-up piano for people making demo tapes and recordings. In any case, a record album was made with the songs we had, and it did surprisingly well. I think we sold several hundred thousand copies globally. Levine entered us in another band contest, and we won. We each got a thousand dollars from it.

Over the summer in 1988, we joined a tour of Europe for about eight weeks. There were four other bands. We each, individually, got two hundred dollars a week. That was a fortune back then, especially considering this was on top of our travel expenses.

My studies were going well, but I wouldn't be able to see my parents until the end of the summer, and then for only two weeks. I told this to Levine, and he asked for my passport. "Oh,

I didn't realize you were that young. I thought you were in your early twenties like the others."

"I just got my diploma. My parents are in Tanzania, and I will have to send them a telegram that I will not be returning on time. There is no telephone access. Also, is there a way I can get a Commonwealth passport? It might make the visa situation easier in Europe."

"Good idea. I'll see what I can do. I'll take care of everything." He hesitated, then said to me, "You're going to be performing in public. You'll have to develop a persona. Do you know what I mean?"

I knew what the term meant, but what *did* he mean?

"You can't wear the turban. Do you have any casual clothes?"

"These are my casual clothes," I said. I was wearing a shalwar khameez.

Levine laughed and said, "You can't dress ethnic. Try to dress more like the others."

I guessed I could get by with t-shirts and button downs. I bought a couple of pairs of jersey work out pants.

That summer, in eight weeks, we visited forty cities in Europe. I found it almost overwhelming. We went between cities by coach. When Levine told us we'd travel by coach, I pictured, in my mind, Cinderella's pumpkin coach, so seeing that it was a tricked out bus was surprising.

The members of the other bands were partiers. There was lots of drinking, drugs, and girls. I was not a drinker, nor did I find most of the girls attractive or interesting. Some of them were very aggressive. Peter was in his element.

I wanted to visit museums, or take tours of the cities. When would I, again, have the chance to do this? Often the others teased me as "too young to party."

We made a lot of contacts with other musicians and entertainers. It was on this tour that I met Jimmy, who would become famous in America. We were back stage at a stadium, somewhere in the UK. Dublin? It was hard to keep track of where I was. The rest of the entourage was gathered around a long buffet table, stuffing their mouths, drinking, and joking around.

I sat on a folding chair, watching them, getting into my performance mindset, waiting to go on stage. This white dude sat down next to me and asked, "How's it going? You look very serious."

I turned to him and said, "All my life, I thought I spoke English, and I cannot understand what these people are saying, or what they keep laughing about."

Jimmy laughed and said, "I know! Right? Then, he mimicked one of them. "G'dy mblbrbl..."

I chuckled, nodding my head.

"They sound like they have marbles in their mouths. I keep asking people to please repeat! By the way, I'm Jimmy Paxon. What's your name?"

"Dayal Singh," I reached to shake Jimmy's hand.

"You've got gorgeous hair. It looks like it's never been cut."

"Thanks. It hasn't."

"Nice tan, too. Are you wearing eye make-up?"

"It's kohl, cultural, and this is my color," I replied.

"You look very cool. No wonder the girls go crazy."

"Huh?" I was oblivious if I wasn't interested.

"You don't hear them? They're not all over you? You're a really good looking guy."

I'm sure I blushed. "Am I? Thanks."

Jimmy laughed. "I'm just saying."

"You're from the states?" I asked.

"Yeah. Where are you guys from?"

"We've all come from Switzerland, but originally I'm from Tanzania."

"Tanzania? That's an actual country? I have no idea where that is."

I shook my head. "Africa, by the Indian Ocean."

"I have no idea where that is, either. What were you doing in Switzerland? Did you go for chocolate, or cheese?"

I chuckled. I may as well have been from Mars. "I was going to school. I *am* going to school!"

"How old are you?"

"I'll be nineteen in a few months."

"Really!"

"Why? How old are you," I asked him.

"Twenty eight. I did this tour because I play both trumpet and guitar, and this gig pays well, but I'm going to be part of an improv ensemble when I go back to the USA. How long have you been performing?"

"Not long at all. Not even a year. We won a radio contest. I'm studying engineering, and I work part time at a recording studio. My life this past year has been surreal," I explained to Jimmy.

We had a pleasant conversation. He told me he loved performing and asked if I was enjoying the tour. I said that except for the language barrier with people I was told were speaking English, and wondering where I was most of the time, I was enjoying the new experiences and seeing new places. I also appreciated the audience response to our music. We've stayed in touch almost 20 years now.

Amazingly, some of the guys in the other groups could barely play an instrument. It seemed they used a Synclavier, which was a synthesizer that created sound by recording and remixing. I was intrigued by it.

While we were on tour, we did a video for "Empty Pages" that I was told played on MTV. Peter did the vocals, but there was a lot of me in my white tux at the piano. When I brought it, the guys laughed at me, but when they saw the video, they told me I looked great.

I was able to see my parents at the end of August. There still were no stores that sold ice cream, but my parents made it because they now had a freezer, and they supplied Mr. Curtis. Baba was always coming up with something unique with local fruit, and he was making money.

I bought some furniture for my folks. I thought Ama was going to cry. It made me happy to finally be able to get her small luxuries. I also had my father show me how to make chapattis.

Back at school, I started to do some research on investing. Now that you can get information on the internet, it's much easier. Back then, if you didn't have at least a hundred thousand dollars, bankers wouldn't talk to you. Bankers certainly weren't talking to a teenager. I went over to the economics department at school and asked if anyone could help, and was told that when I had at least five thousand dollars, I could buy shares in a mutual fund. That was the start of me taking charge of my money.

I started teaching physics as well as calculus, but stopped teaching trig and stats. I can teach calculus in my sleep. For "relaxation," the weekends I didn't work in Montreux, I skied with Adam and skated with Yuki when it got cold enough if she wasn't going to Geneva, where her parents were. She cooked us okonomiyaki, which is sort of like a frittata, and tempura.

Because of the tour, we continued to get radio play, and we were in touch with several radio disk jockeys. We did covers of a few songs I learned to play off records the Glazers brought. There was a group in the 1960s called *The Cryan' Shames* that did a couple of pop songs that I loved: "I Wanna Meet You," and "Sugar and Spice." There was also a group called *The Amboy Dukes* that had a hit with "Journey to the Center of the Mind." For some reason, these groups in the American Midwest started out well, but they flamed out. Were they not promoted well? Did the guys mature to do other things?

We also did some *Beatles*, *Steve Winwood*, and *Neil Diamond* songs: The *Monkees* had a huge hit with "I'm a Believer." Our covers of the *Supertramp* songs, "Take the Long Way Home" and "Goodbye Stranger" charted. Peter's guitar on all was awesome.

I had my name on a couple of patents that year, which resulted in some future earnings. One was for a device that allowed an artist to add or cut sound distortion with a rheostat. Another patent I just did the calculus formula for.

I still had to be frugal. I looked at the course catalog one day while I was waiting for Dr. Schultz and discovered several of my courses counted as master's work. I asked him to switch me into an official graduate program. I told my brothers about this, but I did not tell my parents lest they think I was mature enough for marriage.

Peter bought a stereo system for the apartment, so we were listening to more music. Adam had gotten his degree and was going for a Ph.D. in ethnomusicology. He started teaching and arranging music, and brought home all sorts of music for us to listen to and get ideas.

Levine really liked "She's a Vixen." Both Adam and I had written the melody. It was about Mara enchanting me. Suddenly, "She's a Vixen" was a top-ten song in Europe, and quickly charted in America. As rock songs go, it was pretty good. A little corny, but if you listen to rock song lyrics, most hardly make enough sense to tell a story. I wrote to both Mara and Shayla. Weeks later, Mara wrote me a short letter saying how wonderful it was for me to have this success and she also asked how school was going. Shayla wrote back that she had a baby boy and she hardly got any sleep, and wished we could really visit.

The song was released in January 1990. Levine told us we were going on tour starting May first. We were going to open for *Iron Butterfly* in the Americas, and then come back to Europe. I would have to leave two weeks before the semester was over, and I had to tell Dr. Schultz.

"Singh, you seem to be veering off into music, but you have accomplished so much. The whole department is impressed with your work, particularly how quickly you write code. I'll do your last week of class and invigilate the exam. You'll be back in October, right?"

I had been too busy to miss my parents, but I had to write to them and tell them what was happening. I was making money, and I had to take advantage of the opportunities.

I emailed Sodhi that if he wanted me at the wedding, to plan it for August if he could. I wanted to see my brothers, meet their wives, and have us be together as a family. I also told him that starting at the end of April, if they were to email me, to email me in care of Levine. I had no idea where I would be. I also wrote to Shayla with this information, and told her I would write again when I got a schedule for where we would be in the United States. We would be a night in each city, traveling by a coach bus.

There were 20 of us, with crew. It was like being in a traveling dorm. There was no privacy at all, and I had never been with so many rowdy guys. The *Iron Butterfly* group and their roadies were always high, noisy, and fighting.

America is vast, and although the east coast is hilly and varied, once you get to the Midwest and on the interstate you don't see towns, just fields and flat scrub. The American savannah was calleds *prairie*. We stopped at a lot of truck stops on the highway. They called them restaurants, but the food was indigestible.

We met many trafficked people: runaways, and those brought by others without being told the truth of their situations. This surprised me. We were in America. Both Adam and Oscar spoke Spanish, and they talked to servers, people who worked at petrol stations, and prostitutes. Women were brought by a husband, or a "friend of a friend," from Central America, India, China, and other places. America was not what they expected, but most were either sure there was no way back, or going back was not worth the bother.

Adam and I learned a lot. I wondered if our crew realized this, or even cared. Because of my parents, I started thinking about if these people could be helped.

I had told Levine that I wanted to get some comp tickets for my family, as I considered the Glazer girls to be family. Something got lost in translation with the tour manager. How would the girls be able to get past security without the tickets and security passes? I had been away from family for so long, and as much as I liked my friends, they were not family. I called Shayla and told her there was this glitch, and to buy a ticket and I would reimburse her, and I would personally tell security that I was looking for her in Chicago.

It didn't work out. The face value of tickets wasn't the price. All our shows were sold out and tickets were going for triple face value! It might have been for the best because there was a lot of commotion and fighting in Chicago and several other venues. Police had to be called and several concert-goers were arrested for fighting and drugs. It was in the papers and on local TV news. I was horrified by this, but the rest of the guys thought this was funny. They felt it wasn't a party if there wasn't a brawl, cocaine, and groupies. In spite of the ruckus, our reviews were good.

I had brought some small balls with me to juggle and to alleviate stress. Our crew seemed fascinated, and I taught a few of them how to juggle. "In Africa, all the kids can juggle," I told them. I was showing them and one of the crew guys said, "You're quite the mover!" He winked at me. The others started laughing. I asked Adam what was so funny.

"You do this thing with your hips that's very erotic. I'll get the video people to film you, but you should do it during our solos."

The movement was called "popping." I juggled during Oscar's drum solo, and they were right. The screams! I know there are videos of me, but now there are videos from most of our concerts online. I've looked at them with my children and think now that I was a cute guy.

The crew asked a lot of questions about Africa. Again, so many people knew nothing at all. To most of them, I came from an unknown planet. I kept hearing, "Your English is very good." I told them we speak English in Africa, as well as many other languages. It was as Mara told me: people thought we lived in the jungle, or in trees.

It was a long haul in close quarters. Shayla had given me Mara's phone number, but nobody ever answered. I left messages on her answering machine, but I didn't have a phone for her to call. This was so frustrating. Here I was in America, so close but so far. I tried calling Yuki a couple of times, but the connection was so bad we could hardly understand each other. I sent her postcards.

When we finally got to the West Coast of the United States, we were interviewed by a journalist who wrote for *Rolling Stone.* He wanted to know our thoughts on current music, the tour, and our future plans. "She's a Vixen" was still on the charts. By that time, I was the only musician in the group who could put a lucid sentence together. We had a pleasant chat, but I told him, "We're in school in Switzerland, except Oscar. Being on the road, rehearsing, playing and singing constantly is exhausting. I am not the partier the other guys are. It's a difficult lifestyle for me to adapt to. This is my first visit to the United States. I've seen little except stadiums and the interstate."

In South America, we got everywhere by plane. I telexed Levine and told him to make my ongoing ticket to Singapore, and I would make my way back to Switzerland. That was complicated, too. British Air was the only airline at the time to go from Rio to Singapore, via Guam. ✪

# CHAPTER 6

The tour exhausted me. I had a little over a week with my family in Singapore. My brothers started joking about me being next. Meaning: to get married.

We brothers were able to get together for one breakfast, just ourselves, and I asked them both how they decided to marry, and if there were any marriage contracts. Both my brothers told me that they felt they had a lot in common with their partners, not just religion, although neither was particularly religious. They both wanted to have two kids if that was possible, and they had expectations for middle class lives. They knew they would never live in Africa again.

Both of their wives were college graduates and planned to continue working in their fields. That was very common in Malaysia for educated women. It's also common for Sikh women.

The wedding was a nice affair. There were probably about seventy people. I assumed that they were mostly either friends or family of Anu's and maybe Sodhi's work colleagues, and friends from the gurdwara. Everyone's welcome at a wedding. If you've never been to a Sikh wedding, many are up to a week long. All these rituals are supposed to get the community involved. You can read about them on the internet now.

The morning of the wedding, Anu's female relatives and friends fetched Sodhi to give him the Kirpan, a ceremonial sword (borrowed), and put kohl on his eyes. With a red ribbon, they guided him to the gurdwara which was a short walk. As they got closer, his friends joined them. One was his best man. They used the red ribbon to keep him from going in to the gurdwara, which he was supposed to cut. The women told him to put money in a jar filled with water. This was a symbolic bride price. Nobody knows how that started, and I think he used Tz. shillings, but one of his friends shouted, "Can he put in a check?" Lots of laughter, because there is no specific amount of money, but finally they gave him the scissors to cut the ribbon.

An Amrit (we don't really have priests—just people who've taken Amrit—sort of like a Bar Mitzvah) started the Milni, because of course, neither family really knew the other, so he made introductions and there was more sharing of flower garlands. More rituals, but the most important one was my parents going to Anu's parents' home, to really get to know one another and for Sodhi to assure them that he'd take care of Anu.

My father's friend, Dhillon, who had also been trafficked, arranged the introductions at the wedding. He had become a gem dealer in South Africa, and did very well. We saw each other at the same time.

"Sat sri akaal Dayal! Waheguru ji Ka Khalsa, Waheguru ji Ki Fateh! I haven't seen you on such a long time. You're in university now?" Dhillon said as he did a wai bow.

"Sat sri akaal! Waheguru ji Ka Khalsa, Waheguru ji Ki Fateh! Yes, Baba, in Switzerland. I'm studying engineering. I don't know if my parents told you, but I am in a music group. In fact, I flew here from South America."

"Is it?" Dhillon responded.

"Yes Baba. I am happy to see you, and I need your assistance. I want to marry a woman who lives in the United States. Her father had been Baba's business partner. I believe you've met him. I need you to ask my parents for me."

Dhillon laughed and said, "If she's American, you just ask her to marry and that will be that. Either she will or she won't."

"It's not that simple," I replied anxiously. "There is no way I can marry without my parents' blessing. I need you to intercede. Can you do that for me?" Not only was it a matter of respect, but it was because we were all so geographically far apart, I didn't want more distance of any kind between us, even if it was just emotional.

Dhillon laughed again. "I will do this for you," he said, "but you must know they will want a Sikh girl for you. She's not Sikh, is she?"

"She's a Jew, she's divorced, and she's older than I am. But I want them to know she is my choice. I have loved her for many years."

"You think you love her."

"No," I said. "I *know* I love her."

They were in the hotel suite and I was waiting outside in the hall, and I heard my mother gasp. Then my father said, very sternly, in English, "If he is ready to marry, we will find him a Sikh girl. Tell him that."

I had not even thought of the possibility that they would reject the idea with no discussion. I was so hurt and shocked, I actually felt it in my heart. I could not go against my parents. I was deflated for the few extra days I was with them.

I would be turning twenty in a month. I plunged right back into engineering upon my return to Switzerland. All that travel, being in the United States with a bunch of immature idiots and not seeing Mara had really frustrated me. I felt I was treading water. Was it depression? Exhaustion? I didn't think of counseling. The concept was foreign to me. I remember what Mara had said about my mental health, and continued reading a few pages of the Adi Granth before bed, as meditation. Yuki was a comfort. I cherished our physical closeness and her pragmatism.

I emailed Avi, expressing my frustration and disappointment at our parents' attitude. He just ignored my complaining. I wrote to my parents and told them I had been in love with Mara since I was fourteen, and she had made it very clear she would not even address a relationship until I was out of school.

My father wrote back:

*Dayal, my son, I love you so much, but I beg you to get your mind off Mara. Do you know she lives with dogs, and sleeps with them in her house? Also, she's much older than you are. Don't you want children? We will start looking for a proper wife for you.*

*Love, Baba*

I hadn't thought about having children except to avoid having them. I was just a child myself! I started wondering if anyone is ever actually prepared to have children, but I also thought that if you love a woman, and you want to share your life with her, does it matter? Should it matter? For me, it didn't.

My parents could not articulate why my being with a Sikh woman was so important to them. I wondered, later, neither of them having families, if they both thought it was a mark of social acceptance.

I tried not to dwell on this and concentrated on the projects that got interrupted when we started touring. Months earlier, I had started working on a new piece of sound equipment that a professor had conceived. I was having fun with it as I had now made a prototype. Nobody else had the patience to code the software, and that was what took a lot of time. If you've ever written code, you know that sometimes there are mistakes, and it takes patience and attention to detail to "de-bug." This thing allowed us to control sound distortion. It had a microphone that played into a computer that then "released" the sound, into either a tape or amplifier. It was like a Synclavier, but made for voice. It could manipulate audio signals to make a tone distorted, or fix distortion. To understand how much coding I had to do, there are one hundred milliseconds in one second. So, the orchestral tuning note, A 440, is the musical note that vibrates at 440 cycles per second (which is the same as 440 Hz). This device did not calculate musical pitch by milliseconds but rather by samples. It used 48,000 samples per second instead of 1,000 millisamples per second. We sang into a microphone, but before it went to a tape or disc, by manipulating it via the computer software, we could make the tone seem higher, lower, echolike, or even correct the note.

A fellow student studying to be a voice coach worked with me to develop my breathing, vocal control and range. I had to sing or we didn't have enough voices when we performed. In exchange, I allowed him to play around with this device and re-cord when I recorded myself.

I didn't consider myself to be a singer. Peter was our lead singer. Adam and I would do back up and harmonies. Rarely did Oscar sing, but he vocalized in bass. By using this new device, I felt that we could get the sounds I wanted without making a zillion overdubs. It helped to create multi-track melodies and harmonies without our having to hire or train other musicians. Later, I realized it was a forerunner of *auto tune*, which would correct an off-key singer. A guy named Andy Hildebrand per-fected it twenty years later. Now, there are apps you can get for cell phones that do this. I had to make it so any nontechnical person could use it.

I recorded several songs on my own, including *Sly and the Family Stone's* "Hot Fun in the Summertime," and songs with solo singers where you could easily hear the difference when we used this device. I brought the prototype to the recording studio so the engineers could play around with it. Dr. Schultz wanted comments, so we could adjust it and then patent it.

Levine wanted to keep our momentum going, so he asked for more songs. By this time it was November. The guys had some interesting ideas, but all were half baked. In order to not lose them we recorded what we had, and I sent Levine a copy of the tape, forgetting I had my test vocals on it.

He called as soon as he got it and asked who was singing. I didn't know what he was talking about, thinking it was all of us, of course. Then he asked, "Well, who sang '*Hot Fun*'? The vocals are beautiful."

I started to laugh, and explained, "That was me, but through a sort of synthesizer. It was an experiment. I need the tape back, actually. We can't really use it."

"Why not?" he asked.

"Well, because, really, nobody sounds like that. It can't be replicated on stage live, at least at this time. I wish I sounded that good!" I was a purist and didn't think we should record anything we couldn't perform onstage. The rock band, Queen had the same policy.

"I want you to re-record those songs, with piano, as you sound. If you want, add bass and drums, but do them as separate tracks for now, and send them to me, and the Elvis Presley song "A Little Less Conversation." Do you know it? You're a better singer than you think."

That was flattering, but I didn't believe him. I felt my voice was hollow. I didn't like listening to myself. Peter and Adam had an issue with the song choices.

"Look, you guys," I said, "This was an exercise. Let's redo what was on the original tape and send it to Levine. I don't really care who sings. I have plenty to do. I don't want to argue. If you're not on board, I'll just send Levine a tape of me singing solo accompanying myself. You guys don't understand that we're in the music business, not just goofing around in a rock band."

Considering I had to continually remind them of this—particularly Peter—I wondered how long we'd last. I liked Oscar as a drummer, but none of us really knew him at all. He played with a lot of bands. He'd commit to touring with us, as well as recording, but otherwise he was on his own. He was the first non-engineer I knew to have an email address and cell phone. He was serious about being a musician. He listened to a lot of music and practiced. There was no question with Adam. He took advantage of every opportunity to learn music, new instruments, and improve his playing. What he did with the bassoon was intriguing, and we both wanted to try to incorporate it more into our sound.

We finally had a discussion about this. I said to Peter, "Do you have a plan to graduate, or just keep playing music? Is there a particular style of music you like?"

"I'm leaning towards American blues, but whatever you guys decide is fine. I'm having fun," he responded.

I liked a lot of classical music, and Jazz, but we were a rock band, or were we? We charted in top 40, and contemporary adult.

That led to a discussion about our adult futures, getting married and having kids. They hadn't thought about it. Peter said, when I questioned him, "I'll know when the time is right." I thought, *"What a luxury to go through life and let it just happen and not plan for a future."*

One day, after getting back from working on the auto-tune device in the lab, I found all three guys in the apartment with champagne and joints, partying. I wanted to just decompress for a few minutes, but they all started talking at once: "Did you hear it? "A Little Less Conversation" is on the charts! It's being played!" Adam yelled.

My gut reaction was, *"Fantastic! But now what? Do we have to start touring again?"*

That song shot to number one in Europe and less than a week later it was top 10 in America. I sent letters to both Shayla and Mara. It took at least a week for my letters to get to them, and a week or so for their responses. They both had heard it! ✪

# CHAPTER 7

I used to check the Prodigy account once a week, on Saturdays, but I had to get with Levine. I would have called, but I felt it was too expensive and the phone connection was often poor. In any case, I emailed him and asked him what was happening, and he emailed back telling me I had to check the Prodigy account every week. Our song was hot: "Billboard with a bullet." It stayed in the top ten for over a month.

"I dread going on tour again," I emailed. I had to acclimate myself to a new place every day.

"Until you guys have a ten or twelve song album, you can't tour. You have to get it together. We have to start planning now for spring or at least summer as headliners. I'm getting a lot of queries, especially from America," Levine responded.

I was in a quandary. I made a list of issues we guys had discussed and emailed Levine. The logistics of getting around bothered me the most. I didn't want to go by coach, but could we afford to fly between cities? What were the possibilities of renting a Steinway in every city? Did it make more sense to use Yamaha keyboards and bring a Synclavier? I also wanted to learn how he costed out everything, and who decides what royalties we got.

"No issues. Check your bank account in a few days. I'll teach you as I learn. We don't make money on touring. We make it on sales we generate," Levine responded.

I was after the guys to come up with six more songs. I decided to work on a Swahili song, "Malaika." It was written by

Adam Salim in 1945, and it was timeless. The problem was that even though the tune was beautiful, the words were in Swahili. It could be on the album, but I wondered if it could be released as a single because nobody would understand the words except in my small corner of Africa—where people didn't have radios or phonographs. I had to translate it into English.

I was happy with what we were doing. Then, Yuki told me she was leaving. Her father's assignment was up, and next year she would go to college, if not in Japan, in Singapore. I felt ambivalent about her leaving, but I had known we'd not last forever. I found I was more attached to Yuki than I thought. I just busied myself with music, school, and working with Adam on arrangements and production.

Adam did almost all the song arrangements. Peter and Oscar just showed up when we told them to, and we'd rehearse and then record. Then I'd work with the engineers to start mixing. After I was happy, I'd call the guys back to approve what I had done. I asked Levine for production credits.

When I checked my bank account the next month, I found I had thousands more than I expected. This made me feel like it was worth the effort to record. This wasn't a game. We were doing well also because Levine was licensing our songs for advertising use globally.

As Mara had told me to do, I started looking at real estate ads in the paper. I didn't think I wanted to stay in Switzerland permanently, but I thought it would be a good idea to build equity. Yet, this money I had was from being an entertainer. I wondered if I could do as well as a professor or as an inventor.

By this time it was January. My bandmates had gone home for Christmas. I was used to not going back to Africa, and I was afraid my parents would bring up the subject of marriage. I skied, spent time in Montreux for extra cash, and a couple days on my own in Nice and Monaco, playing the table games at several casinos.

I collaborated with Levine, via email, on the show production. I didn't think we could do anything nearly as elaborate as what other big groups did, but I could synchronize lights to music. I asked Levine how he chose cities for a tour.

"It's by your fan base. Here's how it works: ASCAP, when getting royalties from airplay on radio stations (this was how it used to be done: the radio stations would send a list of songs they played once a month to ASCAP, and we'd get like a penny per airplay), and record sales from stores tell us the potential of how much audience we'd get at live shows. We have nothing else to go on. After I cost what the venue is to rent, plus our transportation costs and insurance, we also ask for sponsorship from radio stations. I don't think anyone but solo performers make any money touring. Our profit is from selling records, which comes from touring and from the merchandise: t-shirts, stickers, and those balls you juggle."

We were set to start touring in May, first in Europe, then in the United States, Canada, three cities in South America, Asia, and the east coast of Australia. It was an eighty-day tour. We only flew between continents. We had to go by coach, and the crew took a huge truck.

Our venues were usually sports stadiums that held about 30,000 people. I started thinking about the mathematics of this, and how much we were making per seat after expenses: Not much. The irony, to me, was that we needed large venues to be profitable, but sound distortion was a big problem. People weren't hearing us at our best.

I wrote to both Mara and Shayla about the tour date in Chicago, and told them to be in touch with Levine for passes. I was in Copenhagen when I got a message from Shayla. She was excited to be able to see me, but said Mara was out of the country.

Everyone else on the tour again was having a blast. Adam and I worked on playlists and arrangements together. The in-ear monitors really helped us communicate onstage, because there was always so much noise. The acoustics were terrible. I don't think most audiences realized that we often couldn't hear each other on stage.

We addressed the audience between songs, and both Peter and Adam decided to always introduce me as "the perpetually sun-tanned Dayal Singh." We couldn't see the audience unless we moved the lights around.

We had to do promo spots with local radio stations as we traveled. We were supposed to go as a group, but it was like herding cats. I'm sure it made for great radio, but I was ready to throttle Peter any day of the week. He seemed to be stoned eighty percent of his waking hours.

Security was a big hassle, but since I kept reminding them to look for her, I got to see Shayla in Chicago. I introduced her to the guys, but they were in party mode, so I took her back to the hotel with me. Being able to laugh with her and pour out my feelings helped me so much. She brought me up to date on her family. Her son was starting to talk. Anya was in high school. Where was Mara?

"Mara's in West Africa, Ghana, I think. She's taking overseas consulting assignments as they come, because she doesn't want a real job," Shayla explained.

"I'm still in love with her, but my parents are opposed."

Shayla smiled and said, "Zed," and we both started giggling.

"So, how's being married?" I asked her. "Is the sex what you hoped it would be?"

"Well, it was, but now I have a kid, and I can barely keep my eyes open. This is the latest I've stayed up in months."

"I'd do you just because you're a good friend, and always have been. You two have been an anchor to me." I reached across the table and kissed her, and she kissed me back. We just looked at each other for a few seconds. Then, she said, "If you have rubbers, let's do it. It's not like you're some random guy. We really do care about each other. It's just that I can't stay. I have to get back, and my drive is over thirty miles." No mention of a husband. It was the first time I had had intercourse in about two years. Yuki and I had always done oral.

Shayla was still such a comfort. I put my face into her cleavage and I felt calm immediately. I was feeling her heat, and I was in ecstasy. We were both laughing and I had to keep pulling out because of her vibrating with laughter. What was more important than anything was that I was with someone I cared deeply about. After Shayla left, I had the best sleep I had had in several years. The afterglow lasted several days.

The videographers were pretty discreet, but one of them said to me, "Dayal, flirt with the camera." The *persona*. I was concentrating on playing the piano and singing at the same time. A cameraman cued me to look up, and I smiled and winked. When everyone saw that, if I winked, from then on, it made it into every video. They also taped me juggling. My hair would come loose and be flying. They ended up producing several music videos which played on MTV. We were bona fide rock stars. I had never seen so many photos of me.

In concert I explained more about the songs, particularly about "Malaika" being a Swahili song. I got more comfortable being more conversational.

We developed a routine. More crew guys started running with me in the morning, but they had to set us up in every city, so they didn't go exploring with me. I always wore a turban and shalwar khameez when I went out, and I noticed that people stared, but didn't think about it until I was in a museum, standing in front of a painting, and I heard a child behind me say, "Mommy, is that man a terrorist?" I heard the woman gasp. I reflexively turned around, and they stepped back. I smiled at them, but only the woman returned the smile and I could tell she was nervous. I moved on.

Again, I learned, from talking to the hospitality staff at hotels, that so many people working in the USA in these positions were trafficked. Many had children in their home countries. One told me and Adam she left her husband because of excessive drinking. Many had been terrorized by police and gangs, particularly from El Salvador, and their governments did nothing. So many women told us they had faith. They were going to pray for salvation in their next lives. I realized that fatalism among less educate people was universal. They had nobody to turn to, except the people they worked with.

We did the dates in Canada, flew to Brasilia, Buenos Aires, Santiago, up to Seoul, then Hong Kong, Tokyo, and on to Kuala Lumpur where I got to see my brothers and their families. We did shows Australia. then I flew to Arusha and saw my parents and friends for about a week before heading back to Switzerland. Nobody broached the subject of getting married. I was tense any time my father and I were alone, except when we were making chapattis together. I felt bad about this, but the whole marriage thing was the elephant in the room, to use an expression.

I saw that they were building a road north of town. Baba said it was supposed to surround Arusha. My primary school, which had been about a half mile out of town (a kilometer or so) was now in town! The market was also being moved.

I was now 21. School was one music class a semester, teaching and coding. I started every calculus class this way: after we played a video game for a few minutes and then opened the code, I told the class, "This class will take a lot of your brain power. If you aren't comfortable with trigonometry, statistics, geometry, and physics, I urge you to reconsider whether you want to take this class. You will be inventors, so you have to have a project in mind. The endorphins you will get from the physical feeling of accomplishment will be similar to how you feel after having sex."

It was always guys, and there was always nervous laughter. I just wanted to weed out pretenders.

Levine emailed and showed, on a spreadsheet, month to month, record sales and royalties from licensing, radio play and videos. Clearly, revenues were up when we toured. We were making a lot of money from videos and selling merchandise.

I wondered if there was some way we could live stream our concerts to smaller cities, like sports promoters did. Levine said he'd look into it. When Peter, Oscar and Adam were back in Switzerland, we recorded the newer, English version of "Malaika." It charted immediately in both Europe and the Americas. Levine started planning a tour starting in May that would go through August. Milwaukee was the closest we'd get to Chicago. Levine said he wanted us to have a break from some cities so we wouldn't be overexposed, but our concert would be shown live in the cities we didn't get to.

I called Shayla when I got to the USA, and she came and spent the night with me in Milwaukee. Making love with her was always very satisfying, because we knew each other and could take our time. She told me she was separated from her husband, and Mara was, again, somewhere in Africa.

One day, Levine joined us in Kansas City. He handed me an envelope from my father. It was not an aerogram. For my father to get an envelope, I knew it had to be important. It was about *this girl*. She had just graduated from high school in Mumbai, but was living with her family in Dubai. He explained that her father had been on safari, and while Baba was talking to Mr. Curtis at the hotel he saw this guy in a turban having coffee. So, of course he went over and introduced himself and they started talking. He included the girl's address and asked me to contact her. He also asked me to send him and Ama postcards from where I was.

Talk about being overwhelmed. This situation would change my life forever. I had to sort out my feelings. I still loved Mara. Or, did I just love the memories? She had not encouraged any devotion. I had to admit that to myself. In fact, she had discouraged me. She was mature. She knew the truth of my situation. There was no sense delaying. I was of two minds. I felt anxious, but I was ready for a partner.

The girl's name was Sita. I started by drafting a letter, which I wrote by hand. It took me several drafts, but I decided to write this:

*Dear Sita,*

*We don't know each other. I am 21. Not nearly old enough to be married, I don't think, but I want a partner, a wife. I think we need to learn about each other as this is what our parents want. I am studying engineering in Switzerland, and my studies will take a couple of more years at least. However, I am writing you from the United States of America. I am also a musician and I have paid for my expenses, as well as many of my parents' expenses, by being a musician. My parents are not wealthy. You probably know they live in Tanzania.*

*I have a scholarship to university and teach, but I also earn money by playing piano. I am touring with a musical group called "The Pleasure Seekers" and we will be on tour for another couple of months in the Western Hemisphere, then on to Asia.*

*I don't know what to tell you. I am a very simple guy. I study, I go to work, and I exercise. I do not smoke or drink. I learned to ski on snow. It's cold where I live for most of the year. I am not religious at all, but very much culturally Sikh. I sometimes find it difficult dealing with Christians, but that is the world we live in.*

*Were you told I live in Switzerland? Have you ever been to Europe? Part of my job involves travel. How do you feel about that?*

*Please write me back and send me a photo of yourself and tell me about you. I am interested in getting to know you. Send your response in care of my manage, Mr. Levine, in London, or I won't receive it for months. I will try to send you a photo of myself.*

*Sincerely, Dayal Singh*

I included Levine's business card in the envelope. I did not say anything to my bandmates about this because really there was nothing to say. I was writing to a stranger and it would be too complicated to explain.

Levine stayed with us for about two weeks. He had break-fast with me every day, as the others were sleeping in because they partied so much after shows. We talked about a lot of things. "I'm getting a lot of inquiries about the group's future plans, and there's interest in a film from what the videogra-phers have. They'll be with us until the end of the tour," he told me one morning over a typical diner breakfast of toast, eggs, and coffee.

I nodded.

"You're looking even more serious than usual. Are you ok?" he asked.

"That letter from my father you gave me a few days ago? He wants me to meet a potential wife in Dubai."

Levine smiled and stopped eating. "I thought you had a girlfriend."

"I did, a girl I was seeing, but she returned to Asia. I was in love with an American, but she was older and she knew my par-ents would do this, so she discouraged me."

"How much older?" Levine asked.

I hesitated. "Eight years."

He started laughing. "How did you meet an American girl eight years older and find yourself in love?"

I was not laughing. To me, this was not funny. I told him about my father being bought by Mara's grandfather, how I al-ways knew her and how she influenced me. How she told me she wouldn't have me and I had to stay in school.

"Her sister, Shayla, was with me when we were in Chica-go and Milwaukee. That's the story. I made it worse because I asked my father to allow me to marry her now, and he said if I was ready to marry, to marry this young woman I haven't met yet. It's at least a year off. My parents will continue to make it an issue. I love my parents. They've done their best for us. I trust them. I can't go against them."

Levine was looking at me with a bemused expression on his face. He finally said, "That's very interesting. Mara sounds like she really cares about you. I'm a Jew, too."

"Is it?" I responded. "Are you married?"

"For about seven years. She was the daughter of a family friend. I always liked her, or at least I didn't *not* like her. It's a good marriage. We have two daughters. We got reacquainted at a Hanukkah party."

"What's that?" I asked.

"It's a celebration of Jews winning a war in ancient times. We celebrate in winter, around Christmas."

"Really? I'm sorry I never thought to ask about your family. Our big holiday is Prisoner's Release Day, which is sort of Sikh New Year. The Sikh community, unless two young people find each other, the parents move to arrange things. You know, I never meet other Sikhi. Were it not for my feelings for Mara, I would not balk at all. My father picked my mother off the dock at Dar es Salaam. Just on her looks alone. She had nobody, neither had my father. I know my father would have waited had I not had a friend intercede on my behalf. It was stupid of me. My father knew I wanted Mara because he knew I had seduced her. I think he was hoping I'd forget about her."

"Well, maybe you'll like this girl. Maybe she'll be suitable. Is that why you don't party with the others after the shows?"

I rolled my eyes. "NO. I don't party because being on the road is stressful. Also, I never liked the idea of casual sex. I want a permanent partner, a lover who knows me and understands me. In a way, Mara spoiled me. She demonstrated to me that you get better sex if you know and trust your partner. That's what I want. How many times do the guys get up with head-aches and say they don't remember the night before? What's the point of that?"

Levine burst out laughing.

"You find that funny?" I asked.

"No. Ironic. I do want to address something as long as we're being honest. You're a vibrant, sexy young man. No chance of you shaving, is there?"

"Oh, no. I can trim my beard if you think it's too straggly. It's always a big issue in our community if anyone cuts their hair."

"Some of the Orthodox Jews are like that, too."

"Is it? Well, somewhere along the line God must have said something very profound about hair."

I was glad Levine had taken the time to talk with me, because I felt I was losing the emotional ties I had with my bandmates.

When we were ready to leave for Asia a few weeks later, Levine joined us again, and he had a letter for me from Dubai, from Sita.

I could feel my heart racing. I carefully opened the enve-lope and unfolded a two-page letter. A photo fell out. It was a snapshot of three girls in school uniforms. On the back it said, "Mindi, Sita, Nikki October 1986."

I assumed they were sisters. They were pretty girls, but you couldn't tell anything about their bodies in those uniforms.

The letter read:

*Dear Dayal,*

*Thank you for your letter. I have just graduated secondary school and I am taking a certificate course in child care. I live in Dubai with my mum. We like it here because it is very quiet, clean, and there aren't any beggars.*

*My father told me he met your father in Africa. He was on safari with his second wife. He and my mother are not divorced, but they are not together, either.*

*I, too, feel I am too young to marry, but I am not extending my education, either. The girls in the photo are my sisters with this mother. My father has two boys with his second wife.*

*I learned English in school, but I mostly speak Hindi. I don't know if you know, but my father produces Bollywood movies. I was interested in being in the movies, but my father does not want his daughters performing.*

*I do not play any musical instruments, but we do have a stereo and we listen to music. Mostly I watch television and read magazines. We also go shopping, and we go to the beach, or movies. There is a lot to do in Dubai.*

*I think I would like to travel. I have never been anywhere but Dubai and Mumbai.*

*When can you come to visit so we can meet each other face to face?*

*Fondly,*

*Sita*

I didn't really know what to make of her. I had to think what to write her in return, and get a photo of myself as I really looked. The videographers had many photos of me. I hadn't even thought to ask, but when I did, they showed me dozens of me singing, juggling, and playing the piano. I told them to pick one for me that I could send to a girl, and the woman cameraperson, Alicia, asked, "Oh, like to send an autograph?"

I shook my head. "Not exactly. Actually, give me a few. My parents really don't have many photos of me." They had hardly any photos of us except for passport photos. I wondered if they'd be upset seeing photos of me with my hair loose, but this was how it was.

I had Levine mail these to my parents, and I sent them a brief letter, telling them I was in touch with Sita, and she had asked for a photo. I realized they didn't have any photos of me, and there were lots of me and my band.

I then composed another letter to Sita:

*Dear Sita,*

*Thank you for your nice letter and the photo. I am enclosing in this letter a couple of photos of me performing. We have records that I bet you can get in Dubai.*

*I am very busy. I sometimes watch television in the hotel room, but mostly, when I am not exercising or performing, I try to go to museums and galleries and see the cities I'm in. I was able to go to the beach in Malindi on the Indian Ocean with a friend several years ago, but I rarely have time to just sit and do nothing. With my fellow bandmates we sometimes play Scrabble. Do you know the game?*

*Our performance tour ends at the beginning of August, and I can probably arrange to come see you from Kuala Lumpur before I go back to Africa, then on to Switzerland. How does that sound? Can you send me a photo of yourself in everyday clothes? Do you have internet access? Can you cook? Do you think you'd mind living in Switzerland for the next several years?*

*I look forward to your reply.*

*Fondly,*

*Dayal*

Trying to be optimistic, I was hoping that when we met in person there would be an immediate physical attraction that would overcome all my doubts.

Peter developed a sore throat and a cold. I took on singing on some of his songs for the next several shows. Our margin was so small, and people paid a lot of money for tickets and wanted to hear us at our best. Our audience might think we were having a good time, but our job was performing, and making it look effortless, like we just got together to do this with friends. Whatever it was Peter had could spread through us all. We also needed every last warm crew person. As it was, with five guys with us, the odds of something happening were high.

We got through South America again, then went on to Asia. It was great to see my brothers and their wives. They came to the show in KL, and everyone got to meet everyone. My mates and crew said how much alike we looked and acted. Both my brothers were happy in their marriages. My sisters-in-law were funny, outgoing women. I stayed with Avi and Siri for several days and had a set of shalwar khameez made of silk. I took them out to dinner, but we mostly stayed in due to the heat.

Sita's father had internet access, so I emailed him that I would be arriving in Dubai on the second Monday in August. We'd have a break because European dates picked up at the beginning of September. I was getting anxious about meeting Sita, and I planned to spend five days in Dubai. ✪

# CHAPTER 8

ubai now, is actually a city, but back in the early 1990s there wasn't much to it. The airport was at least ten miles away from the town, in the desert, miles and miles of sand. Sita's father had instructed me to take a taxi to their apartment and they would find me accommodations. The flight had been over twelve hours. I had dozed but had not really slept. It was probably about 2:00 in the afternoon by the time I got to their building.

What you noticed as you drive in is that, except for potted plants here and there, there is no greenery. It's all sand and concrete, even in town. In the middle of what seemed to be nowhere, there were two 30 story buildings. I noticed about half a mile off there seemed to be construction going on, but again, all was sand.

There was a doorman and a security person, who called up to their apartment to announce my arrival. He told me which elevator to take and said my bag would be brought up. It was, again, like being on another planet.

I was so tired, but wired with anticipation. There were two apartments per floor, but a maid in a uniform had one door open.

I noticed, looking out the wall of windows after I had entered the apartment and been brought into the sitting room, we were very high up. The twentieth floor? Thirtieth? I was not sure. I could just see sky through windows from the front door. The place looked right out of a magazine, perfectly decorated. The maid whispered for me to follow her, and she had me sit on a sofa and wait. The whole room was white and cream, with pink accents. Pink pillows on the sofa and a faux painted ribbon border on the wall across from the window. The tables were glass, and the lamps were crystal. I was looking around, taking it all in. In a few minutes I heard footsteps and an older woman, very pretty, came into the room and reached for my hand to shake it. I stood up, of course.

"Salaam, sat sri akal Dayal, so nice to finally meet you. I am Fatima, Sita's mum. She's not here right now. She went to get her hair done. Please sit."

Fatima sat in a chair across from me and said, "Would you like something to drink? You look exhausted."

Before I could say anything, she picked up a bell and rang it, and the maid came back. She said to the maid, "Please bring us two Cokes with ice, Maria." Turning her attention to me, she said, "Is that OK? Would you like something stiffer?"

I shook my head and said, "Oh, no. A Coke will be fine."

"We bought your record a few weeks ago. You have a lovely voice, very enchanting."

I smiled. "Thank you." I didn't know what else to say. Maria brought us the Cokes.

Fatima was staring at me. "You're really very handsome. You could be Hrithik Roshan's brother. Have you seen him? The Bollywood actor? You have the longest eyelashes I've ever seen on a man. Is that kohl you have around your eyes?"

I'm sure I blushed. "Thank you. Yes, kohl."

Fatima nodded. "Sita is very nervous, as you can imagine. She feels she is too young to get married. I didn't marry her father until I was 22, but I was in college. Sita has expressed no interest in going to college. She wants to dance in her father's movies. She's a bit of a social butterfly. She likes to be with her friends."

"She told me she likes to read magazines and watch TV. Does she have any other interests?" I asked.

Fatima hesitated, then said, "Does shopping count? All these girls are waiting to get married. They go shopping, they get their hair done, go out for lunch. Perhaps at some point she'll develop charitable interests, as I have, and maybe join a book club."

We sat in silence for a few minutes and then I heard the front door open and Sita called for the maid, "Maria, can you help me with these parcels?"

Fatima got up and went to her, and started speaking to her in Hindi. I stood up to greet her, smiling nervously. She came around the corner and I could see she was very pretty. She was shorter than me, maybe 5'4", and had a lovely figure. She was wearing a T-shirt with embellishments and embellished jeans, very tight. She had sandals on her feet. Her toenails, I noticed, were polished like her fingernails: a metallic pink. She also had large dark eyes, a great deal of makeup on, and her hair was put up with some fancy clips. Her eyes met mine and she smiled and came to shake my hand.

"This is so exciting! I am so happy you're here. How was your flight?" she asked.

She sat down next to me and maintained eye contact, a good thing.

"I am happy to meet you, too. The flight was very long, as you can imagine. I've actually been traveling for weeks, as I believe I wrote to you."

"We have your record. Did Mum tell you?" Sita asked.

"Don't you think he looks like Hrithik Roshan?" Fatima asked her.

Sita blushed, looked down, and responded, smiling, "He does, doesn't he?"

I had no idea who they were talking about. I had seen some Bollywood movies, but I found them contrived. "So, what do you have planned for the next several days so we can get to know each other better?" I asked.

They both looked at each other. I was looking back and forth at both of them. I don't know what I had expected. Finally, Fatima said, "We'll get you situated in our 'guest suite.' I thought you might want to rest after such a long flight. We'll go out to dinner around eight."

"Will Mr. Makkar be joining us?" I asked.

Sita laughed and Fatima said, "No. He's with his other family. It will be just us. Sita, take Dayal to the guest suite."

Sita walked me down a long marbled hall that had Persian rug runners on the floor. We passed several open doors. The apartment seemed huge. When we finally got to the "guest suite," I looked around. It was a nice-sized room, the walls were dark blue, there were dark velvet drapes on the windows, and a double bed with a blue velvet cover on it. I could see there was a bathroom attached, nicely tiled with a deep tub, and I couldn't wait to get into it.

I turned to Sita and said, "I think I'll soak in the tub. Every place we've stayed for months, the tubs have been shallow."

"We have bubble bath, if you want it!" Sita exclaimed.

"That sounds interesting. I've never had a bubble bath." I took off my turban and shook out my hair, then pulled off my tunic. She gasped and started to back out of the room.

"What's wrong?" I asked her. She didn't say anything, but she was clearly embarrassed.

I took a step towards her and reached for her hand, and said, "My dear, we are going to have to get used to each other. This is for real now. We can't have secrets. Tell me what's wrong."

"I have never seen a man naked. I have never…"

"I'm not naked. I've just taken off my shirt." I moved a step closer to kiss her. She allowed that, but did not reciprocate. I stepped back. I realized that this was probably the first time that I had kissed a girl and wasn't hard. *Bad sign*.

"I see we have a lot we have to talk about," I said. "Are you not attracted to me? Because, if you aren't, we should not even think of marriage."

She looked down and blushed again. "I've never kissed a man before."

"You just had an opportunity." I sighed. "After I take a bath, I want to rest for a while, but I hope at dinner we can talk about our expectations. How does that sound?"

She nodded but would not look at me. "Do you want to stay with me and talk now while I soak?" I asked her.

Her eyes got wide. She made a squeaky sound and said in Hindi, "No, I couldn't," and turned and fairly ran out of the room.

I nodded off in the tub, then got up and collapsed in the softest bed I had ever slept in. I was really exhausted, physically and emotionally.

Maria woke me sometime between 6:00 and 6:30. I dressed in the new shalwar khameez I'd had made, put my hair up, and came out to the living room. I sat there for a few minutes, still trying to get my bearings, and Maria came out and offered me a drink. There was a small TV on a buffet and the international news in English was on.

Fatima and Sita joined me after about half an hour. Fatima had on a sari, gold brocade over green. She looked sexy and exotic. Sita was wearing a nice, simple pink shirt with a scooped neck and a short black skirt, which showed off her figure. She was also wearing a lot of gold jewelry. Maybe it was the style then to look ostentatious. I told them they both looked beautiful, and we went down in the elevator to a waiting taxi.

We went to a hotel which was not far from the apartment, for dinner. Even at dusk the weather was still stiflingly hot. Thankfully, it was cool in the restaurant. We ordered, and I started asking questions because it was clear that Sita didn't know what to say.

"So, you have sisters. Is that correct?" I asked.

Fatima nudged Sita, and she smiled shyly and responded, "Yes. Mindi lives in America now with her husband, and she has a boy and a girl. Nikki is in London with her husband. She's pregnant."

Fatima asked, "You have brothers, right?"

"Yes. They're both in Kuala Lumpur. They went to boarding school in Singapore and stayed on through college and got jobs."

"So," Fatima asked, "How is it you live now in Switzerland?"

I told them about Dr. Schultz, how he had educated my brothers in Singapore, and he suggested that I continue in Switzerland, where he also taught, and he took care of all the details.

"It ended up being a good move, I think. I've been working on interesting projects and I met my bandmates."

Sita still had nothing to say. Fatima said, "You must meet many interesting women on your travels."

I looked at her, wondering what she was getting at. "I meet many interesting people traveling, but it can be a bit rough being a nomad, moving from place to place. I'm not really a party person. My bandmates are, but I see what we do, entertaining, as a business, and somebody has to make sure we stay on track. Do you understand?"

"Don't you have a manager do that?" Fatima asked.

"Well, yes, to a certain extent, but somebody has to *liaise* with the manager."

"Have you ever had a girlfriend?" Fatima asked. Sita blushed at the question.

I hesitated. What to say? "Yes, but I am not interested in casual encounters. I always knew that my parents wanted me with a Sikh girl. That was important to them. What's important to me is that I share interests with my partner, and that she be attracted to me and be interested in sharing a life with me. I have a question for you two. How is it you are living here?"

Fatima laughed. "We've only been here about three years. As you saw on the ride over, there's a lot of construction. Mr. Makkar has invested in building here. We had been in Mumbai, but you know, Mumbai is not very hospitable to Sikhs. I really didn't like Kuwait, either. Women are not allowed out on the street without a male escort. We believe we can feel more at home here."

Still, nothing from Sita. I said to her, "Sita, I'm trying to learn about you. What was the last book you read that you found interesting?"

She looked at me, and seemed to be thinking. Then she said, "*Little Women*. That was interesting. I'm reading *Princess Daisy* now. I like the Harlequin romances from the United States. Love stories. I can read English, but nothing complicated."

She did not ask me about books I had read, which was probably for the best. The last couple of years they'd been about engineering, coding, investing, or African history. I tried again.

"Have you seen any movies you've enjoyed?"

"We loved *Dirty Dancing, The Breakfast Club,* and *Pretty in Pink*," she answered, looking at her mother. "I like movies about girls like me."

I hadn't seen any of them. "Do you want to know anything about me?" I asked her.

Sita was still pondering a reply to that question when Fatima asked me, "How did you learn to play the piano in Africa?"

I told them about raising money for transport by bartering, Mr. Curtis offering me the piano, and finding someone to teach me.

We ate for a bit in silence. Then Sita asked, "So how did you get into a band?"

"The guys heard me practicing. We were also in orchestra. Adam is studying ethnomusicology. That's music of different cultures."

We were silent again, and then I asked Sita, "Where did you go to high school and what did you study?"

"I went to Saint Rita in Mumbai. It's a Catholic school."

"How did you choose the school?" I asked.

Sita looked at me, and Fatima answered, "Her father chose the school for all the girls. He wanted to make sure they could all speak English. Even I went to a Catholic school. We all got better educations than we could have gotten in Indian-run schools."

"So, how was it being Sikh in a Catholic school? I ask because in Singapore, religion didn't matter at all. In Switzerland, nobody bothers me, but I'm often asked if I know Jesus. I wear the turban and I have to wear western business clothes, including a tie, to classes, but when I work in the lab, nobody cares, so I always wear a shalwar khameez. It's more comfortable."

"In school we had to wear uniforms," Sita said. "You saw the photo. We all thought they were ugly, but it was to equalize us, so nobody stood out as either rich or poor."

"We have a dress code in my school, too. How was the food? Was it vegetarian?" I asked.

"Are you veg?" Sita asked.

"Mostly. I guess that's 'no.' I was just wondering. My room-mates are European and they eat a lot of meat. In Africa, my mother and our cook, Hassan, often made lentils, and potatoes, cabbage, rice, and greens. We ate ugali, which is cornmeal, at least half the week with a sort of stew called 'relish.' Sometimes we have chicken. I really like fish. You see, I ordered lobster, and I love prawns."

"I got used to eating meat in school," Sita responded.

"Can you cook it?" I asked.

She giggled, and said, "No! I can't cook at all. Maria cooks for us."

I looked at them both. "Where I live now, with two other men, we have a cleaning service that comes in once a week to clean the apartment, but we all cook. Not well, but we can feed ourselves. Do you plan to learn to cook, Sita?"

She looked at me, seeming baffled. Finally, she said, "I guess, if I can get lessons. Do you not plan on having a servant cook?"

I shook my head. "Servants are very expensive in Europe. The cost of living is probably as high as it is here, but servants don't often live with you. There are no servants' quarters. I am not rich enough to be able to afford someone just to cook."

"But you are rich enough to support a wife, and your parents have a cook?" Fatima asked.

"My parents, although considered middle class, do not have running water in their home, and barely electricity enough for lights. Hassan, their houseboy, lives in servant's quarters. He also has side businesses. I am making a good living and can support a household that is not extravagantly run. Where I live now, everything is walking distance. In any case, that's why we are getting together to talk now, about expectations. I have been very independent for a very long time, away from my parents. That means if I had a problem, I had to solve it myself. I have always budgeted and planned. I live frugally. I give myself an allowance. Where do you get your money, Sita?"

Fatima started to say something, but Sita just jumped in and said, "My father gives me an allowance."

"What do you do with the allowance?" I asked.

"I buy jewelry, and clothes, and I go out with my friends."

We were finished eating and just waiting for the check. "You have no savings? What if you want something particularly expensive?"

"Like what?"

"I don't know. Say, to take a trip?"

"I'd ask my father for money," she replied.

I took a deep breath. I looked at Fatima. She was looking at me but didn't say anything. I could not read the expression on her face.

"I think we should talk about this in the next few days we have. I am sure living with me would be a big change for you. I can't have a frivolous wife. I'm looking for a partner."

I paid the dinner bill with a credit card and we left. When we got back to the apartment, I went to the guest room and just crashed.

I awoke probably around five in the morning to a vivid erotic dream. In the dream, Mara woke me by kissing me. She said, "Ndugu, do me now." I put my hands on her breasts and said, "Zed," and she laughed and said, "Zed, y, x, w, who cares? You make me burn…" and I woke up to find myself hugging a big pillow and very hard.

I jerked off, rinsed off, and decided to stretch. I hadn't exercised in about three days. I dressed in a T-shirt and workout pants and went to the kitchen. Maria was up, listening to a small radio, drinking tea. I told her I was going out for a run and would be back for breakfast.

I ran about two miles and then I could feel the air getting hot, so I ran back.

Fatima was up by this time. She said, "Did you have a good run? Do you want me to wake Sita?"

"My run was fine. I'll wake Sita."

She started to say something, but I said, "We can't be formal. She needs to get used to talking to me alone. This is important, or I can leave now. Just tell me which room is hers."

Fatima nodded and said, "Second door on the left."

Her room was painted pink, a real girl's room with a canopy bed, and stuffed animals all over. There were a couple of Bollywood posters on the walls and clothes were strewn about. I walked over to the bed, sat on the edge and leaned over and kissed her lightly on the lips. She looked so much younger without makeup on. She slowly opened her eyes.

"Good morning, my dear. Tell me how you feel about this whole situation. Our lives are about to change, if you want me."

"Does my mother know you're in here?"

"Oh, yes. I told her I wanted to talk to you alone. If you are ready to marry, we must communicate. We have a lot to talk about in the next several days. I am looking for a true partner, a woman who shares my values, and who wants to build a life with me. I don't want to disappoint my parents, but I am very busy, and I'm just two years older than you are. I have plenty of time. Are you ready to have children now?"

She sat up. She was wearing these ridiculous pajamas with some sort of cartoon design on them. Not sexy at all. I started to unbutton the top, and she re-buttoned it. She said, sternly, "I thought you were a gentleman."

I smiled. "Sorry. I am: A *horny* gentleman."

She looked away from me, took a deep breath and sighed.

"Sita, I'm sorry. I was trying to be playful. Have you ever taken care of a baby?"

"At school we had a nursery. I've fed them and changed nappies."

"Is that what you want to do?"

"I don't mind working in a crèche. That's why I'm studying for a certificate. Mum says I can't go on without responsibilities."

"Well, in addition to what you don't mind doing, I want to hear about what you want to do. Let's go eat breakfast, and then we can go out and talk more, OK? Please, dear, don't put on so much makeup. You're very pretty naturally. Maybe eye-liner or lipstick, but in Africa and Europe, only low class girls wear so much makeup. I don't like it."

Waiting for Sita to arise, I returned to the kitchen for breakfast. Maria was fussing around.

"I'd like to make toast. Can you tell me where the bread is?" I asked her.

"I'll make you toast. Go sit in the dining room, Mr. Singh," Maria responded.

"Oh, Maria, you don't have to call me mister. Singh is fine, or Dayal, whichever. And you don't have to wait on me."

She turned around and looked at me. She had a thoughtful expression. "Yes, I do have to wait on you. That's my job."

"Where are you from?"

"Originally from the Philippines, but I came here from Kuwait, I think three years ago."

"Is it? How is that? I mean, how is it you got to Kuwait, and then here? I'm from Tanzania."

Maria's English was pretty good. She told me she got to third grade in the Philippines, but left school because her parents needed school fees for her brother. She married, worked cleaning bars and a guy from her church told her she'd get better wages in Kuwait. She had no idea where she was, but they placed her with a family that treated her badly. The Makkars attended a party at the family's home and Mrs. Makkar asked to borrow her and brought her to Dubai.

"My parents were trafficked to Africa," I told her.

"Your parents?"

"Yes. My father was sold to someone who brought him with other children to east Africa to be resold as servants."

Maria motioned for me to sit at the table and brought me toast.

"I was taught by Peace Corps Volunteers."

"Peace Corps?"

"Yes, they come from America. If there is an atlas here, I'll show you."

"What's an atlas?"

"It's a book of maps."

Maria smirked and responded, "I don't think I've ever seen a book in this house that wasn't filled with personal photos."

"When I go out with Sita today, I'll see if I can find one. Have you been back to the Philippines?" I asked her.

"No. Maybe this year. I've been sending money for my children, for school fees. Now I'm paid enough that I think I will be able to fly home, I'm not sure."

"Are you treated well here?"

Maria shrugged her shoulders. Finally, she said, "Yes. I'm not beaten. I can go out on the street. There's nothing out there, really, but I have freedom."

After breakfast, when we went out, I asked Sita where Maria's room was, and she told me servants quarters were the first two floors of the building, over the garage.

Sita and I took a cab to another building, a mall, and Sita relaxed, but as we walked, I reached for her hand and she pulled away and said, "We can't hold hands in public."

Just like Africa. Men can hold hands, women can hold hands, but men and women? As if they are having intercourse in the street.

I apologized, "I'm sorry I offended you this morning. I'm very attracted to you. I need to know you feel the same about me."

She nodded, but didn't say anything.

"Sita, did you ever think about what you'd do once you finished school?"

She hesitated and smiled, "I like you, but I never thought about being attracted to a man. In school, we were warned that men would use us. I don't think anyone asked how we'd be used. Truthfully, I've never been alone with a man. I wondered if I had any options, but I hadn't thought about staying in school. I'm interested in fashion, but I have no idea where to learn how to start. I've never worked a sewing machine. I was hoping my baba would let me dance in his movies, and act, but he said I'd have to live in Mumbai, and I just couldn't. It's a very dirty, crowded, dangerous city for women. And, really, I knew they'd get me married. So, I didn't think about it at all. I knew I didn't have much choice."

I didn't know what to say.

Finally, she said, "Dayal, I was always told I would get married and be a mother. My mum was only in college until she married Baba. I don't even know how they met. Now it's my turn."

"I didn't really have a plan or dream, either. I was curious about how things worked. An older friend told me to stay in school as long as my way was paid. I want to tell you, while inventing is important to me, and I also love music, I want a partner. I want a sex life."

Sita blushed. We walked around through the mall, which was on several floors: lots of jewelry and clothing stores. We passed a heavily curtained store and Sita told me, "That's a beauty salon. In the back, they have a yoga studio."

"How would anyone know what this is?" I asked.

"You see that little sign, in Arabic? It says 'Hema's Place.' It's really by word-of-mouth. You know, this is a mostly Moslem country, and they don't want to attract strange men."

I bought Sita a necklace she liked and then we went to a bookstore to find an atlas and small globe for Maria. There were no books on sex, not even in the religious section with the other Vedas.

We went into a carpet store and I bought an intricately designed red rug for my parents. It caught my eye immediately, and I knew my mother would love it.

"I didn't know Maria could read English," Sita remarked to me on the ride back to the apartment.

"I'm not sure, but she can look at the maps and other photos," I told her.

That night, Sita asked me if I wanted to watch a movie on TV. That was also a new experience for me. I only watched TV if one of the other guys had it turned on, and rarely was anything in English. Even when we toured, I usually just watched the news.

We were sitting together after Fatima went to bed. I kissed Sita and lightly sucked her earlobe. She turned to me and I cupped her chin and started kissing her. When she didn't pull away, I started delicately fondling her breasts. I sighed, and put her hand, which had been on my chest, on my erection.

She drew back, her eyes wide, and said, haltingly, "I'm not ready for sex."

"We're just being affectionate. We're not going to have intercourse," I replied, trying to reassure her.

"In school we learned that touching was wrong."

I had to address this: "Well, nonconsensual touching is wrong. I'm hoping we can get comfortable with one another. Please tell me that you don't believe in some Christian nonsense that sexual pleasure is a sin. Have you ever read the Adi Granth? It's 1400 pages, and nothing about what sex is or isn't allowed. We are not naked and ashamed. Our religion is so different from theirs. God is not inconsistent. Our gurus went to prison over this. My only concern is pregnancy. I'm not ready for that and neither are you. We can give pleasure to each other, without intercourse. I want that. I need that. This is how I want it to be in our marriage."

We sat in silence for a while, and she kept her arm around my waist.

"After my European tour is over in a few weeks, I want you to visit me in Switzerland. We have to get to know each other privately, intimately. Do you understand?"

Sita nodded, but she didn't say anything.

The next morning, I told Fatima that if she really wanted our marriage to work, she needed to make Sita much more independent and encourage some introspection.

We walked around another small mall the next day, and met some of her friends for lunch. There was too much giggling and colloquial Hindi mixed with English and Arabic for me to follow their conversations. I excused myself to browse the bookstore, but most of the books were in Arabic, and nonfiction. I stopped into a hardware store and bought my father a set of screwdrivers in various sizes. In the evenings, we watched TV and kissed, but she was still very nervous.

The last night, after Fatima had gone to bed and left us alone, I said to Sita, "I leave tomorrow. Let's just sit in the dark, in the quiet."

We sat for a few minutes, hugging, and I whispered to her, "Do you at least enjoy kissing me?"

She turned to me and brushed her lips against mine and whispered back, "I do." She put her hand on my face and stroked my beard. I took her hand, kissed her palm, and put it back on my face. I was getting hot. I thought of asking her if my beard bothered her, but decided not to make an issue of it.

We continued to make out. I slowly lowered my hand from her shoulder to her breast. I could feel her tense up. She was breathing as if she was excited, so I just quietly blurted out, "Let me touch you. If it doesn't feel good, I'll stop. We're not having intercourse. If it feels good, I want you to reciprocate."

"How do I do that?"

"As I stroke you, I want you to stroke me."

We spent over an hour fondling each other, and I said to her, "Listen, I need a woman to cuddle and hold and laugh with, to share ideas with. I need that woman to enjoy me, to appreciate the pleasure I give her, and to want to give me pleasure in return. Do you want to be that woman? Because I want you to be that woman if you want to be my wife."

I was succumbing to a cute girl, and I wasn't really thinking. She was looking into my eyes, and seemed to relax, but then, she moved my hand a little and whispered, "Keep doing that." I was stroking her, and she was so wet. We continued to kiss as I stroked her. Suddenly, she tensed a little and exclaimed, "Oh! Oh! Dayal!" She hugged me tightly and was moaning. I felt we had crossed a boundary. She was surprised and said, "How did you know to do that?"

I shrugged. "Now, I'm going to take care of myself, in bed. Do you want to watch me? I'll want you to do this in the future."

She accompanied me to the guest room, and sat on the edge of the bed. When I pulled my pants off and my erection sprung out, her eyes got wide and she tried to stifle a laugh.

"What's so funny?"

She shook her head slightly, whispered "*sweet Jesus*." and got an odd expression. "Nothing's funny. I've never seen a real ling. I wonder, I mean…"

"Please, touch me."

She very lightly stroked me, then let me hold her hand as I jerked off. When I ejaculated she gasped, and blushed, but she kissed me sensuously, more than I expected, and lingered a few minutes hugging me.

"Do you understand that sex is more than intercourse?"

"I had no idea. You know, there isn't even any kissing in Bollywood movies." Then, she whispered, "I'd better go to my own room." ✪

# CHAPTER 9

The next morning, I left for Arusha and spent a week with my parents. I had brought towels, the rug, and the tool set for my father (which caused a delay at customs). My parents were fine, but I still had to take care of some issues for them. They had trouble getting parts for their Toyota truck, and apparently it was a communication problem.

"I wrote a letter and listed the parts I needed and sent an international money order. Just last week, I got a letter and they returned the money order. They said one of the parts was back ordered, the belt had gone up in price, and to reorder," Baba told me.

I made a list of things I could take care of in Switzerland that were too cumbersome to take care of without a private phone number. I also emailed a list to Avi. This was so aggravating.

In Arusha (and in just about all African countries) to get a landline phone, you had to apply with the post office. Just like anywhere in the world, the post office was its own entity, and they moved at their own pace. If you had a contact, or possibly a politician as your *patron*, you could 'grease the wheels' and move things along, but that didn't mean the phone would work. This was one of the few things in Africa that didn't have as much to do with race or politics as just nothing working. Also, the line workers could make it so someone else could tap into your phone line: they could make and receive calls, and you'd be charged. Same with electricity: You had to monitor your bill for spikes. There weren't any cell phones until about 2004, and the Sri Lankans brought them in! My parents were among the first to have a cell, but even then, my brothers had to bring batteries as shipping them from South Africa was expensive and they'd often become 'lost' in the mail.

On my second day, Baba and I went for a walk. That was something we had never done, but I noticed a lot of changes around town. I mentioned the amount of construction.

"Yes, you can see the companies from the emirates and Malaysia are very interested in us. The World Bank has funded a lot of infrastructure. They're paving the road to Dodoma."

"Dodoma? They're still thinking a new capitol will be in the middle of nowhere?"

Baba chuckled and responded, "Nobody is sure what they think. The wazungu don't ask what we want or need. They have their own plans for us. We notice that the Americans have plans for our farmers without understanding anything about how productive the land could possibly be. They want us growing cash crops. They hold meetings every now and then. Their presentations are like a performance."

We walked in silence for a bit.

"So, tell me, how was your visit with Sita?"

I sighed. "Baba, she is a very simple girl. She is sweet, but… ."

"There's a problem?"

"She is of a wealthier class than we are. Sita is used to having servants and having everything taken care of for her. She's very pretty, and I hope she'll be a partner, but I don't think a marriage should be so much work. I will tell you that if we go through with this, I'll have a marriage contract written up by a lawyer so her father knows I'm not jumping in blindly."

Baba was silent. Finally, he said, "That's probably a good idea, but… what is it you want?"

"You know what I want. I want Mara. I've compared every girl I've ever met to her. It wasn't just sex. She knows about managing money. She has so many interests, is independent, and never expects anyone to do for her."

"No. She is divorced and has never had children."

"There is no logical reason. Khadija was 15 years older than Mohammed. I want a partner, not a baby machine. I still have at least two years of studies. Our music is making money. I do not need a wife to cook for me. I want a partner to bring something to my life I do not have now, and that is *joy*. *I do not have joy*. I've told Sita to come visit in October if she wants to continue on this path to marriage, and I've told her I will not keep her the way her baba does. Her pastime is shopping. Do you understand? I am making money, but I am not wealthy yet. If she is ready to have children and care for them, that is OK. I do not intend to have a wife who insists on having nannies raise our children."

My father did not respond, but we had not much else to say.

I spent the next few days visiting the Maasai and my Chagga friends. I brought them books for their children. I stopped by my old school and brought a world map and a chart that had a skeleton with body parts. I also visited Mr. Curtis at the hotel, whose son was now the manager. I spent an hour everyday playing the piano, and I had clothes made. More and more, I appreciated that there was no way I could have such fine things tailored in Europe.

I had about three weeks back in Switzerland before we went to England and the Nordic countries. There was a lot of mail waiting for me. Shayla had written, telling me she had enjoyed our visit. She told me Mara was not back yet, but would be home by September, which was now. I got a letter from Sita, too, thanking me for visiting and telling me she was looking into flights herself, and to tell her good dates to arrive.

Pete and Adam asked me why I went to Dubai. I wasn't prepared to start a conversation about this, so I just said, "I went to see a friend from Singapore who had moved there." I knew I'd have enough explaining to do soon.

Then Peter asked, "A girlfriend?"

"No."

He started to say something to Adam. I noticed by the kitchen sink, where we kept the vitamin bottles, there were two small pill bottles. I picked them up and saw that they were antibiotics for Peter. I looked at him and he stopped talking.

"Pete, what are these for? Don't you use rubbers? Are you out of your mind?"

"What do *you* know? You don't even have sex!" Pete yelled.

"Matter of fact, I had sex in Milwaukee with a friend."

"You did," Peter responded, sarcastically.

"Yes. Just because I'm discreet and don't brag doesn't mean I'm a monk. Do you know what discretion is?"

"The better part of valor?" he responded.

Adam burst out laughing. I said, "I'm careful. "

I wanted to contact Mr. Makkar, Sita's father, so I told them I was going to my office in the engineers' building. Adam said he'd walk with me.

"Uh, Dayal, not to gossip, but this isn't the first time Pete's had the clap."

I stopped walking. Peter was a goat. "It isn't? Has he not heard of AIDS?"

"I think he thinks it's a gay guy's disease. I don't know. When it comes to sex, especially casual sex, that's the kind of sex he enjoys."

"So it wasn't a cold he had on tour. Wasn't he seeing a girl before we left?"

"Yep. He hasn't seen her since we've been back."

"Aren't you concerned about his behavior?" I asked.

"Sure. But what can I do?"

"Not to change the subject, but, what are you doing with your earnings? I'm thinking of buying a condo."

Adam chuckled and said, "I don't think they'll let you do that until you're twenty-one. How old are you now?"

"I'll turn twenty one in a few weeks. Listen, I've got to contact a guy overseas. I'll get back with you later. Let's try for dinner together. Seven or so?"

"OK, meet you at the apartment."

I composed a message:

*Dear Mr. Makkar,*

*I had a very nice visit with Sita, and I'm sorry I didn't get to meet you while I was in Dubai. I think a marriage will work out if we can agree on a few details. I hope that she understands the weather here is very cold and dry, much different than Dubai.*

*She told me that you give her an allowance, and she spends it all. How much do you give her every month, and why?*

*I hope that I can persuade her to get a job or come up with something to do while I work and am at school, at least until she's ready to have a baby.*

*She's told me she likes to shop. There are not that many places to shop around me.*

*I've told her my schooling will take a few more years. I am buying a condo, but we don't have servants quarters in Europe. We can't afford a live-in servant.*

*Also, I help support my parents in Africa. They can't contribute to the wedding.*

*Finally, my band travels several months a year. It can be stressful. I wanted her to understand this.*

*I plan to have an attorney write up a marriage contract. I will send a draft to both of you. My personal wealth at this point is under half a million USD. My wealth hinges on performances and record sales. I've been living on my scholarship as well as a small allowance I give myself. I intend to give Sita a limited credit card until she can demonstrate fiscal responsibility.*

*I have found she has been negatively influenced by the Catholic nuns. I hope with time she can get around this.*

*Sincerely,*

*D. Singh*

I sent it off, thinking to myself that it would probably be what he expected of a prospective son-in-law.

I composed another email to Levine:

*I have returned to Switzerland to find that Peter is being treated for gonorrhea which he contracted on our recent tour. He did not have a cold. I hope you will have a private chat with him when we see you.*

I wrote to Shayla:

*I enjoyed our visit. I just got back from seeing my parents, and went to Dubai to meet the girl my parents wanted me to marry. She is Sikh, of course, and I believe we can develop a* relationship. *I have not heard from Mara in months. I know she doesn't want to marry me. I want to be with a woman, and this girl will make my parents happy. If we can work out the details regarding our expectations of each other, we'd probably marry in the spring. I'll let you know and send you an invitation.*

I remembered what Mara and I had talked about years before. What I wanted was the closeness of a woman. I knew I would have to make compromises, but for me, it was worth it. I just assumed every woman wants the same. I also assumed a Sikh woman would understand. I was naïve, but optimistic. ✪

# CHAPTER 10

I arranged for Sita to visit the week after our return from the European tour, for two weeks.

When we got to London, the first stop on the tour, Levine broke down margins for us. He agreed with me that, for our next tour, we should add a synthesizer. I was pushing for a Synclavier, which was very expensive, but I offered to have the cost come out of my royalties.

He wanted to know when we'd have enough songs for another album. I liked the Phoebe Snow song "Poetry Man," and I had a draft of a song I was calling, "Don't Hustle Me." I wanted to do the Ides of March song "Vehicle"—that was perfect for the bassoon. We also added more Don Fagen. I loved "New Frontier" and his interpretation of "Ruby," the Leiber/Stoller song. We had enough songs for a two-hour show, with the old and the new.

Things went smoothly on this tour. I felt it would be easier for all of us, especially if we had other musicians on stage to use Lavalier microphones for vocals so we wouldn't be tripping over cords all the time. What I learned was they were better for a hall seating 1,000 or fewer. They were not powerful enough with amps to deliver a distortion free sound. Sound distortion remained a huge concern for me.

Many of the places we performed in had terrible acoustics, and amplifying our sound did not overcome this. In fact, it made us more distorted. The other guys didn't care, but I told Levine that I would work on panels we could mount to cut echo and distortion. I ended up just getting corrugated box boards that could easily be clipped and hung to rafters. They cost less than a dollar U.S. apiece, and we could easily move them, and it didn't matter if they got bent or torn. I also worked on microphones for our instruments that could be wired to specific speakers, which would definitely enhance the listening experience for people in remote parts of the halls, where distortion tends to get magnified. I patented the idea in Europe, but it's easily enough replicated.

The reviews were great and the audiences seemed to know a lot of our songs. Freddie Mercury and Brian May, Queen, used to remark how important it was to hear the audience response, and it was.

This tour was sponsored by Carlsberg Beer. They paid for a lot of promotion: T-shirts and other merchandise for sale at concerts. (This was becoming a large side business for us—a significant source of income besides record sales).

When we returned from the tour, I got together with Dr. Schultz about the course plans. I told him I was going to continue to use video games to teach calculus, as they were getting very sophisticated. He wanted me to come up with a dissertation project. I wrote up a paper detailing hertz and stage geography to avoid interference and feedback. This was counted as a master's thesis. I needed something bigger for a dissertation to "add to the body of knowledge."

I also started seriously looking for a condo. I would have preferred to continue to live with the guys, but I knew Sita would never tolerate it. We kept the place relatively clean, but it was still what anyone would call a "bachelor pad." I just wanted to cost things out. Switzerland is mountainous, and housing was limited.

Dr. Schultz suggested a *pension* that a friend of his ran where Sita could be in a more intimate setting than a hotel. It would be cheaper, and was in our neighborhood. It wasn't luxurious by any means, but more of how we'd really live.

I started contemplating moving to a less taxing country. Since I was legally a Tanzanian citizen, my tax situation was different from the others. Also, being an enrolled student helped. But I would not be a student forever, and my change of status could increase my taxes by over 40 percent. In the past year I had made close to half a million dollars, including from our rendition of "A Little Less Conversation," which was being used in some sort of television advertisement in the United States.

I figured Sita and I could easily live on two thousand dollars a month even if she had to have her hair and nails done every week and buy a new outfit. This was back in 1991.

A few days before she arrived, I told the guys that I had invited her to visit, because I planned to marry her. I wanted to get all the 'shock and disbelief' out of the way. Peter, immediately, started laughing and asked if I had knocked her up. They all seemed incredulous. "But why?" Peter asked. "You never even mentioned seeing anyone!"

"Why am I getting married? Well," I explained, "As you are all aware, I thought I wanted Mara, but apparently Mara doesn't want me, so I've moved on. My father met her father, and her father felt she was ready to marry. I am not sure she is. For me, what's important besides the attraction is that she's Sikh. We aren't getting married tomorrow. We barely know each other. She will be staying in a pension. She can't stay here. It would be improper."

Peter looked baffled. "I still don't understand…"

"If you're worried about us as a group, that won't change. As long as we're successful, I intend to put my heart and soul into The Pleasure Seekers. I told her that I want to finish my schooling. As long as we keep producing music, I don't know how I can explain this to you. I don't want to be with a woman having religious and cultural beliefs are different from mine."

I took a breath and explained, "Maybe I'm making a mistake, but I've thought about it. I'm ready because I want a sex life, and I want to be with one woman. We've met. She's nice. You never know until you're into a marriage."

Peter still couldn't believe that I was marrying someone I barely knew. Someone I hadn't had actual intercourse with. I almost couldn't believe it myself, but didn't dwell on it. I didn't want to get into it with him. To Peter, sex had nothing to do with affection. It was recreation. He stopped talking to me for several days. I guess he felt strongly that how I lived my life was too weird. It wasn't that I was horny, or lonely. Looking back, maybe I was. I never liked chasing women. I had too much to do. I wanted to be comfortable with one girl. I also tried to convince myself that how I felt about Mara was because she was my first lover, and I would ultimately have a great emotional bond with Sita. I was just too busy to spend any time being introspective myself. I was sure once we were comfortable with each other, things would not be awkward. My upbringing and expectations of life were very different from those of my bandmates. I've discussed this with others over the years. You just never know how a marriage will play out. Looking back now, I realize I was being optimistic, but I should have been more realistic.

Sita arrived the last week in October without gobs of make up on. I was relieved. She liked the pension. She told me she felt very safe, and she was able to speak French with the proprietress. But there *was* a problem. After I took her to the pension to get settled, she asked me, "Do you know where the Catholic church is?"

This bothered me "Why do you want to know?"

"Two of the teaching sisters at my school wanted me to greet some of the sisters they used to work with. They gave me some gifts to bring to them."

"You don't plan to go to church after we're married, do you? It's important to me that you see yourself as Sikh."

"Probably only for Christmas Midnight Mass."

I let it go, because there was no gurdwara, or even a satsang (a group of Sikhs) in Switzerland, and even if there was one, how much mumbled chanting can one take? I also knew that both Adam and Michelle did this.

"I will fetch you after breakfast but I have to teach every morning from nine to eleven. I can sign you up for a tour of Bern or Zurich, or cooking, art or exercise classes, if you'd like, but I know you don't want to watch me work in the lab. It's boring."

"Do you have any brochures that I can look at?"

"Sure. You can come hear us practice if you want. We can go out for dinner, and then to a movie, or to hear music in the evening if you like. If you want to watch TV and just chill for a few hours with me, that's fine."

"Can I walk around Zurich?"

"Of course, the central business district is very walkable. Also, Bern has a very charming old town. We'll go to the studio in Montreux on the weekend, and we could go on a boat ride on the lake. How does that sound?"

I gave her brochures from a cooking school and an art center. Adam had been seeing Michelle, who was very outgoing and curious, and she was delighted to spend time with Sita. They went shopping and I guess did other girl stuff.

I still hadn't gotten a reply from her father, but I let it slide for the duration of the visit. I was anxious about this situation. When we went on the train to Montreux, I started questioning her. "Sita," I asked, "What do you think? I know it's cold here, but will you be ok living with me here for a few years, until I finish school?"

"I think so, if I can go back to visit my friends every few months."

"That should be ok, maybe two or three times a year, or they can come visit us. And, you know, of course, that if we have children, I want them to be raised as Sikhs. This is important to me."

"Of course."

"Adam was raised Catholic, and he's told me enough about his own education. I don't believe in heaven. I don't want our children confused about this."

She looked away and didn't say anything. I went on: "This isn't a problem, is it?"

She sighed and finally said, "No, I understand. But the Christian Bible has some interesting stories…"

"Their Bible is full of stories and contradictions. Our scripture is different. I'm not religious, but my family and I read the Bible and the Adi Granth, and while it's mostly poetry, it is very direct: Same God as their God without the contradictions. Did you ever read it?"

"No."

"But you've read their Bible."

"Parts of it. More New Testament than the Old. They taught it in school. We never had an Adi Granth. I understand what you're saying, and I know the Sikh holidays. I just want my children to understand right from wrong."

"Good. Now, have you gone to a doctor and learned about contraception?" I asked.

She blushed. "What? No, Not yet. I will."

We stayed overnight in Montreux, and Sita was nervous about this. I, again, reassured her that we would not have intercourse. After we walked around the town and had dinner, we went back to our room. I invited her to take a shower with me. She was clearly uncomfortable, but followed me in. She glanced at my penis and said, "Your ling is very big. Bigger than David's."

"You told me you had never seen a naked man. David who?"

"Michelangelo's statue."

I burst out laughing. "Oh, well. I guess I've been blessed with more surface area." I didn't tell her he was not aroused. I hugged her to me and took her hand and put it on my erection, and slid my hand between her legs.

"We are not going to have intercourse until we are married. I just want us to touch each other."

"I'm trusting you," she responded, trembling.

It wasn't just that I didn't want to risk pregnancy. It was my display of patience and self-control.

We got into bed, and we spent a lot of time kissing and touching each other. I laid back, took her hand, and put it on my erection.

"You're so hot!"

"You make me hot," I whispered. I slid down to eat her. "Is this ok? The right place?" I asked.

"What are you doing?"

"This is oral sex. I think you will enjoy it. If you don't, I'll stop. Just tell me."

She laid back and sighed. I stopped and said, "Tell me, should I move my tongue? Faster? Slower, Up? Tell me."

"Keep doing what you're doing. It feels good."

She reached down and caressed my head, started breathing fast and moaning, then suddenly went rigid as she exclaimed, "Oh!" and I could tell she was having an orgasm. I slid up to her, put my hand over hers to jerk me off and ejaculated onto her. I quickly wiped up my cum with the sheet and hugged her, and we drifted off to sleep.

The next day, before getting on the train, we went shopping. She didn't buy that much except for chocolate to bring back with her.

On the day she left, she asked me to visit at the Christmas break. I told her I would check my schedule, because I knew I would probably have to catch up on school work and practice learning new songs, but I would try to call her every week, and I also told her to look into buying a computer, and that I would pay for it.

After seeing her off at the airport, I called her father. His secretary kept me on hold for several minutes, but finally he came on the line.

"Sat shri akal, Mr. Makkar, did you receive my letter from September?"

"Jo Bole So Nihaal. Sat shri akal. I did, but I'm sorry, I can't talk right now. Can I call you back?"

"I am very busy, too. Can you please get your calendar and schedule a time to call me? I don't want to go back and forth on this if you want Sita married."

I wanted him to treat me seriously. I knew that some business people, to avoid unpleasantness or knowing they would come out on a losing deal, would stall and stall. If I was aggressive, he would work to get me off his agenda. It took Mr. Makkar over a week to return my call.

"Thanks for getting back to me, sir. I know you're busy, so let me be direct. What do you usually give Sita for an allowance?"

He was evasive, so I asked, "Just a 'ballpark' amount."

"Oh, I guess it would be about one hundred dollars a week, US," he responded.

"Why so much?"

"Is it so much? Really?"

"Do you have any idea what her expenses are?" I asked him. "She told me she has saved none of it."

"You know," he said, after a moment's hesitation, "I do not live with Fatima. I have a younger family. I want the girls, to be happy and not bitter. When I see her, I'll ask her why she isn't saving money. Is that OK?"

"When do you think you'll see her?"

"Probably in a day or so. She'll want her allowance."

"Has she ever lived without servants, or traveled away from you and Fatima for any period of time? Am I going to have to teach her how to work a washing machine and how to cook or wash dishes?"

Mr. Makkar laughed heartily. "I believe they taught her at school to do housework, but cooking? I'm not sure."

This was aggravating. "As I wrote to you, I plan to have a lawyer draw up a marriage contract. I do not mind you reviewing it or even suggesting changes, but I want everything spelled out. I'm particularly concerned about her education."

"What do you find problematic about her education, Dayal? She got the best education in India."

"The first thing she asked after I got her settled was where there was a church. The church has no place in my life. I want my children raised Sikh. There's a reason Marx called religion the opiate of the masses."

Mr. Makkar laughed again. "I agree with you there, son. I'm sure she knows she's Sikh.

"Fatima told me she was also educated in the convent."

"That's one reason we aren't divorced."

"But you weren't married in the church, were you?"

"No, of course not. But her education has her believing that divorce is a sin. I wanted sons, and polygamy is legal in India and Dubai."

"Yet you sent your daughters for a Catholic education."

"Son, there are trade-offs. I wanted them to learn to speak English and have a working knowledge of mathematics and the western world. Her sisters are in the United States and England. They're not dependent on me, so I consider this family a success."

"I understand. I'll have a solicitor start working on a marriage contract, and after we agree, we can set a date. How does that sound?"

"Fair enough, Dayal."

This was one complicated family. Sikhs do not believe in polygamy. We also believe women are equal to men. I suppose it was cultural influences that caused him to value sons.

On the weekend, I emailed Levine and asked him if he could suggest a lawyer to develop a marriage contract for me.

"You mean a prenuptial agreement? You're marrying?" he responded.

I then wrote a letter to Mara:

*Dear Mara,*
*I haven't heard from you in months. I've been very busy, with touring and teaching, but I also met a Sikh woman. Her*

*father had met Baba. Her name is Sita, and I believe she will
be a suitable wife. I am not 'in love' with her, but she is nice
and I'm sure love will grow. When we set a date, I will invite
you to the wedding. I still love you, and always will. I don't
know what else to say.*

*Love, Dayal.*

I felt sad writing to Mara this way, but I felt it was the ethical thing to do. ✺

# CHAPTER 11

Levine emailed to tell me he was setting up summer tour dates and wanted a master for an album. Finally, we were getting more than eight weeks' notice. We were able to use the recording studio after I was finished working, and we recorded all rehearsals. That way, we could compare every take, and piece together better parts if need be. Levine also told me that Carlsberg was sponsoring our European and North American tours again, and we were getting additional sponsorship from our record label. We were thrilled, as our expenses would be lower and we could stay in nicer places. We would kick off at the end of May this time. Adam agreed to do the charts and audition side musicians. We'd mostly play sports stadiums, along with several music festivals.

I made a point to go to a Philips store and got a TV with a VCR so they'd be compatible. When I saw the videos, especially of myself talking, I felt I looked ridiculous. Adam and Peter were happy, however.

I had set up a regular time to call Sita once a week, but our conversations were very general. She told me she practiced speaking French with a friend.

I told her I might not be able to call her when I was traveling. This was still the era of phone cards. I suggested she might want to come for a few days to the West Coast of the United States cities if she wanted to see me perform. She said she'd think about it, but probably would not because of the expense. I knew that if I was to pay, I'd have to pay for both her and Fatima, so I considered this. I had to get out of the mind-set of being overly frugal. I just had so many other things to think about.

The attorney sent a prenup contract, and I sent copies to Mr. Makkar and Sita. I had emailed both my brothers about what to put into the document, and while both thought I was looking for problems that didn't exist, I reminded them that she and I were from different backgrounds and probably had somewhat different expectations. Also, Sita didn't really have any concept of saving or planning, and her parents were pushing her into the marriage. I thought it was very straightforward and Sita made no objections.

I told Adam what I was doing, and he questioned me about having a marriage contract. "You make this sound like a business transaction. Michelle and I agree on so much that it hasn't occurred to me to write anything. We talk everything out."

"You're both students, from similar backgrounds. I did a marriage contract for several reasons. I am addressing how we will live. She has been used to a very elite lifestyle. I'm hoping our values and dreams for our future will be enough, but I want her family to understand what I think the issues may be."

I saw Michelle look sideways at Adam.

"What?" I asked.

Michelle took a breath and shook her head. "Dayal, I don't know. Just from being with her, you know, she's really into fashion, and I'm not sure she's ready for marriage."

"It's not going to be tomorrow," I responded, somewhat defensively. "I told Sita that we couldn't move from Switzerland until I attained my Ph.D., which is at least five years off. I had to make our situation clear, with no ambiguities. Jews have Ketubah's—marriage contracts—and in my part of the world

it is common for families to hammer out some sort of agreement. Even if you have a love match, the parents always get together to sort out economics: where you'd live and who would
pay for what."

My parents were in no position to do this. How many of our
African friends were always fretting about not having enough
cows, or having to work for the English to earn cash?

I was hoping to get married at the very end of the tour, in
August, but Sita told me that Fatima was having our horoscopes addressed for an auspicious date. That was a very Indian
thing to do.

The song I wrote, "Is This OK?" was a hit. We got it out as
a single, and added it to shows. We started in Boston and zig-
zagged through large cities in Canada, the USA, and Mexico,
then to Spain and France. We broadcasted live shows to the-
aters around the USA, San Jose, Lima, Buenos Aires, Sydney,
Perth, and Brasilia, and Japan. I wrote the Glazer girls, but
there was no way I could see them.

At the end of the tour in August, I flew to Dubai for a week.
We hadn't seen each other since December! I couldn't imagine
where Sita got the idea that there was so much to do in Dubai.
Was she comparing it to Mumbai? I noticed the town was growing. There were triple the number of buildings, many quite tall.
We got out to the desert for camel races, where I saw my first
Salukis. I thought they looked like Mara's dogs. They ran a few
races, and were so graceful. We went out to eat, saw movies,
strolled the mall, the beach, met her girlfriends (she knew no
guys and did not socialize with the girls' brothers or husbands),
had dinner with Baba Makkar's other family, and we talked

more about our expectations. Again, I asked her if she had explored birth control methods, and hit a road block.

"You know, a lot of women use the rhythm method based
on their cycles and it works," she said to me.

"Do you know how it works? I will use condoms, but you
need to know your options."

We had no arguments, but our conversations were never about anything controversial or deep. She wasn't wearing a
lot of makeup anymore, at least not when I saw her. She told
me she had started saving her allowance, and was even going
through her wardrobe to decide what clothes she would really
need, as the weather would be different in Europe.

We weren't sleeping together in Dubai, but we could bring
each other to orgasm, and I was happy for that.

I asked Fatima about how the wedding planning was going,
and she told me she was thinking of next March.

Seven months more? "Why are you delaying this?"

"Your horoscopes… ."

"This is nonsense. We've known each other over a year. I
have a school break in November. Make it for then." I found this
irritating, but when I was stressed, and back then, it was almost
all the time, everything was irritating.

I really wanted to see my parents. I was halfway there, being
in Dubai, so I asked Fatima and Sita to come with me. Mr. Makkar agreed to pay for their flights if I would pay for a place for
them to stay, which was at Mr. Curtis's hotel. A few other small
hotels had been built, but Curtis' place was still the nicest.

I surprised my parents (I *did* send a telegram). I sent Sita
and Fatima on several safari runs, suggested they have my tailor create some clothes for themselves, and took them around
in the truck to see Alfred. I brought him a solar lantern, a few

books on alternative energy, and a football and badminton set for his three children, who were giddy about the gifts.

Fatima and Sita were surprised at how far out from Arusha Alfred lived. When we pulled into their compound, Fatima asked me, "They speak English?"

"Alfred was in primary school with me, and he often guides safaris, so I know his English is good. I'm not sure about the rest of his family." I spoke to his wife and children in Kiswahili.

Alfred and I discussed putting in a rain catchment system on his house. He had managed to build a burned brick house with a cement floor and tin roof, but still had his rondoval. His wife and daughters still had to fetch water. I told him I'd loan him the money if he agree to pay it forward.

Sita and Fatima seemed uncomfortable with the goats, chickens and dogs approaching us in their curiosity. Alfred's mum offered us chai and *mandaazi*, which is a fried pastry. I saw that Fatima and Sita were hesitant, but I whispered to them, "Everything's boiled or fried. You won't get sick."

On the way back to town, we stopped at a Maasai encampment. I just wanted to greet them, and I had bought them a few plastic buckets. We didn't stay long. The flies were too annoying, and there was no place to sit.

On the drive back to my folks, Sita and Fatima commented how remarkable it was that people could live like they did and be so happy. Sita asked me, "How is it you have a relationship with such *primitive* people?"

Her question shocked me. "They aren't primitive. They're just poor. You know, they haven't had the advantages we've had."

"What do you mean?"

"The Maasai like living the way they do. They are free. Their children do all the chores. As for Alfred, I had my older brothers to help me learn. Alfred was the eldest child. He had nobody to help him. Also, his father had two wives, so resources for the children were spread thin."

My parents were cordial towards Sita and Fatima. However, I knew from the way they were acting, that *they* weren't comfortable. There was a real class difference between *us* and *them*. Baba pulled me aside and asked, "They knew they were coming to Africa. Why didn't they dress more simply?"

I remembered the time Avi and Sodhi came home after guiding safaris one day, and were counting their tips in various foreign currencies. Sodhi remarked that most of the tourists on his lorry were French, and Avi responded, laughing, "Today mine were all Italian. They always dress like they're going to a photo shoot. The women, always silk shirts unbuttoned to show cleavage and gold necklaces, tight silk pants that look painted on, and stiletto heels. Not just high heels—pointy six inch heels. They tottered and had to be boosted into the lorry. I can't imagine what they were thinking. That the ground would be hard so they wouldn't sink in?"

My future wife and mother-in-law were dressed as if going to a business luncheon, and I wondered if they owned any clothes that didn't need to be dry cleaned.

"Baba, these people live in a tall building. They don't even have a garden. These are their 'simple' clothes." He understood this because he had visited my brothers.

I had been living in Europe as a *European* and just accepted that some people never did any *real* work. This was also why I took time to address expectations with Sita.

Hassan had brought one of his wives to live with him, and she was helping Ama with baking. Fatima expressed surprise that my mother could bake such amazing things over a grill in a covered pot.

Fatima picked a wedding date and it would be in Dubai. I tried to not think about all I still didn't know about Sita, how my life would change.

Upon my return to Switzerland, I was lucky to find a two bedroom condominium apartment and sent photos to Sita. I bought us a queen-size bed and linens, but no other furniture. I thought Sita would want to choose what she wanted. Often, the expats leaving had sales. I was only in the apartment to sleep, anyway. The only other big thing I bought was an upright piano from the university.

Mr. Makkar and Fatima planned everything. We didn't do all the rituals. We did the maitan mandala, in front of the gurdwara, the exchanging of garlands, the formal meeting of families, and I agreed to read two pages of prayers, but I had to learn them phonetically. Sita had a mehndi party, and at the end, my brothers and I crashed it and had the women do our hands.

It was at the wedding that I learned that Fatima was estranged from her parents. Mr. Makkar's parents were deceased. Fatima's sister and brother came with their families, from India, and Mr. Makkar's brothers barely knew Fatima or the girls. Mr. Makkar was at least 20 years older than Fatima, and his second wife was just a bit younger than Avi. His sons, Farid and Bala, were in primary school.

The Gurdwara Nanak Darbar, where we held the wedding and party, was large, modern, and although not air-conditioned, cool inside. I paid for all the flowers and a photographer.

My parents, brothers and their families (they each had a son now), my bandmates, Dr. Schultz and his wife, and Levine and his wife, came for the wedding. I had Mr. Makkar negotiate for a block of rooms to make it somewhat more affordable for everyone. Dubai is one of the most expensive cities in the world. It's right up there with Zurich, Paris, Hong Kong, and San Francisco.

On the Makkar side, there were many friends and business associates. I had invited the Glazers, but none of the girls came. Shayla wrote and said the airfare alone was too much, let alone a place to stay, but they made a donation to "Save the Children" in our honor. I wondered how bad things could be in America if everything they earned went to just staying afloat.

Sita had many school friends, and nuns. I wondered how the nuns could afford the trip from Mumbai. Adam whispered to me, 'Manchote.' That is what the French call nuns: penguins.

There were probably about three hundred people. The band knew all the wedding songs people always ask for. Sita looked lovely in a white silk sari, even with too much makeup and jewelry. Later, she changed into another white dress with a fitted top and flowing skirt. It would have been more traditional for her to have worn red (which my mother commented on), but this was the Christian influence. I gave Sita a star sapphire pendant to rest in her cleavage. She gave me a mother-of-pearl pin for my turban.

When we got to the reception, there was a receiving line, and I shook hands or bowed to everyone. I noticed Sita never curtsied, which she should have, to the older men. I also noticed that I didn't see Maria.

"Why isn't Maria here?" I asked Fatima.

She looked surprised. She hesitated and asked, "The maid?"

"Yes, of course! Didn't you invite her?"

Fatima laughed and turned away. I felt bad. I thought for a few minutes, and then went to a pay phone, called the apartment and Maria answered.

"Maria, this is Dayal. I am so sorry. I just assumed you would be here. I am sending a taxi for you."

"Excuse me?" she replied.

"Maria, our wedding! Do you have a nice dress?"

"For church."

"That would be fine. Our wedding is over, but we're at the reception. There's plenty of food, and I want you to meet my family and my friends. I'm sending a taxi for you. Not to the service entrance, to the front of the building. It will be there in about 20 minutes. Go down and wait. Tell the doorman you are waiting for a ride if he gives you any problem. I'll have the taxi bring you over here."

"Are you sure?"

"Yes. You've been very kind to me and I want you to be able to celebrate and have some fun."

I kept an eye out for her, and when I saw her, I took her to meet my parents and my brothers, then my mates and the others from school. I told them all that she worked for Sita's mother, and that she was from the Philippines. When we talked during dinner, I told my parents that she had been trafficked, and for some reason, I guessed because she was a servant, and not Sikh, she wasn't invited. I knew Fatima and Sita were a bit miffed, but too bad. I was beginning to realize they had elitist attitudes. Most Sikhs include their whole communities when there's a wedding, regardless of economic status.

I had persuaded Sita to honeymoon in Paris, which I felt was one of the most romantic cities I had ever visited. I loved the art museums and the cafes, and she had never been there. In fact, before she visited me, she had never been anywhere except Mumbai, Kuwait, and Dubai.

I noticed that she was very quiet on the plane, but attributed it to exhaustion and that she had been drinking. When we got to the room, I immediately undressed and beckoned her to join me in the shower. I whispered to her, between kisses, "Sitaji, we are going to have intercourse. I will take as much time as you need, but this is for real." I really wanted her first time to be good, but I had been told that for many women, the first time is painful, so I tried to be gentle.

She decided to wear a negligee, and I was wearing nothing but the steel bangles.

"Lights on or off?" I asked her.

"Oh! What do you prefer?" She responded, nervously, as she slid into the bed. She was shaking.

"On, this time. I want to look at you and admire your body. I've always thought you were beautiful."

She blushed, but smiled. We had been naked together a few times, but now I saw her vulnerability, and in a split second, I saw the yin-yang of us: I was about forty pounds heavier than she, and broader. She was very pale, so I looked several shades darker in comparison. As I caressed her, I asked, "Where do you want me to touch you?"

She responded, hesitantly, "What you're doing feels good."

I had been feeling her, but moved slowly down to eat her. She started to relax as I kissed her and stroked her, and she surrendered herself to the sensation. I felt her tense a bit, then undulate. She moaned, "Oh, Dayal," when she came.

I moved up and reached for a condom from under the pillows and handed it to her. She trembled and fumbled with it, so I sat up and took it from her and put it on myself.

"I want you to put it on me next time. I want you to touch me and stroke me. Tell me what *you* want. Talk to me."

I started kissing her again and slowly started to enter her. She was very tight. "Do you want me to stop?" I whispered.

She groaned, and grabbed my arms. "No, I knew it might be painful."

I started saying to myself, automatically, *Zed, Y, X…* I was so excited. I hadn't had intercourse since I'd been with Shayla.

She was moaning. She gasped and whispered, in Hindi "What are you saying? I feel how hot you are!"

She put her hand on my chin and pushed her tongue between my lips, then then tilted her head back and exhaled, "Ah!"

How soft she was, and I loved the feeling of her breasts against my chest. She arched her back slightly and plastered herself onto me. I could feel her shuddering. I felt we were one.

We slept cuddled together. I wanted another go at her in the morning, but she was hungry.

That first morning, she put on a pantsuit and very high heels. I said to her, "Sitaji, you can't walk in those shoes. We are going to be out all day."

"All I have is my wedding flats."

"Wear those."

We went to the museums and in the evenings, we tried different restaurants and she practiced her French with the waiters. In the evenings, we made love. She was still hesitant, but willing to try different positions. Mornings after some play and breakfast, we shopped. She (or, rather, I) bought a fur coat, several pairs of shoes, a pair of very nice leather boots, some lingerie and, well, we had to buy another suitcase to bring it all back.

Upon our return to Switzerland, I bought a Fiat so we could get around. Sita started working two afternoons at a crèche. I was doing all the cooking.

She didn't say anything about decorating, which surprised me. After about a month, however, she seemed subdued. I kept asking her if she wanted to talk about what was bothering her, but she continued to tell me it was nothing. "I am just getting used to my new life. I miss my friends, and my mum."

I hired a cleaning service to come in once a week to clean, but I was doing the laundry, cooking and grocery shopping. I insisted she go grocery shopping with me so she could learn prices of everyday items, maybe learn Swiss German, and have some say in planning our menus for the week. I dragged her to rehearsals once a week. On Saturday nights, if I didn't have work in Montreux, we went to the club. I started wondering what I had gotten myself into. She was not affectionate. She rarely started a conversation with me.

When I had time to just contemplate my life, I felt sad that Sita was not the partner I was hoping she would be. She did not want to shower or be in the tub with me. She didn't help pre-pare meals unless I asked her to, and certainly didn't help clean up. We had a mechanical dishwasher in the apartment, and there was no reason she could not load that, and make the bed, and learn to put groceries away or do the shopping. It was all I could do to get her to put soiled clothes into a basket. I showed her how to separate clothes and use the washers in the laundry room several times, but she was obviously bored by the idea.

She would allow me to hug and kiss her, and she accepted sex play but never initiated it. This was definitely a case of the Swahili "the man makes love and the woman has love made to her." I kept telling myself to be patient. This was normal. I had uprooted her. Her somberness affected me.

I kept a regular routine: school, work, piano practice, run-ning, working out and taking care of her and the apartment.

From what I could see, she would get up in the morning, eat what I left her and go to the crèche, or if she didn't have work, watch TV or call Michelle. After a few weeks of this, I told her I thought she was depressed. "Sitaji, tell me. Is it something I've done or not done and what can we both do so you'll be happier?"

She sighed, and didn't make eye contact with me. Finally, she said, "Nobody has ever before asked me what made me happy or unhappy. I was sent to school and told when I had completed high school that I would marry. I would learn to love my husband. Now, here I am. It is not you. It's me. You are doing your best. I know, I just have to get used to living in a new country and speaking a new language. I have to get used to the cold. You are very caring. I will love you. I know I will. But…"

She started sobbing. I felt so bad. My initial reaction was shock at her sadness. I got her a tissue and put my arm around her. I didn't know what to do. In my life, I had never been with anyone, adult, that is, who cried and wasn't mourning a death. I was with men. Here was my wife, so unhappy.

"You were right, Dayal, about my schooling and the church. But the church and Jesus gave me comfort for so many years. The nuns talked of faith all the time. You know, there are no people like us here. Not even a satsang. I don't know how to find what I want to do, what will occupy my time. I have no idea how my mother found peace in her own life, or if she ever loved my father. I don't know if my father loves his new wife. I miss my sisters, I miss my mother, and I miss my old life. And, you know, what was my old life? Frivolous, really. I think I want to have a baby."

I was shocked, but I shouldn't have been. I just hadn't thought about it. I was *not ready* to have a baby. The main reason was that Sita could barely take care of herself, so that's how I addressed it to her.

"Sitaji, I understand everything you're saying. I was sent off to school, living with people not like me. I had to adapt. I know it's been difficult for you. Together, we will explore different things you might become interested in, maybe art or making jewelry. There are so many opportunities in Switzerland. I'll teach you to use the computer so you can email friends. We can get a computer for the house. I'll do whatever it takes. But you must learn to take care of the house before we have a baby. You must talk to me more. When I hold you in bed, I don't want to hurt you. I want to give you pleasure and I want you to give me pleasure. I want us to be partners."

That evening I insisted she choose the restaurant for the kind of food she wanted. It was a pity that there were no Indian restaurants in our area. Our only choices were some varieties of European food.

Sita chose a French restaurant that served crepes, and she told me how much she really liked them. They were like roti. I told her that it wouldn't be difficult to learn to make them. I could already make chapattis. We decided we would both learn, and we would check out some cookbooks. Of course, finding cookbooks in English was difficult, so we asked her sister to send us one she thought would be easy to use.

I taught her to drive. This took about a month practicing every day. She was nervous because our roads are winding and you can't see that far ahead, but she really didn't have much trouble with the actual driving part. It was merging into faster traffic, parallel parking and backing up that gave her trouble, which makes everyone nervous. Learning to drive, however, gave her a lot more confidence to explore and go out on her own, and our lives seemed to go a bit more smoothly for the next several months. Still, I had to cajole her into housekeeping chores.

She wasn't interested in learning to ski, but she went ice skating with Michelle. I still skied with Adam several times a month. ✪

# CHAPTER 12

I told Sita in March that we were going out on tour starting in May. "It will be a ninety-day tour. This is even a bit much for me, but we're going to start with three dates in England and one in Copenhagen, then Sweden, then go to eastern Canada. Then we'll zigzag through the United States, a few cities in South America, then Asia. We're going to be in the western United States for about two weeks to get a little break and attend some sort of awards show. Adam is bringing Michelle. There will be a gym and a pool at every hotel, and we can tour most cities. All the hotels have internet access, too."

"Is This OK?" was nominated for Grammys in America, for song of the year, and the album it was on, "Magic Fingers," for album of the year. Adam and I were also nominated for producers of the year.

Living the reality of touring, constantly moving, unpacking and repacking, and trying to keep something that resembled a regular schedule was rough. Adam and Michelle were more likely to chill at the end of the day. I knew Peter and Oscar would party with the crew and whomever they picked up.

A few days before we were to leave, I asked Sita, "Did you remember to tell your mother and friends to send any mail via Levine's office?"

"Oh, no! We're leaving on Saturday?"

I had her sit down and write or email anyone who she thought might want to contact her. I gave her a tour itinerary, which listed our hotels as well. Then, I asked her what she planned to take along in terms of luggage. She had three suitcases of clothing, plus another large bag of… what? Cosmetics, toiletries, shoes?

"Sitaji, this is way too much. Two suitcases. You can buy anything you need as we travel. We're going to the USA. They have everything there."

I didn't think of it at the time, but she did not bring one book. I had four with me.

"So here's what I usually do. I arise around 7:30. I go for a run, and I hope you'll join me either running or going to the gym in the hotel for exercise. We'll have breakfast. I will do a sound check with our guys and rehearse. You could go with me then or do something else. You can check with the concierge about what's available. I will return to the hotel around 1:00 in the afternoon, and we can go to an area restaurant for lunch, which would usually be our main meal, and then we'll go either to a museum, an art gallery, or possibly a movie. I might decide to take a nap. Sometimes, we'll play Scrabble, sometimes cards. We might then have a snack, but we have to be back at the venue by 21:00 because our shows start at 22:00. We'll return around midnight. I really want you to be with me, but I understand if you don't want to be at the show because it will be the same every night. We might switch the order of songs, or add or subtract a few, but we have a routine. I rarely go to an after-show party. You can if you want, but they are usually wild, and I don't drink."

"Dayal, this sounds really regimented," Sita replied.

"I have to keep a regular schedule or I get headaches. It's stressful for me to move around being in different places all the time. I hope it isn't that way for you. I'll give you $100 a day for spending money. Is that ok?"

"I think so."

Things started out fine. Sita told me enjoyed being on a treadmill or bicycle, but preferred we do yoga together in the hotel room. When I was busy, she wanted to go shopping with Michelle. Michelle told me that Sita seemed obsessed with jewelry.

After the show in Montreal, I returned to our room. I was exhausted and trying to wind down. Just making conversation, I asked Sita, who had been watching TV, "Did you do anything interesting today? What did you buy?"

"Why do you ask what I've bought?" she responded, hesitantly.

"Curiosity. Michelle told me you really liked to buy jewelry, so I would think you'd want to show me what you've purchased and what you plan to wear it with."

She got up and went to the closet and brought out several small bags. She slowly emptied the contents onto a table. I got up and started looking through the pile, and it was a pile. Then I started separating pieces. Most were gold tone, but not real gold, of course. In fact, there were a lot plastic bangles, necklaces with plastic beads, and a few rings.

"You've bought all this since we came over, or did you buy some in Europe? Do you have nothing at all like this already in your collection?"

She looked at me, sort of questioningly, and said, "I bought a few bracelets in Europe."

"What do you feel when you buy this? I ask, because I bought you a star sapphire, very rare, for a wedding present. My friend knew I was looking for something unique, very special. When he showed it to me, I knew it was perfect. I notice you never wear it."

"Oh, Dayal, it *is* special: Too special to wear. I never think about what I feel when I buy jewelry. I'm giving most of these to my friends as gifts." She didn't seem quite sure herself.

"This is junk from China."

She started to cry. I felt bad, but I wanted to get to the bottom of this.

"Sitaji, I think you have a shopping habit."

"I've never seen anything like these in Dubai or India," she said, still sobbing.

"Probably because the shops you usually frequent only handle more expensive items."

She continued to sob, but I would not comfort her. I was tired. Sikhi call this *maya,* or *moh*: an attachment to worldly things.

"Come, take a shower with me," I said, taking her hand.

She pulled back and said, "I don't want a shower."

I had so many negative feelings all at once: Rejection, sadness, feeling disrespected, anger, and alienation. I just never imagined the woman I was with would be this way. Our love was not growing. I didn't want to go to bed angry, I would never sleep.

I got down on my knees and took her hand again. "Please," I said, "come with me. I'm sorry you don't want a shower. I want you with me. I want to touch you. I need to be soothed. Please."

She came with me but would not make eye contact. I turned the shower on to warm up the water. I undressed her, and then I undressed myself. I put my arm around her and brought her into the shower and started washing her. I just wanted to touch her. There was no other way I could initiate affection. She just stood there, sobbing. I put the soap down and hugged her to me. She was slow to return my embrace. I wanted to make love to her.

I started to lift her, holding her rear end, and she stopped crying and asked, "What are you doing?"

I said, "Hold on to me." I slid my hand between her legs. She clung more tightly to me. I leaned her against the wall, and started stroking her as I kissed her. She lifted her face up to me, and she returned my kiss.

As I entered her, she said, "Ooooh," and gave me more of her tongue and moved her arms around my shoulders. I broke the kiss and whispered to her, "Is this OK?"

She whispered back, "Oh, yes yes, keep going."

So I kept going and I could feel her get tighter, if that was at all possible. She shouted out, "Oh, yes! Oh!" and a bunch of Hindi.

I allowed myself to come, and felt my love for her. I enjoyed making love to Sita, but I wondered why there had to be so much drama.

We went directly to bed and cuddled. As I was drifting off, I realized I hadn't used a condom. Ah, well… .

We would be in Chicago, again, in about two weeks. I had sent both a letter and a telegram to Shayla, inviting her, Anya, and Mara to the show, and I had specifically requested that Levine send Shayla passes.

When Levine joined us in Philadelphia, he gave me a letter from Shayla. She wrote that all three girls wanted to come to the show. She sent along Mara's phone number, and I tried calling. It was like one of those bad dreams. The call would not go through, or I got a recorded message to "try your call again later," or I got an answering machine. I left several messages about the hotel where we'd be staying, and begged her to call on those dates. I called Shayla and begged her to make sure Mara got the message.

The tour was going well enough. We went to Atlanta, did a festival in Florida, where it was very hot and humid, and I was grateful for the T-shirts we had made, because I had to change several times during a performance to be comfortable. We implemented the panels and microphone ideas so our sound would not be as distorted. I convinced the guys that we didn't need dramatic visual effects if our music was clear, but I was glad we had the extra horns and percussion.

Our performance was part of a festival in the park along the lakefront in Chicago with a lot going on: food tents, amusement park rides, and an art fair. After the sound check, I went back to the room. Mara had left a message! I called her that evening and she answered the phone.

"Mara! Habari yako!" and suddenly I was overcome. I burst into tears.

"Ndugu? Dayal? Is that you?" She sounded shocked.

"Habari, Mpendwa! I've been calling you forever. Calling and calling, leaving messages. Where have you been?" I could feel my heart beating in my chest. My emotions were so mixed.

"Oh, Dayal, I've been trying to have a life."

I could tell she was weeping, too. "What do you mean?"

Mara gave a bitter laugh and explained, "I'm not even supposed to be here. I got back two weeks ago. If there's any way for my government to make things worse in the world, they do. I was working on community-based recycling in Malawi, in the Traditional Housing Areas. You know, squatter communities. The Europeans wanted to institute recycling for import substitution, but they didn't bother to take into account if any BTUs would be saved. It's the idea that counts, right? Getting the community involved, so later they'd be able to tell their elected ministers what they want. It was funded by the U.N. So, we had to do household surveys of the type of garbage they generated. To do that, we had to schedule community meetings. Apparently, our elites have no inkling what 'dictatorship' means. I had to figure out where the most influential people in the communities were. It's always grandmothers. But the economy is, well, Banda owns everything. In any case, of course we needed Malawi Congress Party permission—which I was told by the British that we had…"

"You mean, like TANU?" TANU was the Tanzania Africa National Union, the single party in Tanzania.

"Yes, but the week I started, the auxiliary, you get what I'm saying? —a bunch of Malawi Young Pioneers got the crap beat out of them… ."

I had to laugh. These sycophants were in every country, shaking down regular folks.

"*That* never happened before," she went on. "It was in the newspaper, which was confiscated quickly. Everyone knew. People were very paranoid. So, the European Community decided to freeze aid until Banda allowed a free press and scheduled elections. As if. The ODA, with the Europeans, had been threatening him, which was why he allowed this project. You know, to make it look like bottom up organizing was allowed. The only reason they needed me was so a mzungu would be in charge and no Malawians would go missing for daring to start something."

"Is it?"

"Yes. Nothing was happening, and within days ODA, the British, told me the project was on indefinite hold, and I had to return. The pay was ok, I got it all, but the per diem was $90 a day, and how much does it cost to live in Malawi? Five dollars a day? So I lost that. So, I returned and just took this job because some dog groomer was on vacation."

"So, you're still readjusting," I remarked. "I'm playing tomorrow. I want you to come to the concert, and I want to see you. I'm staying at the Palmer House downtown. Do you know where it is? Can you come?"

"They're calling for a transit strike. And I have to go to work. I'm booked a month out. I wish I had known sooner that seeing you would be a possibility. I can't not show up because it makes a lot more work for everyone else I work with. My reputation is that I show up no matter what. That's how I get temp work. It's going to be a big transportation mess downtown. I can't drive down there. There's no place to park. Can you possibly come up here? I'm only about eight miles north of where you are."

"I can try to come up there. What's a good time?"

"I work out in the western suburbs, so I won't be home until three. Please come, It'll be so great to see you. You have your wife with you, right?"

"Three is too late. We have to be at the venue by six. And I can't bring Sita."

"Why?" she asked.

"She's very insecure. We're still not in love. I want us to be. Especially now, I think she might be pregnant."

"Oh. I don't know whether to say congratulations or sorry."

"I know. I have mixed feelings myself. But I have to see you."

"Call me later, then. Tutaonana," she said and hung up.

I started weeping. I realized I had never stopped loving her. My gut feeling was that she had started me on my path to adulthood. Not just sex, but how she talked to me.

That conversation meant so much to me. She spoke of Africa, and who else would care about how foreign aid wasn't making things better? She really cared, and she knew I'd understand.

The next morning, I went to breakfast with Adam and Michelle. Sita was still sleeping. That was how it had been since Montreal. That was why I thought she might be pregnant. She was having morning sickness. It had only been a little over two weeks. I didn't say anything to the others, though. It was just a feeling I had.

"Did you hear the news?" Adam said. "There's a transit strike. Can you believe it? This is going to be a nightmare."

"I heard," I responded. I started eating, then asked, "Are Pete and Oscar up yet?"

"I doubt it. They partied hard last night. They went to Buddy Guy's Blues Club on the south side," Michelle responded.

"That's where the Rolling Stones go when they're in town."

"Right. I bet they closed the place," Adam replied, yawning.

"You mean they didn't spend the night fornicating?"

Both Adam and Michelle laughed and Adam replied, "They may be now."

Pete and Oscar, both hung over, were a little late to the sound check. I didn't really think about it because this was so often their state. We started rehearsing, Peter was dancing around as he does when he plays guitar, not looking where he was. He fell off the stage. I couldn't believe it. Chaos ensued. We had to call an ambulance, and with the transit strike, Chicago was one giant traffic jam. It took over half an hour for the ambulance to reach us, and over an hour to get to the hospital. I went with Pete, and his big concern was whether the guitar was ruined. He had cracked a couple of ribs and fractured his leg. I called our road manager at the hotel and told him that we would go on with the show because we had enough musicians with us, but what a mess. I left a message for Sita at the hotel that I would most likely not be returning before the show, and would explain later, and a message for Michelle to turn on the news. Then I left a message for Mara and told her there had been an accident, it would be on the news, I would probably be back at the hotel after midnight, but to still try to come to the show.

Mara and I never got together. I called her around mid-night. "Mpendwa, habari. Sorry it's so late."

"How was your show?" She asked in a very sultry voice. I knew I had woken her.

"Have you seen the news reports? Most people could not get to it. I hope that they can turn their tickets in and get refunds and a discount for next year's show, if we have one. Peter's in the hospital. It was a very stressful day."

"How is Peter?"

"He'll be laid up for a few days. Something is always happening to him. But listen… I've just missed you so much…" I was overcome and started to weep. I was in our hotel room, but I had taken the phone into the bathroom to not wake Sita. I realized how tired and stressed I was. "When this tour is over, I want to see you. I'll fly in from Europe."

"Well, let's think about it. We'll see how it goes," she said, sounding somber but calm.

"Don't you want to see me?"

"Dayal, you're a married man now. I am not Shayla. I can't separate love and sex."

"But you did!" I whispered fiercely. "You told me to!" My heart, I could just feel myself all twisted up. "I need you in my life."

She was sobbing, I could hear her. "That was a totally different situation. This is the punishment I suffer for having fun with you. Should I still write to you at your address at school?"

"Yes. If you send a letter to the engineering department, at school, I'll get it. Do you have email?"

"No. Not yet. I use a friend's email. I'll send a letter soon, OK? I do miss you and I do love you, but think about your wife."

We left it at that. I felt horrible. I joined Sita in bed and I cuddled her. I wanted to get up, find a taxi, and go find Mara, but traffic was still insane even outside the hotel after midnight. We had gotten away from the show venue by taking a circuitous walking route. It was nuts. I couldn't help but think fate wanted us apart.

The next morning, I was still stressed and went down to the gym, and watched local news on TV while I was on the treadmill. The strike was settled around noon, and by 2:00 P.M., traffic started to clear. We went to Madison, Wisconsin, by coach, only four hours away. We had a good show up there, and Adam explained Peter's absence. Peter was the one who usually sang "Poetry Man," the Phoebe Snow song. Such a beautiful song, and he did a great job of it, with his facial expressions and intonations. Adam and I rehearsed it at the sound check and we were passable with harmonies. Peter joined us two days later in Tulsa. He had a cast on his leg and his body was all taped up. He could not sing. He could barely play the guitar. We went on as we had with our backup musicians.

Sita was pregnant. She seemed happy, but tired. When I came in after a show and suggested a shower, she joined me eagerly.

We played in Omaha, then Phoenix, then went up to Las Vegas, where we got to see Jimmy Paxon with a small group. It was great to connect with him. Sita's sister and brother-in-law, who lived in Colorado, joined us as they were gamblers. Then we flew to Los Angeles, a very short ride, where we were nominated for the awards.

We had to rehearse a song to open the Grammy Awards. Peter was still not a hundred per cent, but he could play. Of course we opened with "Is This OK?" Sita got to wear a lot of her jewelry and a beautiful pink sari, which I had to pin her into. She looked incredible, and several people said she looked like a Barbie doll, which Michelle had to explain to me. I was told several entertainment news shows and some of the tabloid magazines ran photos of us. I was surprised that we got the awards both for song and album of the year. Adam and I got the award for producer of the year. The trophies were nice, but the recognition was what was important.

We played a date in San Francisco then we went up to Seattle, and then flew to Seoul. It was there Sita miscarried.

She told me she knew something was wrong because she had missed a period, but thought it was due to travel. When she soaked through a pad in an hour, she was concerned, but didn't want to bother me. Then, she fainted. She was in the hospital in Seoul overnight. I was grateful the doctor spoke English. He told me it was not a viable pregnancy, there was no fetus, just a blob, and it was not uncommon.

Sita accepted the explanation, but it took a lot out of her. I was glad the tour was almost over. Still, I suggested she go rest in Dubai and I would come to be with her in a couple of weeks. We only had seven more shows.

All the excitement took a toll on me, too. I had breakfast with Michelle and Adam the next day. They could tell I wasn't my normal self. Adam asked how I was doing.

"It turned out it wasn't a viable pregnancy, but it was scary for both of us. I don't know if you know, but we Sikhi, Africans, too, actually, don't celebrate pregnancy. You're not a baby until you're born. We think it's bad luck. I hope she didn't start fantasizing. Still, I know it was rough on her. I was thinking, how do you know when it's a love match?"

"How do you mean?" Michele asked.

"Well, I feel so bad for her. She was forced into a marriage with me."

"Oh, Dayal, don't say that. She wasn't!" Michelle shot back. "You asked her if she was physically attracted to you and told her what your lives would be like. She told me that. She told me she was getting used to you. She also told me…" She and Adam started giggling.

"What?" I asked.

"She said you were a good lover, patient and gentle."

"She said that? Still… what choice did she really have? If not me, it would have been anyone. She was never allowed to meet boys."

"And it wasn't the same for you?" Adam said.

I looked at him and smiled. "Come on, you know it wasn't. I had had sex." I was far enough away from my parents that I could have stalled for years.

Michelle said, "Ah." She had studied psychology and sociology and was doing women's studies. "Most women in the world have no choice. You know the African women, the ones in plural marriages, bond with their sister wives, and even take lovers. Also, you know so many leave husbands and go back to their parents' communities? The girls who get married off to older men, they really don't have a choice, but most seem to get over it. They maneuver. I think it's women who think they've made a love match and assume so much that do the worst. The fantasy bubble is busted once the first issue comes up."

"So, how did you guys know?" I asked.

They looked at each other and grinned. Adam said, "When you want to see the other person the first thing in the morning and the last thing at night. When the conversation never ends, and you want to share experiences other than sex and you can and do, and ask, 'Is this OK?'"

We giggled at that.

I said, "I don't know that we've reached that milestone. I do love seeing her morning and night. I do want to share experiences with her. She just seems reserved with me. She hardly ever starts a conversation. We share few interests. Maybe when she's pregnant again, we'll grow closer. We were getting there, I think. It just bothers me that she self-soothes by buying stuff. We're so different that way. I grew up without stuff."

Michelle laughed and said, "I had an American roommate for a while, and she got a letter from her sister who had been married for just six weeks and was getting divorced. The reason doesn't matter, but she said, 'You don't really know someone until you've gone camping with them.'"

Adam chuckled and nodded his head.

"What does *that* mean?" I asked.

"You've never been camping. You have to cooperate. You have to select a spot, pitch a tent, gather firewood to cook, and then cook over a fire and have to take care of everything," Adam explained.

"Outside? Sleeping on the ground, like the Maasai?" *I wondered why anyone would do that.*

"You know," Adam added as he was cutting his food, "You guys never lived together. Not really. You didn't know each other, not the habits you both have."

"I just felt that we'd work it out, like my parents did." I shook my head, trying to explain. "The whole Catholic thing bothers me, too. I meditate. I think she prays. "

"She does," Michelle admitted.

"You know that?"

She took a sip of tea, put her cup down, and looked straight at me. "Yes. She asked me not to tell you, but she's asking Jesus to help her. She's under as much stress as you are."

"I'm surprised you haven't known. I told her that didn't work for me. They fill you up with quotes from the Bible, but it ends up being about faith and believing with no evidence. She believes what they taught her because they were nice to her. She takes no responsibility. She doesn't question." Adam added.

"What do you mean?"

"When I was an altar boy, just 11-years-old, two priests molested me. I was shocked, of course, but I put it out of my mind until one of them started pestering me about going to confession. I asked what I had to confess to, and this guy says to me, 'For enticing me.' That was the end of my faith. Right there."

I took that in. I had no experience with homosexuality.

"Why did you send her to Dubai?" Adam asked, interrupting my thoughts.

"To let her rest and be taken care of for a few weeks."

I still felt I was not ready to take care of a child. "Do you ever feel ready to have children?" I asked, addressing them both as I finished my tea.

They both chuckled again. Michelle said, "The only people who think they're ready are the ones who haven't thought things through. People who don't think about sleepless nights, or nappies, or juggling work and a child, or ever consider their child could be born handicapped."

We all raised our eyebrows at that thought and grew quiet.

The rest of the tour went smoothly—no mishaps, no drama. Levine met us in Jakarta and gave me mail. Shayla had written about how frustrating it had been to try to get to see us. Dr. Schultz had written that he wanted me to teach an introductory course on sound engineering the next semester and to send an outline.

I missed Sita. I didn't like sleeping alone. I went to several of the after-show parties, but I didn't have fun. When you're sober, drunk people look like fools.

I flew to Dubai as soon as I could after our last show, and found Sita to be quite well recovered. She had had a grand time visiting with her friends and going out shopping. I tried just being with her, doing nothing for two days. At least at night I could hold her. I wanted to get back to Switzerland and what I considered *normal* life. I had also wanted to go to Tanzania to see my parents, but this would have to wait. When I got back to Switzerland, I mentioned my vague plan to Sita. I wrote to my parents and asked if they would like to come for the Christmas-New Year holiday. Baba wrote back that he and Ama would love to do that, and perhaps my brothers would as well. At least I had something to look forward to.

Michelle told Sita she saw an ad in the paper for a jewelry store looking for a clerk, so she went in one morning with Michelle to check it out. They hired her on the spot.

The store had many international customers because, in addition to regular jewelry like rings, necklaces, and watches ( the watch store seems ubiquitous, like in Hong Kong), they sold Swiss vintage enamel jewelry. The artisans made tiny birds, flowers, fruit, and charms. These items were fascinating, so colorful and detailed. I could appreciate the workmanship that went into the art, but from the point of view of someone who grew up in a place where a family's most precious possession might have been a hoe, the idea that there was a niche market of people collecting these things made apparent our social stratification.

One night we got a bit high while we played cards with Adam and Michelle. I flopped onto the bed when we got in, but Sita took my hand and said, "Take a shower with me."

I was in a stoned fog, but I followed her into the bathroom. She undressed me, then she took the soap and started washing me, and it was enough: The warmth of her, feeling her breasts against me. She kissed me, and soaped my dick and balls. She had never done that. Was a bit of weed all it took?

I had thought I was too tired, but apparently I wasn't. We slept late the next morning, and she stayed cuddled with me, and the thought that she was pregnant again pranced through my mind.

We went to Dubai in November for a few days. It was shocking to me how much construction was going on. I had seen a few buildings when I had fetched her at the end of our tour, but now there were at least 50 large ones under construction, and some new roads. There was a small recording studio Levine wanted me to visit. While Sita was with her friends, I spent several afternoons with these new sound engineers, helping them with design build-out for the future. They wanted to be able to record artists who could not record in their own countries. The Pleasure Seekers had no presence in Moslem countries. I really wondered if anyone heard us there, but these guys told me there was an underground sharing of music.

We returned to Switzerland refreshed. There was a letter waiting for me from Mara:

*Dear Ndugu,*

*I am sure the fates have conspired to make our communications difficult. I have sent you postcards or aerograms from where I've been working when I've been in Africa. Have you gotten any of them? I've sent at least a dozen. I've always wondered why you never responded.*

*Being in Malawi messed up my head a little. I've always gotten depressed when I'm stressed, but this experience was surreal. It involved organizing, and it's not like people don't know what to do.*

*I had to go to all the squatter neighborhoods. A Peace Corps architect took me around, and we stopped at this housing estate of about 200 small burned brick houses south of Blantyre. Imagine houses the size of your parents' living room. I was told they were to be marketed to the middle class—high school graduates who had management jobs, and electricity was coming soon, but no water infrastructure. Buyers are expected to put in a water tank and dig and line pit latrines, so they'd be pumpable.*

*These houses weren't even big enough for two, let alone a family of six! And right at the entrance to the estate was a big sign. At the top: World Bank funded, then the architectural firm, the engineering firm, the construction firm. So proud to have their companies listed—and nobody would buy these houses. I asked someone from the World Bank how they came up with this scheme—that's what they are called: schemes—and the guy told me it was based on a model in China! Have you noticed what the World Bank is funding in Arusha?*

*In the USA, the cost of fuel for transportation and heating our homes has become a major concern. Inflation is a problem. Our government has discouraged the development of renewable energy to keep the fuel companies profitable. Just the cost of living was the reason for the transit strike. There could be more efficiencies, of course, but the city is run by a political machine, and the politicians are not for the citizen taxpayers. It's the same wherever you go.*

*I have to be truthful. I have missed you terribly at times, but I try to not think about you. You have a wife now, and your wife should be your main priority. It would do neither of us any good to pine for each other. I told you to not confuse sex with love. I think it is immoral to break up a marriage. If a marriage breaks up for other reasons, that's one thing. But to **steal** someone's partner as a sexual conquest hurts too many people. I would always wonder, that if a man left his wife for me, wouldn't he leave me for another woman? I would not do it.*

*Shayla told me she was with you last time you came through. She has two boys now. You probably know that. To tell you the truth, I wouldn't have wasted time with either of her husbands. Shayla wanted children and being married is the best way to have children.*

*I almost forgot, note my new address. Love,*
*Mara*

I read it over several times, then I folded it up and put it in my sock drawer. I had mixed emotions, but hearing from Mara was a gift. ✪

# CHAPTER 13

My parents, brothers, and their families came for Christmas week. I really hadn't thought this through. Sita had asked where we'd put everyone. Our apartment was just two bedrooms, so my brothers decided to stay in the pension that Sita had stayed in, but my parents stayed with us. What was important was that we were all together, and we had hot running water and a refrigerator.

My mother was fascinated by our kitchen. She knew what a toaster was, but she had never seen a dishwasher, or at least she hadn't noticed the ones in my brothers' homes. She asked me, "Ni nini kitu hiki?"—meaning, "*What is this thing?*"

I told her, "Vitu la kuosho vyombo *(a thing for washing dishes)*." There is no real KiSwahili word for dishwasher. In any case, she thought that was marvelous, as was the side-by-side refrigerator/freezer that you could get both water and ice from the door.

Switzerland was decorated for Christmas: Lots of colored lights on trees outdoors, and the commercial district looked like a fairyland. I had to admit it was beautiful, especially at night.

My parents thought everything was so exotic, including snow. With the help of Adam, Michelle, and Dr. Schultz, I was able to borrow winter clothing for everyone. We went tobogganing, and we also watched some downhill skiing. We took the train to Lucerne to tour the town and get chocolate. We went out a couple of times back in Zurich for both cheese and chocolate fondues and a raclette, which is sort of like an open-faced grilled-cheese sandwich. My parents had never eaten cheese, as nobody makes it in Africa. My mother hated all the cheeses I had her try, but my father liked Gruyere. They liked the chocolate fondue, although they felt it was too rich to eat without fruit.

We went to a yodeling performance. What can you say about yodeling? It was fun. I bought my father a Tag Heuer watch and my mother a cuckoo clock to take back.

I performed in the school concert. They all got a kick out of my white tux. It was the first time my family had heard me play in an orchestra, and they said that they enjoyed it, although both my parents remarked that it was really loud. They never got to hear live music.

Sita worked right up to Christmas Eve and got a good bonus. I encouraged her to save it, but I knew she spent at least half on diamond earrings. Had I known she wanted them, I would have bought them for her as a gift. I didn't want to get into the habit of buying Christmas gifts and celebrating Christmas. This is not what Sikhi do. I rather missed celebrating Vaisakhi and Diwali, but there were not any Hindus or Sikhi where we were, to do it. Vaisakhi is often compared to a New Year or Spring celebration, and that's how the Hindus celebrate it, but for us it's religious significance is of early supporters of Guru Gobind Singh taking Amrit, the confirmation of their devotion to the cause of Sikhi in 1699. Some of our celebrations are similar to Jewish celebrations: commemorating the formation of armies to defend our right to worship. Diwali is a festival of light—a Hindu holiday celebrating the return of Lord Ram and goddess Lakshmi. More cultural than religious, but we Sikhi use the day to celebrate Prisoners Release Day, when Guru Hargobind and 52 princes were released in 1619 by Emperor Jahangir, who had tried to get Sikhi to worship God the Moslem way.

We celebrated Christmas Eve at my old apartment with Peter, Adam and Michelle. It was a tight fit, but fun. They had put up a tree and let my nephews decorate it. This is something I would never do. Years later, Mara told me her father forbade a tree, although the girls had wanted one. He associated it with Christianity, and they were already too assimilated.

Peter told us about Christmas in Holland, celebrated in early December. A guy named "Sinterklaas" comes ashore from Madrid, of all places, with guys known as "black Peters." They leave candy for the children, in their shoes, from the end of November through early December. Totally incomprehensible. In France, Adam and Michelle told us, they celebrate with a huge meal and lots of desserts, including a replica of a yule log in chocolate. We did that Christmas Day.

Adam brought out the Scrabble board. Sita wanted to go to midnight mass, so she, my brothers, sisters-in-law, their children, and Peter went to church. They walked my parents back to the condo on the way.

Just making conversation as we played Scrabble, I asked Adam if he knew where Oscar was.

"He has a family in the Philippines, so I think he's there. After all our tours he headed for Manila. Treasure. This is a triple word score."

"I thought he was from Mexico. I could have sworn he told me he had family in Veracruz. Azure. The zed is a double score."

"Is that so? Maybe. He gets all over. Zone. Put me down for 30 points."

I knew Sita was overwhelmed with all the people in the house, but she didn't have to cook or clean. We all pitched in.

Just after New Year, everyone left. Sita went to London for a couple of weeks. I missed her, but I also relished the calm to do what I had to do. When she returned, she told me she had some recipes that her sister gave her, and started cooking more. She even started cleaning up as she cooked.

By early February, Sita knew she was pregnant. She was ecstatic, and quit her evening glass of wine immediately, but we both agreed to not say anything to anyone until she was in the second trimester. Her doctor gave us information about infant care and Lamaze classes at a local hospital. We started to check out baby cribs and sources of goat milk (in case Sita didn't have enough milk, easier for babies to digest, according to the doctor), and we got into a routine.

I taught two days in class, and I wanted my students in the engineering lab the other class day, so I had to be available. I also had my own projects. Dr. Schultz let me know he'd be advisor for my dissertation and to get things moving because he wanted to retire.

This was early 1993. The music industry was changing. More groups were making videos, and there were many more festivals. It made more sense, financially, to have a venue with many acts over several days, rather than for a manager to book a venue and have a single band pay for overhead. We could only really fill a sports stadium if we partnered with other groups to split costs. It was too expensive because of security, insurance, and in larger cities, union contracts, let alone flying everyone. The other problem, which was really more significant, was that we didn't actually sell show tickets. The venues made deals with resellers, and the resellers boosted the ticket prices. Shayla had told me this was happening.

At this time an opportunity came up which changed my life. Several of our fellow musicians had been offered opportunities to have their music performed if they could have it orchestrated. Adam was now teaching a class on woodwinds, and was doing more arranging. After Freddie Mercury died in 1991, Madam Chabon wanted our orchestra to perform the music from Barcelona—*if* Adam could orchestrate it. Arranging for so many instruments is a huge undertaking.

"You take woodwinds and brass, and I'll take percussion and strings," I told Adam, when he asked me what I thought. I was just joking.

Then, he mused, "Wouldn't it be great if you could invent something like that microphone you worked on that would record and then transfer automatically to notation on a computer?"

It was like a light bulb went on over my head. This guy in the States had been working on "computerized models of music transcription," and he had even cited my work on the auto-correct microphone. It was just a matter of me sitting down and coding and having Dr. Schultz get someone to debug my code.

I started laughing. Even using macros, it would be tedious work. Yet, this kind of software would revolutionize music. People who had the musical talent to think up songs but who didn't know how to notate would be able to play into a computer and have it notated and shared. I wondered if the Synclavier software would work.

Adam had no idea why I was laughing. "Are you OK?"

"Just excited. I can do that. It's going to take forever, a lot of coding. I know I can come up with software."

I don't know what I was thinking. It took over a year to

get it coded enough that it could work, and several more years until I could get it to display quickly. The computers couldn't *think* fast enough at that time. Back then, in the early 1990s, you wouldn't get an hourglass icon or a *please wait* on the screen. The computer would freeze up and I'd have to look for the bug or find more memory. It was more sensible to just start notating the actual music, which Adam did.

I emailed Levine and told him what we were doing, and asked him if he could negotiate a contract for us with the university. I told him it would take at least six months, which was more optimistic than realistic. I had to code enough for the computer to listen and notate. I could code for only about four hours a day at most or it would make me crazy.

I gave Dr. Schultz a draft of my research protocol, and he was as excited as I was.

We told Peter and Oscar that we would not tour that year. It actually took me until the end of 1998, because between coding and memory, I was learning as I worked. Peter seemed relieved. He said he wanted to finish his bachelor's degree. I had told Levine, that he might want to issue a press release that we would not tour this year because of this big project. The only things keeping us in the public eye were our videos. We had three studio albums out, and two live concert albums.

I tried to keep a routine of practicing piano in the early morning, working out for an hour, then coding most of the afternoons I wasn't teaching. Everyone teased me about how I kept a schedule, but I had to or I felt I wasn't in control of my life.

Adam and Michelle joined us for dinner or a board game Friday nights if we didn't go to the club or Montreux. Peter sometimes joined us too, but he still could not find a woman he wanted to be monogamous with. He told us that he called a girl by the wrong name and realized he had hurt her. He ended up writing the song "Players." We were able to produce it in two days. We released it and it charted all over, getting to number five in the USA top forty.

We went to Dubai in June for a week to see Sita's family. Her sisters were there with their families, so it was good getting to see everyone, but aside from the camel races, there was nothing for me to do. I did some coding on a 8/16-bit Toshiba T1100 computer I had recently bought so I could work wherever I was. Not ideal, but that was what was available. I also visited the guys at the recording studio, and they were making wonderful progress.

Dubai had exploded. I could not count the number of buildings now. It was a city, but sort of a ghost town. Aside from the guys working on construction, you never saw anyone on the street.

We went on to Arusha for a week to see my parents. Avi and Sodhi were there at the same time, with their families. My parents were thrilled that Sita was pregnant.

We brothers made a platform bunk-bed for our old room. If we were all going to visit, we'd need more places to sleep. We even started thinking of building a loft on the side of the house.

During these months there was the genocide going on in Rwanda. We noticed that refugees were starting to come in to town, and they were speaking of violence, but everyone was under the impression that it was rebels from Zaire/Congo pillaging. There was very little official news from just several hundred miles away. Back then, we were lucky to sometimes get an *Economist* magazine, or sometimes the Peace Corps Volunteers would have *Time*, but being in the shadow of Kilimanjaro, we only got the BBC around dawn and dusk, and nothing was being reported. We really only got an idea of what was happening when we returned to Switzerland.

I knew Tanzania was getting money from the USA, as it was in the papers, but apparently it was all for military aid. Were we going to go to war with Uganda? Rwanda? Kenya? It looked like the Americans were ignoring what was happening. I laughed bitterly to myself about the absurdity of us getting military aid, when we had so many more pressing issues—like not enough access to basic healthcare. Nobody, not even the UN, was addressing the slaughter in Rwanda.

Sita wanted to go to Dubai to have the baby. The doctor told her it wasn't wise to travel. Her blood pressure had gotten high, and I noticed she had edema in her legs. She had been glowing early in her pregnancy, but now she was looking haggard. I was worried about her and invited Fatima to come stay with us for a few weeks.

Sita had our son, Simran, after a twenty-hour labor on Halloween. I was with her, since we had done the Lamaze. I can't describe the rush of emotion I had when he was born. At first, I thought I might faint, but they handed him to me as soon as they wiped him off, and suddenly, I was ready to be a father. I had the confidence that I could take care of him. Then, the doctor asked about circumcision. I panicked for a moment, but told him that we didn't do that.

The doctor had encouraged Sita to breast feed, of course. She lost the baby weight within several weeks and her blood pressure returned to normal, but she was tired all the time. I didn't realize a baby nursed about every three hours. I hired a nurse to live with us for the first two weeks they were home, and Fatima appreciated that. The nurse taught me how to make formula if it appeared Simran was still hungry after nursing. I decided to contract with a laundry service because the nappies were overwhelming. A Swiss company had come up with a liner paper that would keep a baby relatively dry if you used cloth diapers. I didn't like the idea of disposables unless we were traveling. Sita didn't care either way. It just seemed that for the first four months of Simran's life, if she wasn't nursing, or eating, she was sleeping.

Those first weeks were magical. I went to class to teach and brought as much work home as I could to be with my family and marvel over Simran. When Sita wasn't nursing, I cradled him in my arms while I read or graded homework. I just felt so at peace, and even if he woke me with his cries, I had no problem getting up and bringing him to Sita and just being with them. He started looking at me and I talked to him and he seemed to be listening. I had never been around babies in my life, and I had this little guy. Even though the diapers were disgusting, it was all good.

We went to London for the *Naam Karan* ceremony in early December, and we took a series of trains to get to London. Sita's sister had suggested a gurdwara in London for the *Naam Karan*, which could probably be compared to a baptism. The guru (a community leader) randomly jabs a pointer into the Guru Granth Sahib (our scripture) and comes up with the first letter of the name the baby should be called.

I paid to repair the roof of the gurdwara, and the congregation was most grateful. All Sikh temples have a langar, a vegetarian dinner available every night, so I paid for that night's dinner as well, and sweets, of course. We stayed with Nikki, her husband and daughters. They had a huge house, and two live-in servants, which Sita pointed out to me. I knew she was jealous.

I had a lot going on all at once. Dr. Schultz wanted me to teach coding for acoustics every semester if there was interest. Coding stream was going through my mind like a ticker tape. My sound notation project had taken almost a year, so far. So, my own life was taking care of Simran and Sita, practicing piano, working out, coding and teaching. I'd make love to Sita and I no longer had to say the alphabet backwards. Several times Sita asked me, while we were having intercourse, if I was going to come.

Life was a blur, but I remember the first time Simran smiled at me, and when he vomited on my clothes as I was in a rush to get out the door. Caring for a baby is repetition lost in sleeplessness.

As I got more comfortable caring for my son, I wanted to take him round with me, especially when I went to Montreux. As soon as Simran could eat solid food, I started bringing him if I was mixing. I got this backpack-type of harness to carry him, but I was always amazed at how much stuff you have to carry when you take a baby along. I made a checklist so I wouldn't forget anything.

As he attempted to crawl, I wondered how my mother handled us. There were no playpens in Africa. I wrote her a letter and asked her. She wrote back that one of Hassan's daughters stayed with us the first two years when my brothers were in school because my parents had no extended family. I had slept in sort of a hay manger on the ground (I didn't remember that at all) when I wasn't in bed with my parents, and didn't wear anything more than a long shirt until I could understand to go away from the house to poop and pee. When you come right down to it, it's amazing so many African babies survive. I remember digging in mud, playing in water puddles, and being dragged away from a fire several times. Toys? A stick and a wadded-up bunch of papers or rags for a ball. I remember playing with bugs. My brothers made trucks and cars out of scrap wood and metal.

None of this, obviously, was much help in modern Europe. I bought two playpens: one for the house and one for my office. I even rigged up a barrier at the studio in Montreux. I bought a small toy piano and a xylophone, and my students brought over more toys. I recall buying a bottle of bubbles and spending hours blowing bubbles. I know we spent a lot of time in water. I took him into the tub with me almost every night his first two years.

I was thrilled when he learned to walk, not realizing that the terrifying years had begun. He learned to climb out of the play pen, and started climbing on furniture and jumping off, opening drawers and swinging on them, and pulling out sharp and heavy stuff: All sorts of dangerous situations. Sita wanted to hire a full-time nanny. I preferred sending him to a crèche for a few hours a day if she needed a break. We went back and forth on this for weeks. She was now back to working part time. I knew his language and social skills and his toilet training, would be much better if he was with other children. Sita was thinking a nanny would also cook and clean. ✪

# CHAPTER 14

In December 1994, Adam and I finished orchestrating Barcelona. With the school orchestra, we produced a performance, and split the royalties with the university. I had put a significant amount of time into this project, and it only made sense to monetize it. In January of 1997, I finally got the sound notation project completed where we could play an instrument into a microphone and have notation appear on the screen. I'll never forget the feeling I got when I played a few notes of "Malaika" on the piano and it appeared. It was such an emotional rush. It was still really slow, but I was euphoric for days. It had taken much longer than I had anticipated. I continued working on it until 2001. There were so many instruments with different sounds and tonal depth. It was like hertz didn't matter. I published several papers and went to several conferences. The upside was that I was learning about hardware and software that might speed up display.

The computer, as I coded it, could recognize notes as played, but chords still confused it, and timing was the major hurdle. This guy in Stockholm, Sven Ahlbäck, my contemporary, made it easier to use, but it took until 2000 for a general beta test.

I wanted to go visit my parents, but Baba sent a telegram suggesting they come to Europe because of the commotion with the International Court Tribunal trials of those involved in the Rwanda genocide. Attorneys and their staffs added to the usual safari tourists crowded Arusha to capacity. Several new hotels were built, as well as a new court building.

We went to Nice, in the south of France, for a week. Sita wanted to bring her mother to help with Simran. I was very grateful to Levine for getting us a travel agent who could sort out all the visa requirements. I had a Commonwealth passport, Sita had Dubai/Emirates, as was Fatima's and my parents had Tanzanian passports.

The weather was wonderful, and it was nice to be on the beach and just read and doze. Sita bought a swimsuit that plunged in front and really showed off her figure. She looked gorgeous, but exposed. Her mother wore a more conservative suit with a skirt. I didn't think about this until I saw the shocked expression on my father's face. Both he and my mother wore cotton shalwar khameez, and were totally covered. I was used to how Europeans were about their bodies on the beach.

Simran, his mother, and grandmothers played in the water, and my father collected shells and took photos. We took a couple of road trips inland to visit vineyards. Sita and I were comfortable. I always wished our sex life were better, but I wondered if I was expecting too much.

When we returned from France, there was an email message from Levine. He was signing us up for individual email service, from Netscape. We would have to buy modems and computers for our homes. He also encouraged us to get enough songs for another album, and to consider another tour. I suggested it be summer, July at the earliest.

I wanted to get Sita into the mindset of going with me, so I mentioned we were planning another tour. On the plus side, we'd most likely get to see both of her sisters and their families.

Sita wasn't wild about traveling with a child in tow unless I paid for a nanny. Levine thought that we could hire child care in each city if we arranged ahead of time. He would inform concierges as he had his staff book travel.

Because we started practicing new songs for our upcoming tour, I couldn't have Simran with me. It would be too loud for a small child. I started leaving him at the crèche if Sita was working. I felt bad about this, but at least he was socializing with other children. He needed the physical outlet for his energy. At the crèche they spoke French and Swiss German. At home, I spoke to him in English and Sita spoke to him in Hindi. I remember I asked him once what he did at school, and he replied, *Legos*. I had no idea what he was talking about. Was that French? The next day when I brought him to the crèche, I asked the teacher what Legos were. She brought me to a carpeted area that was enclosed with a low barrier. I saw a million small colored plastic pieces. I probably raised my eyebrows and the teacher started laughing at my expression. "The children love these. They can build with them, but you see, we have to keep them confined."

I started wondering how we would keep him occupied on the tour. We'd have to bring a lot of toys and books. I asked his teachers besides Legos what he liked to play with, and it was the same sort of stuff I was drawn to: cars and trucks, things with a lot of moving parts, but also dinosaurs. That interested me, too, because when I was a child, we didn't learn anything about dinosaurs. I bought a couple of books in French and I knew I'd find English dinosaur books in America.

A lot of the American festivals took place in July and August, and then we would go on to the Orient and Australia. We would do a European tour in September. Several other acts were doing the same circuit of venues. We were the only European group. We were told all shows were, again, sold out. There was a party atmosphere. Peter and our crew loved it.

In Chicago, we were at another two-week-long festival. A lot of restaurants showcased their specialties and there were booths, like African dukas, selling T-shirts and jewelry, as well as beer. There were thousands of drunk, mostly white people, pushing strollers with babies.

I got a message from Shayla that she could not get downtown. Mara was working out of town. "I might be able to take the train up to Milwaukee for your show at Summerfest, but things are nuts around here now in the summer," she told me when I called her.

"Particularly crazy? What happened?" I asked her.

Shayla chuckled, "New governor, so road construction all over! Who'd ever think they'd have to reserve a train ticket just going up to Milwaukee? The METRA won't presell single tickets. It's standing room only on trains."

All trains north from Chicago were booked totally by people who could not get tickets to the Chicago shows. It was even on the broadcast news!

We got to see Sita's sister, Mindi, and her family, who were living close to Boulder, Colorado. We hired a driver with a van to take us out. Adam and Michelle came with us. Mindi and her husband, Sadhu, now had two children. It was interesting for us all to see how they lived. They had a huge five-bedroom home and you could see so far because they lived on top of a mountain. The Rockies are much different from the Alps. They are not nearly as green, and are really rocky on top. Aptly named, I thought.

They had a barbeque for us. It was, for me, like eating African cooking, except their green maize, or corn, was something I had never had. Or rather, I had had it out of a can, but never on the cob.

Levine joined us on the west coast and we were able to have a discussion about the cost of tickets. "Unless we buy out the resellers, and take ownership of the festivals, it is what it is. I'll ask other agents if any other groups want to go in on a buy out with you, but they probably want close to a billion dollars. We're stuck in this system," Levine told me gravely.

Insurance had gotten a lot more expensive, as had transportation. When I returned to Switzerland, I invested in a few insurance companies, and a company that offered fractional ownership of private jets, which we had used several times. This made sense because I knew these companies were profitable.

I loved being with Simran. He was curious about everything as I was at his age. We spent a lot of time in coach busses and on planes, so I'd do counting games, read to him, and sing. He loved banging on things and I wondered if that was a boy thing.

We had gone to Vancouver, then over to Seoul. When it was time to travel to Japan, Sita told me she wanted to go to Dubai. I didn't want to fight with her. I booked her and Simran's travel. It was just a couple of weeks we would be apart.

On my way to Dubai, I stopped to see my brothers in Kuala Lumpur. They hadn't seen Simran, and I explained that Sita was tired of touring and wanted to be in Dubai, and I didn't want him to be with strangers for the many hours I could not be with him.

We only had a week between the Asian and European shows. I went to Dubai to fetch Sita and Simran, and Sita didn't want to leave. "Let me come back after the European shows," she begged.

This frustrated me. "I called every night we were on tour in Asia, and you never mentioned staying. Why not?"

"I didn't think it was important," she replied.

It wasn't that making the extra stop was expensive, but having to arrange the time and tickets, and I could tell she wasn't telling me something. "Fatima, what is going on?" I asked.

"Dayal, I have no idea what you're talking about. Please don't put me in the middle of your disagreements."

"If you insisted she stay with me, and you didn't allow her to come back, this wouldn't happen. Is she staying in the apartment with Simran?" He was playing with trucks in one of the bedrooms.

She hesitated, and tried to change the subject. I asked her again.

"Sita signed Simran up for a crèche," Fatima said.

"Which crèche? I want to visit the crèche," I said.

"I don't know."

In the morning, when Sita was ready to take Simran, I said, "I want to go with you and see where my son is spending time." She suddenly clammed up, so I just joined them in the taxi.

The crèche was in a storefront building next to a Catholic church. We went in, and there were several nuns, and a big crucifix on the back wall. I looked at Sita, and she would not look at me. This was around 8:00 in the morning. There were about thirty kids between the ages of two and four, plenty of toys, and I noticed there was a back door to a fenced play area with a climbing gym and swings. While we were there, one of the nuns got all the children to sit in a circle, and started them singing some sort of song about Jesus.

I was shocked! I felt like I had been punched in the stomach. Sita knew how I felt before we were married. I had even put it in our marriage contract. I shook my head and took Sita by the hand. She resisted, but I put my arm around her waist and guided her out the door. She still would not look at me.

"How could you enroll our son in a Christian day crèche? You knew I would disapprove."

"Oh, Dayal, it's just playtime at this age!" she responded.

"The reason I object to them inculcating my child is because of what they did to my people. They…"

"You talk like the Africans are your people! Why?"

"You really don't understand, do you? Sitaji! I am African! They are my friends and neighbors. You know, only Hindus and Americans see color, and race. Are you like them that you judge peoples' intelligence and worth by how light or dark their skins are? Do you think I am less intelligent than you because my skin is darker than yours?"

She looked surprised.

"The Christians congratulate themselves for ending slavery, but they didn't end it. These Christians, of all denominations, not only took African land by force, they instituted the hut tax. If you didn't pay, they burned your home and even beat you. They destroyed communities in the name of Jesus. The irony is that they converted all these people to Christianity, but then wouldn't allow them to run their own congregations, and burned their churches as well! They still do, with alacrity! Bringing God's word? Bloody Hell!"

Sita respond, "I don't believe that's true. I just don't."

I was overwrought. "I'm going to look for a secular crèche. I will not pay for this. You can get your father to pay the bill. I can't believe you did this."

We took a cab back to her mother's building, not speaking. I had never been so angry, but at the same time, I was so sad that she had tried to sneak this past me. I wanted to take Simran with me and not say anything to Sita, but I knew I could not get childcare on such short notice and we had the rest of European concerts.

Back in those days, you still could not use the internet to search for businesses. The front desk at the condo had a phone directory, with a *Yellow Pages* (same all over the world). I looked up nurseries, crèches and kindergartens and started calling around. I spent the day visiting several, to make sure my son would be in a secular environment. I found one that was not far and seemed suitable, and I made arrangements for Simran to attend.

I gave Fatima the information and told her this was where I wanted him to be for the next several weeks. I told her that if she would not accompany him, to send Maria and I'd pay her.

I then called Sita's father and had to leave a message: "Baba Makkar, you are going to get a bill for a crèche. Sita asked to visit for the last weeks of my tour and she put our son in a Christian crèche. I married a Sikh woman because I wanted our children raised as Sikhi. I am not paying for where she put him. You can pay the bill. I found a secular crèche, 'Tiny Tots' and I am going to insist that Fatima makes sure he goes there."

Later, Mr. Makkar returned my call. "My sons went to 'Tiny Tots,' before they were in primary school, buy please don't be so angry..."

I could barely think. "Do you want your sons singing Christian songs? Do you want them thinking they are sinners and have no idea what they did that was wrong? Or doing wrong and asking Jesus to forgive them? Do you want them praying to Jesus and then wondering why he comes before God? Their Bible allows slavery. Mark tells slaves to obey their masters. My parents were slaves..."

"Your parents?" Mr. Makkar responded, surprised.

"Yes. They were trafficked and that's why they became Sikh. My mother is extremely religious. She considers the satsang in Dar her family. They might not have taken Amrit, but they are believers. She, like my father, had no one. What really upsets me is that Sita tried to hide it from me. She can't have my child believing both ways are ok. They cancel each other out."

"I'm sorry, truly. I'll talk to her."

I hoped we could straighten this out when she returned to Switzerland. I remembered what Mara had said about my mental health. At that time, my way of dealing with it was to think about other things. I had to get my emotions in check to finish the tour.

I wrote to both Shayla and Mara. I just had to express myself to people who would understand. I complained about how hurt, shocked, and disrespected I felt by Sita. The issue was, to me, that in a Christian environment, NOT being Christian defines you. Having to live in a society so culturally Christian, I wanted my children to understand integrity and that we would NOT be forgiven by God if we were unfair to people. We would be in the cycle of reincarnation for infinity. I really feared that Simran would start to think it was normal to ask for forgiveness after intentionally making a bad choice. Adam and Peter had joked about being naughty as children and rationalizing that Jesus would forgive them. Oscar told me the same thing. They thought it was funny.

Sita and Simran returned at the end of October. I wondered if Fatima told her to leave. She was morose, aloof, and there was underlying tension. I finally asked her, "Sita, what's the problem? Is it our religious differences?"

She set her lips and refused to answer.

"You're obviously not happy. Do you want a divorce?"

She started crying. "No! I love you! I want to have another baby."

I started laughing. Another child? If she wanted another child, why did she stay away? It crossed my mind that she was trying to manipulate me. "You know, we have to have sex to have another child. Why did you balk at returning?"

"I was really stressed from the travel," she admitted.

Everything was a disagreement. She wanted cardboard decorations for the Christmas holidays. She brought it up every evening as they went up in the commercial part of town.

"We decorated the jewelry store. It's fun, and it looks so festive."

"What's the point? Simran's things are all over. The kitchen's a disaster area. It won't look festive if the house is a mess. It doesn't make sense."

She pouted.

"Look, if you'll feel better, anything that is not specifically Christmas is ok: snowflakes, snowmen, evergreen boughs, that sort of thing. I'd rather celebrate Diwali and teach Simran about our heritage. Diwali is a simple holiday—a festival of light. Don't you understand that?"

"You know, I've never celebrated Diwali. The nuns said it was pagan."

Well, of course, with a thousand gods, Hinduism would be pagan. But there it was. To the nuns, Sikh or Hindu, we were lesser people. "They brainwashed you in school. You don't know who you are or what you believe," I complained.

"They did not brainwash me. I see no harm in him being exposed to Christianity. This way he can interact with his friends and understand what they're talking about."

"Sitaji, I had no problem interacting with my Christian friends in Africa. At school, as long as they didn't try to save me, I was fine. Simran is too young to understand the nuances. I do not want him growing up with a concept of a deity who would judge him. I don't want him confused about sin, heaven, or hell, and the idea that he could do bad things and ask Jesus for forgiveness."

"That's not how it is!"

"That's *exactly* how it is! Don't you see all the contradictions in the Bible? Let me give you one example. God tells Abraham to prove his devotion by sacrificing his son. A loving God does that? Then, just before the knife comes down, God sends an angel to tell Abraham God changed his mind. He'll just take the foreskin."

Sita looked at me and responded, "It was a test of Abraham's love of God."

"God is never like that in the Adi Granth. There are no inconsistencies. One story I never understood, God tells Lot to get out of Sodom, because some bad men in town want to rape the angels, who are presumably men, not women. God is going to kill everyone in the town, including innocent children, but not Lot and his family, even though Lot's wife and daughters seem to be bad people. A few pages later, Moses parts the sea to allow the Israelites to flee Egypt. God closes the sea on the Egyptians and the Israelites rejoice. God asks the Jews how they can rejoice when his children are drowning. Are the Egyptians, idol worshippers, not as bad as the people of Sodom? Think about it. What kind of sense does this make? Are we to love God, or fear Him?"

"Well, both, like a father," Sita replied,

"Sikhi don't ever talk of God doing this. We're just caught in the reincarnation cycle. Then, suddenly Jesus arrives. He has disciples and the issues change to telling people they must believe he alone is the child of God, and you can't get to heaven unless you ask Him to forgive your sins. To be a good believer, you must save others from eternal damnation."

"Well, yes, that is what they taught me."

"The way you do this is you all support missionaries who go out and confuse people and trick them into changing what they believe! But then tell the Africans they need white people to lead them to heaven. That black people can't lead congregations because they aren't as good as white people?"

"Not Christians. They went to Africa to stop slavery."

I chuckled. "Is that what you were taught? They didn't want Muslims to enslave them, but Christians enslaved the Africans, and burned down their homes if they didn't work for the wazungu. The white Christians."

"Peter's a Christian," Sita retorted.

"Yes he is. Your point? I think this double talk is part of the reason Peter lives so dangerously. He feels he's imperfect, but if he prays to Jesus, he can still sin. He's so promiscuous. He doesn't equate sex with love. He doesn't use protection. It's a game to him. Since prostitution isn't condemned in the Bible, and all women are subjects of men, he doesn't think exploiting women is sinful. His lust is the sinful thing. He believes in your Jesus, and he thinks he will be forgiven for using women for sex."

"And you equate sex with love?"

"I always have."

"Do you love me?" Sita asked.

"I did. I was trying to. Now, I wonder if I can trust you. How much can I love you if I can't trust you? I demonstrated to you before we were married that you could trust me."

She sat silently and didn't respond.

"The reason I went with my parents' wishes to marry you was because you were Sikh, but you're only genetically Sikh. Emotionally, you're a Christian. You don't want to accept responsibility for your beliefs or actions. You want the idea of Jesus to do it for you! I do not want my son believing nonsense. When I was a child, my family read the Bible, both testaments. I will read them to Simran, but remind him that these are stories. He will have to decide what to believe."

Sita sighed and just stared at me.

"Do you believe in heaven and hell?" I asked her.

"Yes, of course. It's a matter of faith," Sita replied, almost defiantly.

"With no evidence. You know I'm a scientist, right? I don't know if we're in the reincarnation cycle. What I do know is that once I'm dead, that's it. There is nothing after that."

"Well, you have to have faith…"

"Sitaji, you are mouthing what they taught you. Faith in what? Our God, same God, tells us to have faith and show it by caring about others. He and the gurus have always addressed that we're all equal, to be fair, to be altruistic, kind, and give back. We've never permitted slavery. Sikh women are equal to men. Why would you decide to have faith in a system that makes it so women are lesser people? That men should control where you go, how you live, how many children you should have, and, in some cases accept being hurt?"

She never responded to my tirade.

In January I got a letter from Mara. She wrote how much she agreed with me, and that their parents fought them being assimilated. At home, her mother continued to tell her that they don't believe Jesus is special, and as she got older, she saw it all as just stories that *goyim* accepted. She suggested that I read from the Bible to Simran and ask him what he thought and to remind him that these are stories, and not true, because he was still too young to understand allegory. "There's no getting away from this. We live in their world. Ultimately, you'll get him to understand that the *goyim* have an agenda."

I tried ignoring my own feelings of pain and disappointment by keeping busy. The shock of realizing that Sita was captivated by the mysticism and rituals of Catholicism affected me physically. I was sad because I realized that her interests and priorities were focused away from us as a couple, and it would be a lifetime of confusing Simran. Had I let my lust for her overcome me?

I was surprised that I felt so strongly, but this was the core of who I was. I didn't believe that God was punishing me, or even trying me. We believe everything is preordained. I wanted to love Sita, and to trust her. I had to find a different way to love her. She had given me a son, and the truth was that she was a very good mother. She talked a lot to Simran. He could count to 30 at the age of three in both Hindi and English. He knew the Latinic and Hindi/Sanskrit letters and knew the colors in French. Hindi, and English. He was starting to dress himself. I couldn't let the emotional turmoil consume me. I didn't want to disrupt Simran's life. I realized that to the rest of the world, at least the Judeo/Christian/Moslem world, our religion was barely a religion at all. Abdulrazak Gurnak, the Tanzanian writer, had a character in his book *Paradise*, address this. When sin is mentioned in the Adi Granth, it is for betrayal selfishness, lust, or attachment to worldly goods. The punishment is being caught in the cycle of reincarnation.

I would have to demonstrate to Simran how I lived my faith. I would tell him that it's dangerous to believe something based on faith, with no evidence. When you just do that, you are easily manipulated. ✪

# CHAPTER 15

In February, Sita mentioned going to Dubai in May, when her sisters would also be there. Then she said, "I think we should have another baby. Now would be a good time to conceive so the baby will be born after your tour."

This was the one thing she did think through. She knew I had applied for a patent for my sound notation program. I was also presenting some papers. I'd be busy right up to our tour dates. Simran was a little over three. Sita and I were OK as long as we didn't discuss religion and I wasn't too sexually adventurous. Yet, there was always *something*.

One day at breakfast, she told me she was thinking of taking Simran for a haircut. I didn't think she meant to needle me, but she surprised me. I said, "No. He is too young. We'll braid his hair if you don't want it in a topknot."

"You trim your beard!" she responded.

She was right, but I had *never* cut my hair, and even trimming my beard made me nervous. I had not taken Amrit, nor had my brothers. We were *Sahajdhari*: culturally Sikh. Like Reform Jews, as Mara described us. It had nothing to do with logic. I was respecting my mother's wishes to be culturally Sikh. I trimmed my beard, because Levine asked me to, then I realized it was easier to take care of and I wouldn't get debris stuck in it. I remembered how it was when my brothers were teenagers and they wanted to cut their hair, to look modern and *hip*, and not wear topknots with a patka, and Ama decided they were mature enough for turbans. When my brothers visited my parents, they kept their heads covered with turbans, lest my mother freak out. Avi told me he was enough of an *other* that he didn't want how he appeared to affect his business relations. Sodhi told me short hair was just easier to deal with, especially since he was going bald.

"Dayalji, your reasoning doesn't make sense. You saw my sisters' husbands. They cut their hair. They aren't being smote by God."

I sighed. I wondered if I'd ever get to the point where my hair, or my son's, didn't matter in the larger universe.

"Simranji, Ama wants to get your haircut. I have never cut my hair because God says we're perfect as we are. Is your hair a problem?"

He had made a ramp from a chair to the floor and was playing with his trucks. "Sometimes big people think I'm a girl," he responded, a bit insulted, as he sent a vehicle racing.

"That used to happen to me, too, but it really doesn't matter. You can remind them that you're a boy. If you want, I'll braid your hair instead of putting it in a topknot. I'll talk to the people at your school. We're different from most people here. If there are people like us, one way they can tell is by our hair. When you're older, you'll wear a turban and get a steel bracelet like mine. We do a lot of things that are different from the Europeans."

The irony was that in my travels, when I was in public, not performing, I always wore a turban and I never met another Sikh.

The next week, Sita had her bangs cut and blond streaks put in her hair. She looked great, exotic, but I felt it was a subtle jab. I told her, "Your hair looks nice, but I thought you were beautiful the way your hair was."

Michelle had gone with her, and when she heard me say that, she rolled her eyes and said to me. "That's a compliment?"

I started to explain to Michelle, but she shook her head and said, "Never mind."

Now pregnant, Sita also wanted to move into a single-family house with a garden. She was very envious of her sisters' homes in Colorado and London, and kept talking about how much space they had. I knew we needed more room, but housing stock was limited between Bern and Zurich. I didn't think there was any place in Europe we could afford unless we moved to a very rural area. Even though I tried to show her bills, she didn't really have an idea of what anything cost. Her lack of interest in our finances bothered me. If something happened to me, her father and Levine would have to sort everything out.

I had gotten used to living in Switzerland. Having traveled all over the world, I could think of very few places that I would move to for a better quality of life, except for the weather. I really liked Kuala Lumpur, and it would be nice to be in the same place with my brothers. The infrastructure was modern, and you could get a very nice home with land for relatively little money compared to most places. Too bad most of the year it was stiflingly hot. I really liked the West Coast of the United States. It seemed the weather was always nice, and there was a huge entertainment industry. Also, the cost of living was reasonable compared to Europe. I just felt it was too far away from my parents. I did not like most of South America or Europe. Every city in South America had infrastructure issues, and it took so long to get to the rest of the world. Also, most cities in

South America had security issues. You needed to hire private security if you lived a middle-class life.

Europe was expensive all over. I knew I didn't want to live in India, any of the Emirates, or, unfortunately, Africa. Most of the Emirates were hot, expensive, and full of concrete. That's one reason why I didn't even consider buying a place in Dubai. Plus, particularly in the Emirates, women were second class citizens.

The infrastructure in most of Africa was terrible, and there was no security. Africa was changing quickly. I still remembered before I went to Singapore, staring out the window at school and seeing the animals grazing. Those days were gone forever. I realized that I hadn't really appreciated what we had, and now we were losing our heritage. Arusha was beginning to look like many of the commercial tourist towns in America.

It made sense to get a larger home and for me to have an office and music room, so I put a lot of energy into talking to estate agents and anyone else who may have heard of available property.

Just before she went to Dubai in May, we put a contract on an attached home with a small garden that we were lucky to find and arranged to sell the one we had.

Packing took several weeks. I got rid of a lot of the costume jewelry, old clothes, and many pairs of shoes that were beyond repair. I knew she'd never notice. I called Sita every night to talk to her and Simran. She never had much to say, but my son, if I started questioning him, could go on for at least an hour. I asked him if he was having fun.

"I got to eat hot dogs with chips and candy floss. I saw a train on a table at a store! I want one. I want a puppy or a kitten. Bala and Farid have a kitten. When are you coming?"

"I'm not coming. You are coming home. Are you reading any books?"

"No. there are no books at Bibi's, but there are books at school."

I really wanted them to return. At least when I called "Tiny Tots," I found he was attending. That was a huge relief.

It took a couple of months to unpack and put everything away. Our tour started at the end of June and we just did Europe and American cities. Sita, Michelle, and Simran visited every zoo and garden in every city we were in. At the end of August, we returned, and Nikki came from England with her daughters. They went to Capri for a week. I was alone, and I missed Sita and Simran, but I needed the respite. I had left the house in shambles when we had gone on tour, and was still putting everything back together from our move. Adam came over and said, "I'm surprised the place looks like this, knowing you." I just looked at him and shook my head.

By the time of their return, Sita was very uncomfortable with her pregnancy. I did everything I could think of to help her find comfort, but her legs were starting to swell again, and she needed her blood sugar checked morning and night.

Levine wanted us to go to Germany to film some videos. We just did a studio video for *How Can I Go On?* the Moran/Mercury song, but Levine and a production company had a script for *Don't Hustle Me*. That video took about a week to film.

Levine, my mates, and the production crew wanted to film at least two more videos, but I felt I had to get back to Switzerland as Sita was due any day. The weeks around Christmas were terrible. Sita was extremely uncomfortable. She was still working part time at the jewelry store, but had to sit frequently. Her boss told her to go home.

Our daughter, Mena, was born January 3, 1999. My emotions, again: I felt like I was having an out of body experience. They handed her to me, and she seemed to look at me! I was so overwhelmed. Here was my joy, a little angel.

Sita had been in labor, again, almost twenty hours. She had a good midwife assist, but she was totally worn out. I stayed with her the next two days after the birth. I was afraid of eclampsia, and her blood pressure was not stable.

We had told Simran a baby was coming. Sita had weaned him when he started talking in full sentences, but he still wanted her to cuddle him while I read him a story at night.

Upon her return, as soon as Sita started to nurse Mena, Simran had a meltdown. "I want to nurse, too!" he wailed.

I instinctively picked him up and realized that he was wailing at Sita in Hindi, but changed to English with me.

I hugged him to me and asked, "What is it?"

Simran shook his head, still crying.

"Are you hungry? Tell me."

He calmed himself enough to say, "Ama's milk is sweet and she hugs me and she's soft. I want her to hug me. Give the baby back."

"I know how you feel. God waited until you could feed yourself and were out of nappies before he gave us Mena. She can't eat anything else, and you can. You're a big brother now. You have to understand. You know something? You're big enough to go skiing. We'll do that in a few days."

I went with him to his room, and cuddled him as I read to him. He fell asleep quickly.

It was a stressful time for us all.

I, again, hired a maternity nurse for two weeks. We then arranged to go up to London in March for the *Naam Karan*. Fatima returned for that.

One hassle I could get out of the way was the whole birth control issue. I decided to have a vasectomy, just after the baby-naming ceremony.

One morning, as I was fixing breakfast, I told Sita, "I don't want to be responsible for birth control anymore. We have two children. Mena's pregnancy was very hard on you. I'm planning on having a vasectomy."

I could see her tense up, but she didn't say anything. She knew what a vasectomy was. She had told me, when she returned from Dubai the last time, that one of her friend's husbands had it done because they had five kids and he wondered if he'd be able to pay for school for them all. It was a big deal because Middle Eastern men didn't do this, but the guy had been educated in America and that's where he wanted his children to go to college.

"Do you want to consider an IUD or a contraceptive shot?" I asked her.

She sighed again. "I can't think about it now. Do whatever you want," she said, turning away from me, which was exasperating. I wanted to be more sympathetic to her, but she would never discuss birth control.

I did not want to spend years and years changing nappies or fearing someone was going to jump off furniture and get injured. I was very happy with two children, but they were a lot of work.

On Sita's next trip to Dubai, which was when Mena was 6 months old, I stayed and had the procedure done, so I could recover in peace. I had mixed feelings about the vasectomy. I didn't want to seem to control Sita's fertility, just my own.

Sita took a long time to bounce back after Mena. She wouldn't have intercourse with me until after she returned from Dubai.

Our schedules hardly meshed. Part of me wanted her to not work, if it meant we could spend more time as a family, but I knew that if she didn't work, she'd also want to spend more time in Dubai. Her school friends were mostly in Dubai, Qatar, Abu Dhabi or Kuwait. Their husbands would not allow them to travel, and apparently had no interest in bringing them to see us. I assumed they were mostly Moslem or Hindu. Men controlling their wives' movements is very cultural.

In July 1999, we did a performance—just us, The Pleasure Seekers—as a beta test of *MagicScore* at the university. We hooked up the computer so it would display on a large screen. As I played piano, the music notation would appear. It was still slow, but good enough. I started with the Liz Story piano solo, *Toy Soldiers*. It was such a beautiful piece that I decided to start our future performances with it. We played *Hot Fun in the Summertime*, the Sly and the Family Stone song, a great showcase for Adam on bassoon, then, the Mitch Forman piece, *Reunion*. We got a very enthusiastic response. To do multiple instruments still bogged down the software. Now, it's called *Anthemware* and *Scorecloud*, but I patented it with the name *MagicScore*.

Dr. Schultz came up to me at the end, as I was putting everything away, and said, "Come to my office tomorrow, *Herr Doktor*. I'll do the paperwork for your diploma and a pay raise to junior professor." He shook my hand.

I felt slightly in a daze and exhaled. Adam was smiling and said, "Let's celebrate!"

Mena was a little character. She loved music and as soon as she could sit up, she bounced to the piano. She made up songs.

She was also a cuddler. However, for the next few years, until she was out of nappies and in school with her brother, every day was a hectic mess to get the day started. I got the kids up, fed, dropped off at school or the crèche, then I exercised for an hour. I taught my classes, from 10:00 until noon. I had office hours from 1:00 until 3:00 unless someone needed a special appointment. On days I didn't teach, I went over student work, wrote, practiced, and coded *MagicScore*. I submitted my patent to the European Community in 2000. I look back at those years, and they are a blur in my mind.

I often prepared breakfast and cooked most nights, We ate a lot of scrambled eggs, or boxed macaroni and cheese with a vegetable. Sita often didn't return home from work until after 20:00, which was too late for the children. I bathed them and supervised tooth brushing, and read to them every night.

In August, 2000, we went back to Arusha with the children. My parents were making more money from selling the tourist trinkets and ice cream to the Curtis Hotel than from export. The foreign brokers were taking over. They had a lot more capital.

Levine scheduled a tour of the Americas and Southeast Asia, including Australia, for our "Greatest Hits" for 2001. We hadn't toured in three years.

When we got to America, we stopped at several schools with music programs, including Julliard, New England Conservatory, Berklee, Oberlin, Columbia in Chicago, and Northwestern. I presented the software and how I had developed it. Computers for sound were still somewhat new, Because Northwestern had engineering, music, and media departments, we had a lot of people at my demonstration. I got a very enthusiastic response, and there were a lot of questions.

I had, again, written to both Shayla and Mara. Shayla met me for lunch one day while we were in Chicago, and was able to meet Sita and the children very briefly, as they were just coming in from a morning at Lincoln Park Zoo. I could tell the children needed a nap. When I introduced them, I told Sita that Shayla's grandfather had owned my father. You'd think she'd have some sort of response, but she just smiled and shook Shayla's hand. Sita never asked me about my parents. Ever.

Shayla told me Mara was grooming dogs at a kennel in Michigan for the summer; remote enough that it would take her hours to get anywhere worth getting to. I called her, and she told me the same thing: she was at least three hours north-west of Detroit in a very rural location. She asked me about my children, and seemed impressed that I was getting another patent. There was so much I wanted to say to her, but I was respecting her emotional distance. The dynamic had changed.

I learned that I was nominated for a technical award by the Recording Academy, which gives out the Grammys. I would have to return to the USA to receive the award in 2002.

One afternoon, as I was readying myself for the evening performance, Sita stormed into the hotel room, a scowl on her face. "I just had the most embarrassing thing happen. My credit card was turned down."

These were the days before you could look your account up online and see where you were in terms of spending.

I said, "We are two weeks into the month. I paid the bill in advance before we left Switzerland. What do you think you bought that brought you up to the limit, and what did you want to buy?"

She gave me a really bold, angry look, and retorted, "You have money. Michelle told me she had a five-thousand-dollar limit on her card. Why do you give me only a thousand dollars?"

"You didn't answer my question. Did you ask Michelle if she reaches her limit every month? Five thousand dollars is a lot to spend every month if you aren't paying for food or household expenses. Maybe she is. And maybe she pays her own credit card bill. Where are the children?"

"Michelle has the children, and she told me Adam pays the bill."

"So what do you want to buy that you need more money for?"

Sita just stared at me, then sighed, turned and went into the bathroom. She came right back out and yelled, "Why do you give me only a thousand dollars?"

"Why don't YOU tell ME what you want the money for?" I yelled back. She glared at me. We never yelled at home. The tension was always under the surface. I didn't want to argue because it was the same argument that never got resolved. I had all these thoughts, and one of them was that she usually didn't need more because she had her earnings from working, and I also knew that she had brought jewelry with her to sell.

"If you loved me, you wouldn't ask," she yelled.

I actually laughed. This was the first time she ever tried that on me. Money equaled love. I was not going to argue about money for trinkets. "Look. I have a performance in several hours. I am not going to spend time discussing this and going in circles. I put a limit on your card because you can't control your spending and for some reason you seem to think that buying things makes you feel that this is how I love you, by you spending money I earn? I have no idea. I own six pairs of shoes, Sitaji. How many pairs of shoes do you have? Have you ever seen me wear jewelry besides the steel bangles? You know I don't just blindly pay the bills. I actually read the statements and see what's on them. Usually, you're under the credit limit by several hundred dollars. Why is this month different? What do you want to buy? Is it jewelry? Because, if it is, and you really want it, I'll give you the money, but I'll ask for the card, and you won't have it for the rest of the tour. Nor will you have it until you can pay me back. We had an agreement."

"Since when have we had an agreement?"

"Since before we got married. You and your father had the contract, which you signed."

She looked at me, made a face of defeat, and sat down, but still didn't tell me why she wanted more money.

"I'm going to take a shower, and then I plan to relax for a bit."

I really hate hotel room tubs. I was just standing under the water, trying to clear my head and calm down, when Sita came into the bathroom, naked. She opened the curtain and started to get in with me. "This is too dangerous, Sitaji. There is not room for two," I said, still upset.

She was going to appease me, obviously. I got out of the tub, and started to towel off.

She turned off the water and said, "I'm sorry. You're right. I saw a silk pantsuit and it looked so comfortable, but it was eight hundred dollars. It was really nicely tailored. I've never seen anything like it in either Zurich or Dubai. I bet I don't have even four hundred dollars on the card this month, but whatever I had apparently put me over the limit. They rejected the card, and I was so embarrassed. Michelle said she'd put it on her card and I could pay her back, but I didn't think that was right, and why I didn't have the money: You know, I brought jewelry with me to sell to some clients, but I paid for that and the insurance out of my earnings. I used it all, knowing I'd get it back, but I won't get it back until we get back to Switzerland. My client paid the store with a credit card."

She followed me into the bedroom and we both laid down on the bed.

"Is the store open tomorrow morning? We leave at noon. I'll get you cash if you really want it." I didn't want to tell her that her name was also on my card. I feared she'd take my card out of my wallet.

"Really? Thank you so much, Dayalji." She kissed me and started caressing me. Then she said, "Tell me what you want."

She took me by surprise. I chuckled. I turned towards her to put my hand on her breasts, and said, "What I always want," and raised my eyebrows.

She lowered her hand to my dick. That was more than rare for her to do. She hadn't touched me below my waist since before Mena was born. She had sort of a smirk on her face. I said, "Suck me off."

She looked at me for a few more seconds, and hesitated, but she twisted herself around and rested her head on my belly, and for the first time, ever, she blew me. We had been married nine years, and it had been longer since I had a blow job. Suddenly, I was thinking with my dick.

No foreplay. It was almost surreal, because I was agitated and excited enough to just go with it. I closed my eyes to savor the sensation of her mouth on me. I felt electrified: "Oh, Sitaji! Sitaji! Your tongue feels so good! Don't stop!" I told her as I burst forth. When I spurted into her mouth, she drew back. As I caught my breath, I asked her, "Did I taste bad?"

She moved beside me and put her arm around me. "Not bad: texture, slimy."

"You're slimy when I eat you, but I love the sounds you make when I please you. It turns me on."

We embraced for a few minutes. Then, she asked me, "Where did you get the idea that you wanted this?"

She had never asked me about the sex I had before we were married, or if I even had sex, and I didn't want to bring it up. I guess the adrenaline affected me. I went into our performance still euphoric.

The next day I went with her to the store. $800 for a silk pantsuit! I waited while she tried it on, and I have to admit, she really looked sexy. As we left the store, I said, "You know, in Arusha, you can get 40 of those made for the same price."

"You can't get Chanel in Arusha."

Several hours later, however, as we were in transit to our next gig, she whined, "I'm so tired of traveling. Do you really mind if I take the children to Dubai?"

"We have just two more weeks. We're going to see my brothers."

She stayed with me but grew unhappy as time went on. She said every place she went with the children, there were so many other children, and they all seemed to be either crying or overwhelmed, and she was now, too.

The children were interested in everything. We went to some art galleries and a couple of children's museums with interactive toy exhibits with Michelle and Adam.

I was happy that my brothers got to be with my kids, and the kids got to be with their cousins. Sita was impressed by my brothers' homes, but she agreed with me that it was too hot. I didn't think it was hotter than Dubai, but it was more humid. Also, the malls in Malaysia cater to a Chinese market. The fruit was much like Africa's, and I hadn't enjoyed such an abundance of pineapple, mangoes, and star fruit in a very long time.

Levine joined us in Singapore. "Whenever you guys tour, record sales are up, over 30 per cent, as are requests for your videos."

When we got to Dubai, it was September. I didn't want to spend more than three days there, because I wanted to take the children to see my parents for a week in Arusha. Sita didn't want to go to Africa. She wanted to stay in Dubai and see her friends. I felt it was an insult to my parents, but I didn't argue with her. I took the children and we went.

Every time I went back to Arusha, so much had changed. My parents' home, which had been on the outskirts of town, was now practically in the middle of the commercial area. Those big World Bank signs were in several places. I saw Alfred and he told me that our friend, Boniface, who had been working for a tour company and doing wildlife research, had gotten trampled by an elephant, and killed. My father told me so many drivers died of AIDS. The word, of course, was that it was TB, but everyone knew it wasn't. Mr. Curtis's son told me that the safaris had to go farther out to see animals. There was a lot of poaching and the government turned a blind eye.

At tea one afternoon, Baba told me, "Someone from the Local Authority (this would be 'city hall' in America) came by and mentioned that our home might be worth selling. No formal offer, but you can see what's happening. They moved the market beyond the ring road. I'm not concerned, but did you see the Petronas telecom shop? And total has opened petrol stations at both ends of town. They took over the Shell stations."

"Is it? Did Avi say anything to you? Petronas is a Malaysian company. I know he's done some work for them. I noticed, Baba, that Mr. Curtis has taken down the cottages and the land was dug up."

"He told me the local authority wanted him to put in a water sanitation system."

Arusha was entering the modern age. It was no longer a charming little town.

I went to the Philips store and bought my parents a microwave oven and a better entertainment system that could play CDs as well as tapes, and could also get short wave. I had clothes made for the children and myself. ✪

# CHAPTER 16

W e returned to Switzerland. I was disappointed that Sita had not returned. When I called Fatima, she told me Sita was waiting for me to return with the children. It was another three weeks before she joined us, so it was just the kids and me. I got them into the routine of putting things away, laying out their clothes for the next day before bedtime (Mena was so cute. Very serious about choosing what went with what. Simran was like me: whatever), setting the table for meals, and sweeping the floors. The children were much more eager to keep a routine when Sita was not around. Simran even offered to help me prepare dinner.

Because it was just me and the kids, we spent a lot of quality time together. One morning, Simran came into my office while I was practicing piano. I was teaching myself the Mulgrew Miller song, "Dreamin." Such a beautiful piece, but a challenge.

"Why do you play the piano so much?"

"I have to practice and learn new songs. I have to keep my fingers limber, and also, my fingers know where the keys are, so it stays easy for me. You know people pay me to do this."

"How old were you when you started?"

"I was about 12. A man in Bibi's and Babu's town—you met him—Mr. Curtis, at the hotel, asked me to help him sell a piano, and I decided I wanted to learn to play it. I found a teacher to teach me, and I practiced every day until I was good at it, and then I kept practicing."

He sat down on the bench next to me and watched me play. "Do you think you want to learn to play?"

He was slow to answer. He looked pensive. "Was it hard to learn?"

"At first, it was very hard. But I practiced every day, and after about three months it became easier. I just loved the sound. You have to want to do it. You have to enjoy practicing and making progress. It took me over a year before I could play complicated songs with chords, like this," and I played a few chords so he would understand that I was playing three notes at once.

"Would you teach me?"

I was overcome. I hugged him. "Simran, I can teach you some things, but it would be better for me to find someone to work with you. I will ask at school if anyone is interested, and we'll try it for a month and see how it goes. You might not like it. It takes self-discipline. You have to be responsible for yourself to learn to play. I won't nag you. I'm too busy. If you decide you don't like it, or want to try another instrument or have another interest, that's ok. How does that sound?"

He nodded his head. Soon after, I went to my office and enquired of the music department if they knew of anyone who might be interested in working with a young child, and what the hourly rate would be. A girl named Alison left a note in my office. We arranged for her to come over after school twice a week. After a month, Simran decided he wanted to take a break, but I noticed that he still practiced on his own, and after three more months, he asked if he could start formal lessons again. I was pleased that he found an interest for himself. He later had Peter teach him the guitar.

Simran was now in standard three. He came home from school one day with French grammar fill-in-the-blank worksheets. I never felt so illiterate. I immediately called Adam and Michelle.

"Can you guys come over this evening? I'll make dinner," I said to Michelle.

"You? Cook?"

"It won't take long. Simran has homework I can't help him with.

"The genius can't help Simran with homework," I heard her say to Adam.

Adam took the phone from her, laughing, and asked, "What could you not figure out?"

"French grammar. I'll make a pizza."

They arrived and immediately started goofing around with the kids.

"Homework first, then we eat, then you can play. I'm also steaming green beans," I told them.

Mena immediately said, "Haricot verts."

"Oui, haricot verts avec parmesan cheese."

"Je'n'aime pas les haricot verts."

I looked at her. She had never told me she didn't like something. Also, she never spoke French to me. She was becoming a thinking person. In French as well as Hindi and English! I chuckled and responded, "Vous faites! Tu les manges tout le temps!"

She looked at me, seriously, and responded, "Pas avec des pizzas." Not with pizza.

I shook my head and responded, "Juste manger trois."

Adam started laughing and said, mockingly, "*Juste manger trois*."

While I prepared dinner, Adam read the sentences to Simran, and he responded and Adam had him fill in the blanks. This went on once a week for the semester as the verb tenses got more complex. I realized that I probably sounded like an idiot when I spoke French. I think Mena realized this, too.

I received a letter from Mara. She wrote about the few months working in Michigan, putting a new porch on her house, and how she had gotten a dog that was sweet and very smart. She included a photo of them together. She asked about the children. I wrote to her about the special Grammy. I so much wanted her to come to Los Angeles and meet me there, and said I would pay her way. She didn't respond.

Sita ultimately returned, but something wasn't right. We were polite to each other, but we weren't having conversations. One morning, just before our anniversary, Sita got up with me and the children, which was extremely unusual. I knew something had to be on her mind. The children didn't have school, so we lingered over breakfast as we listened to the news on the radio. Then Sita said to me, "I've been thinking. Can we buy a single family house in Dubai? In Al Barsha."

I shouldn't have been surprised. I had never told Sita how much I disliked Dubai, how surreal a place it was to me, a land out of science fiction. I experienced culture shock coming from Switzerland every time I visited, but even more going between Arusha and Dubai. The contrast affected me emotionally in so many ways. Dubai wasn't a town, or community, it was a bunch of buildings. There was never anyone on the street. Even on the beach, people avoided each other. You'd never meet anyone by chance.

Sita was staring at me, waiting for an answer. I had to think, and replied, "There are so many things I have to consider, including finding another job. Truthfully, I don't want to raise our children in Dubai. I want them to be in a more socially and racially integrated community. That's why my brothers stay in Malaysia."

I saw the expression on Sita's face change from optimistic to disappointment. "You weren't thinking of living in Arusha, were you?"

It was often on my mind, but I responded, "No. I couldn't make a living there and... ."

"You can get a job teaching in Dubai."

"I don't want my career to be like Dr. Schultz's, six months there, six months in Europe. I was thinking of applying for jobs in England, but the taxes there are so high. I was also thinking of the Eastern United States. The weather is good, the cost of living is low, and they have an international airport in Atlanta. You haven't been praying we'd move to Dubai, have you?" I was being sarcastic but I could not take her blind Christianity seriously. I didn't mention Chicago.

She looked away from me, got up, and replied, "Dayalji, I can never explain to you what faith is. I don't want to live in the United States, and I don't want to stay in Switzerland unless you reverse your vasectomy."

I sighed, "That's not going to happen, either."

"Why not?"

"We discussed this after Mena was born, or, rather, I told you I was getting it done because I didn't want to use rubbers anymore. I asked you about other methods of birth control and you didn't want to discuss it."

"Why?" she asked, totally surprised. She looked like I had told her someone had died.

"You're asking me why? Why? You wouldn't discuss any other forms of contraception, ever, and you knew it was important to me before our marriage. We have two children. If we want any more children, we can adopt. There are so many children who need families, if it's more children you want."

I was thinking of children in Arusha, and of setting up a fund to pay school fees for the children whose parents had died of AIDS, malaria, and accidents.

"Why didn't I have a say?"

"You *did* and said you didn't want to talk about it when I told you I planned to do it."

Sita was really angry. I was perplexed. *She didn't remember the conversation? Or, she did and believed she'd get me to change my mind?* I was not affected emotionally by her anger. I brought my toast to the table and sat down. I could hear the children in the other room talking to each other while they watched television. "Sitaji, that was over three years ago. How old is Mena? "

She looked dumbfounded. "We never discussed how many children we'd have."

"You're right, we never did. I never cared if I had children. I love the children we have, with all my heart. In Africa, where I saw so many children like myself die, it was a fact of daily life when I was a child. Just the last decade, if a child lived to be five, he'd made it past all the hurdles. But people are dying of AIDS and leaving children. The world is not running out of homeless children. When a child needs a home, what difference does it make if we share genetics?"

"I don't want someone else's children. You're controlling my fertility."

I smiled. "Actually, I'm controlling *my* fertility."

That was the end of the conversation. I was disappointed at her reaction to adoption. What kind of crazy Christian education did she get? They make such a big deal about loving everyone, and helping the poor. The ironies of living a Christian life: disliking others. I just didn't get it.

Sita pouted for a few days. Then, when she returned from work one evening, she announced, "I want to take the children to Dubai."

"Now? No, they're in school. You'll have to wait for the winter break. In fact, I want us all to go to Germany at the school break because the Germans decorate the holidays. I thought *you* would enjoy it."

"I don't want to spend Christmas in Germany. I want to be with my mother and friends. If you don't want to go with me, I'll go alone."

"Don't you have work? Isn't that your busiest time?"

She was silent for a few seconds, then responded, "I'm taking time off. I need to think."

"Fine with me." I was really tired of the conflicts. She left a few days later, before our anniversary. She ended up being gone over eight weeks.

Just after Christmas, I stopped into the jewelry store to see if I could get any information about how she was able to take so much time off. I had been in to fetch her after work many times, but never had a conversation with her manager.

When I walked in, I looked around. The place was very busy. I wondered if people were exchanging their gifts or using gift cards.

"Ah, Mr. Makkar! So nice to see you. Do you know when Sita will be returning?"

I was taken by surprise. "Oh, no, I'm not Makkar. She's Makkar. I'm Singh Do you happen to have her end of the year tax papers?"

"Certainly. You do know the store sends them automatically to the government. Just give me a moment."

A woman, a co-worker I presumed, approached me and asked, "Would you like something to drink? You're Sita's husband, aren't you?"

I nodded, and before I could formulate a sentence in French, the manager returned with an envelope.

"Please tell her when you speak with her that her customers miss her and can't wait for her to return."

I took the papers home and was shocked. In American dollars, she had been making over $50,000 a year for the past few years, mostly in commissions. She was making about $10,000 more than I was at the university! She could have paid for full-time servants. I remembered the argument we had over the summer when she wanted to buy the pantsuit, and I gave her the money… she had the money. She was playing me.

I called Michelle, and asked her, "Do you have any idea how much Sita was making at the jewelry store?"

She burst out laughing. "Dayal, sometimes you're obtuse. Sita can be manipulative, but you are in your own world. Didn't you ever discuss money?"

"I tried to so many times to show her where all the accounts were and what we had. I even wanted her thoughts. She wasn't interested."

"She built up a client base and you know, she models the jewelry and the matrons believe they'll look like her. She also sells to a lot of men. Watch collectors. You never asked, so she didn't say anything."

"Why would I ask? It was her money." I sighed. "Am I really that bad?"

"We don't know how you've stayed married as long as you have. Two ships passing in the night, with totally different ideas about where you were going. Sita to a palace in Dubai. You? Nobody was really sure if you planned to return to Africa to live."

Michelle was right. Now, having learned how well she was doing, I felt that nothing I could do would fix this. She argued with me like it was a hobby. She took no interest in my work or my music.

We didn't have a tour scheduled until summer, but my mates got together at least twice a week to practice and discuss song ideas. It was disrupted for December, but when school started again, we got back into the routine.

Peter, just making conversation, asked me how things were.

"Sita went to Dubai. She still hasn't returned," I said, as I sat down at the piano and started fooling around.

"Why this time? Did you cut the limit on her credit card?" Peter joked.

"No, she wants to buy a house in Dubai and for me to reverse my vasectomy."

He started laughing. "When did you do that?"

"I did it right after Mena was born. Now, she thinks she wants another child for me to take care of. Simran and Mena are finally at the stage where they're independent. No more nappies, no more tantrums, they can help with housework. In fact, Mena and Simran are really good about helping in the kitchen. I guess they're trying to improve my cooking. I suggested we could adopt a child in need if she wanted another child. That's not what she wants. She wants a baby from her genes. So… let's play some music."

"How are you feeling?" Peter asked, genuinely concerned.

I feigned a smile. "Well," I said, "there's a lot less tension in the house. Let's play. Have you got anything new?"

"I want us to see what we can do with Al Kooper's "I Can't Quit Her." I just love it, especially the base, and I think it would be good for the bassoon."

I loved the song, too. It was my favorite Kooper song

When Sita returned, at the beginning of February, she was still aloof. She returned to work and gave me the silent treatment. She turned away from me in bed

I was now in turmoil. I knew that this was not all about me, but I also knew no matter what, Sita would not be happy unless we moved to Dubai and had servants. This was giving me headaches. I decided to file for divorce.

It was going to be complicated. We were married in Dubai, and I was not a citizen of Dubai. I also wanted custody of the children. It wasn't that I didn't want her seeing the children. I just didn't trust her to make day-to-day decisions about their educations.

Sikhi don't divorce. Because I had never lived in a Sikh community, I wasn't privy to gossip, but had overheard my parents talking several times about this couple or that, how a husband almost killed his wife, or how a wife inexplicably disappeared. Sikhi are like Catholics that way: you might not live together if things go bad, but you didn't get divorced.

One morning about two weeks after Sita's return, I came home after bringing the children to school. She was still in bed because she didn't have to go into the store until noon. On days I didn't have class or office hours, I often did paperwork in the morning so as not to disturb her, but this time I started right in on the piano. When I heard her get up, I stopped and followed her into the kitchen.

"Would you like tea?"

She didn't respond. I heated water and poured her tea anyways. Then I sat down across from her and said, "Sita, we're at the end."

She looked up. I didn't call her *"Sitaji."*

"I'm filing for divorce. If you don't have a copy of our agreement, I do and I can make you a copy which you can take to a lawyer. I intend to find out if I can file here, or if I have to go to Dubai."

She started crying. "But I don't want a divorce!"

"Sita, you don't want to be married, either, at least not to me. There is no affection between us. I am tired of living like this."

"Well, if you would reverse your operation, we could have another child and then…"

"Then what? You'd be happy? No, you wouldn't be. Simran and Mena are amazing little people, and you spend very little time with them. Why you would want a third, I have no idea. I have tried to be a good lover, a good husband and a good father. I have never cheated on you. I want to find a woman who desires me. You can go back to Dubai."

She was sobbing. "Can't we just live apart and see how it goes?"

I laughed. "We've been living apart! You went to Dubai and chose not to be with us! I think you don't want a divorce because you've been taught it's a sin. Believe me, I know my parents will have a meltdown. That's unfortunate. We spend enough time apart that this should not affect the children. I will move or you can move out if you want. I won't pay for you to live elsewhere. I will give you title to this place, but you have to pay the monthly service fee. I know you've been doing very well selling jewelry. I'm not leaving you destitute, but you will have to take more responsibility for yourself. "

"How long have you been so unhappy that you wanted a divorce?"

"Oh, let's see. When you asked me how I could consider black Africans my people, I was shocked. I wondered if we should marry, but I just felt you didn't know any Africans. When you didn't invite Maria to our wedding, I wondered if I really knew you. When you enrolled Simran in the Catholic crèche, and tried to keep it from me. That hurt my heart so much. You could never find anything of interest when we toured. I went into the store and found out you've been making more money than I was, yet you have always asked for money, as though I was depriving you. You could have paid for servants."

"I didn't think you'd let me, and, you know we were raised differently… ."

"Yes, but we are both Sikhi. What Sikhi believe about God and afterlife are fundamental to who we are. I so tried to make you happy. You never told me what you wanted, except servants. It seemed to me all you wanted to do was buy things. I always felt so bad that your parents forced you into marriage. We've both been terrible at communication, but I thought I was clear with you from the start."

With that, I had nothing left to say. I went to my office at school and emailed Levine to see if any of his colleagues could suggest a lawyer to initiate the divorce.

I hadn't been introspective about marriage to Sita. I was in denial myself. She never got over not living a pampered life. Once she had visited Africa, she appeared to think she was of a higher social status: Very unSikh-like. For so many years I didn't think this was important, but it was.

Sita's father hired a lawyer on her behalf, and of course, he wanted her to have half of our accumulated wealth. My notation software patent for *MagicScore* was still pending, and that and my auto tune microphone were partly owned by the university, so I didn't have to include that. Also, our royalties meant nothing until they accumulated. We were paid quarterly.

Her lawyer wanted her to have custody of the children so she could get child support. On this, I would not compromise. My only compromise was that, if she stayed in Switzerland, she could see them whenever she wanted, including overnight.
I wanted them to be educated in the west, not Dubai. If she didn't want to live in Switzerland, she could have the children on school holidays only. So, until the divorce was finalized took almost two years.

I moved in with Adam and Michelle. The children seemed to take my moving out in stride because I saw them every afternoon.

They both complained that Sita didn't get up to fix them breakfast, and they had to do it themselves. I told them I would come back on the weekends to either fix breakfast or take them out until their mother decided what she wanted to do. Mena said to me, "But Babaji, you never yell at each other. Some of my friends, their parents yell at each other all the time!"

I had to suppress a laugh. "Do they? Well, that's how some people are. I don't like yelling. Yelling would not accomplish anything."

Then Simran asked, "So why do you have to live with Adam and Michelle?"

"It's hard for me to explain, but by being in the apartment, with you, it makes Ama sad, and I don't want her to be sad. I just want to live my life in a different way."

I thought that was the end of the discussion, but then Simran asked, "A different way? Are you gay?"

I was shocked. I couldn't help laughing. "No! I'm not. There's nothing wrong with being gay, though. Where did you come up with a question like that?" My kids were aged five and nine. Something like this would have never occurred to me at that age.

Simran and Mena looked at each other, then Mena said, "Our friends Moira and Clifford, their father left their mother, and he told them he wanted to live his life in a different way, and he got a boyfriend and now they're together."

I took a deep breath and pondered this. "Well, no, I don't have a boyfriend, and I don't have a girlfriend either. But after we're divorced I will have a girlfriend. It will take some time."

"Well," Simran reasoned, "if Ama doesn't want to sleep with you or fix us breakfast, why doesn't *she* move out?"

"You'll have to ask her."

I really wondered if I had been unkind to Sita. When we first got together, I interpreted her reticence to us just learning about each other. We just weren't a good fit. Obviously, religious beliefs and values were important to me. I felt sad and relieved at the same time. I concentrated my thoughts and energies on what I had to do to take care of my children.

I took the children down to Arusha for a couple of weeks, to see my parents. There was so much construction going on in Arusha, it was shocking to me. They were putting water pipes into the street in front of my parents' home. There was now a three story "shopping center" with multiple shops and an ice cream bar across the street, where they had knocked down some houses. In fact, my tailor had moved in and was now creating dresses and suits on spec. I asked him how it was going, and he told me he got a microloan that helped him get the buildout and mannequins, and it was working out.

I mentioned to Baba how much construction there was, and he said, "A man from Philips took me out for tea. He was from England, and he asked me about the history of Arusha. Oh! I almost forgot! Did I tell you we now have a satsang? Some of the Sikhs from Moshi and north of there join us."

A satsang is a group of Sikhs who get together even though they don't have a gurdwara building. "Is it? Where do you all meet?" I asked.

"Curtis lets us use his big room Sunday mornings if nobody has booked it. We take turns reading from the Adi Granth, sing, play board games, and cook lunch, a langar. There are only about 20 of us, but it's nice we can get together. We don't have to travel to Dar or Nairobi. A few sometimes come from those cities."

I wondered what it would cost to build a gurdwara in Arusha.

My brothers arrived a few days later, with their families, and planned to stay longer. My parents were happy with all the grandchildren there. Everyone asked about Sita, and I said she was in Dubai.

They noticed the water pipes and decided we should dig a trench so we could get my parents city water. My brothers and I started digging from the kitchen to the street, and laid pavers around the shower with a better spillway so it would be easier to get water to the garden and wouldn't be muddy so close to the house. We had been using gravel. I don't think it was an accident that a guy from the Local Authority came by and asked what we were doing.

"We're digging a trench so we can get city water to the house," Avi told him.

"Sir, you need to go to the Local Authority and get a permit if you want city water."

"Since when is this?" Sodhi asked very surprised.

"Last several years," the guy told us.

We three went to the Local Authority office the next day, and the city manager told us we might want to consider actually selling the plot because it was worth more than the house no matter what we did to it. "What do you think the plot is worth?" I asked.

"I'm not really sure, but, in pounds sterling… ." It was about $30,000.

"Where can my parents could go for that amount of money?" I asked.

"That's not an issue for us. They can only stay until 2033 anyways, because they don't actually own the plot, it's a 99 year lease."

Confusion ensued. My brothers and I were shocked. We had never thought about this. We thought he actually had a deed, but we were shown the contract in the files. I realized later that we were so discombobulated by this news that I didn't even read to the bottom to see if the plot was in my father's or Glazer's name!

"We have until 2033, right?" Avi asked.

"No, about a year. I know Philips has sent a man to talk to your father. They're very interested."

I made a mental note to find a solicitor.

I had addressed the issue of long tours with my bandmates and Levine but the issues of economics and sound quality remained and were getting worse. Levine knew this was on my mind, and he had a reporter for *Billboard* call me at my office at school. This was just before Skype came into use, so for me, it was a bit uncomfortable doing this over the phone.

She was surprised, maybe slightly flummoxed, because of course, she called the engineering department, and they forwarded the call, and I answered, "Dr. Singh."

"Oh, I'm sorry. I'm looking for the musician, D. Singh…"
I chuckled, "That's me. You've found the right one."
"You're a doctor?" she asked, incredulously.
"Of engineering, yes. Levine told you to call, correct?"
"You're teaching? How long have you been teaching?"
"Oh, gosh, since I got here. Over 10 years now. I started teaching when I got my scholarship. Teaching is how I give back to the community."
"You don't think entertaining is giving back?"
The question surprised me. I hadn't thought about it. "Not like preparing the next cohort of engineers."
"Which do you like more, engineering, or creating music?" she asked.
I had to stop and think. "I think, for me, music, like the visual arts, are emotions played out. Does that make sense? I'm not a psychologist. I came to music because of my fascination with physics. I was curious about how we got such beautiful sounds from musical instruments. That's what captivated me more than telling a story. But to be able to play with sound, you have to make it compelling to others or they won't pay you. Just like any other art form.
"The way we Sikhi view the evidence of God is much different from how Jews, Christians, and Muslims view God. We have a concept called *qudrat*, or creation, which God did and does. Although our scripture addresses God as "he," we see "him" as a force. Calculus is the evidence of God, as are flowers, animals, and music. How wondrous it is that humans evolved as a species to create art and music, which gives us so much pleasure. I am humbled by the thought."
She was silent for a moment. "Wow. That's deep. In America, we call that way of thinking 'spiritual.'"

"Is it? I suppose it is. We Sikhi don't tell ourselves stories, except for how Guru Nanak decided a new religion was needed when he saw his sister was not treated as an equal to him in Hinduism, and then how the other gurus came together to defend the freedom to worship God."

"Sorry, I'm getting a bit off track, but I think your fans would like to know more about you."

"Well, OK. I got interested in piano because I liked the sounds and it was a machine, and someone offered me one. I found a Peace Corps Volunteer to teach me to play... ."

"Peace Corps? Where was this?"

"In Tanzania. Arusha is my home. It's where the safaris start. Then, when I got to Europe, I started working in a recording studio, and the engineers taught me how to produce, and because I wanted to produce music, I kept learning, and I've invented a few things, but that's another conversation."

"Levine said you might not tour anymore."

"When we started touring over a decade ago, I hadn't thought about costs. Not until I got my first check. I realized that I had to take an interest so I could know what was worth doing. I was really shocked when a friend told me what she paid for a concert ticket. Should you have to spend a day's pay to hear two hours of entertainment? I am very appreciative of our fans who do this, but there is no doubt in my mind that ticket prices are going to get beyond the reach of the average fan. It may be more like a week's pay."

She was surprised that I knew what tickets cost.

"That's why Levine told you to call me. You should really interview other performers. I wonder if many care. I do, because it's a matter of integrity to me if those paying to hear us live aren't getting the best sound quality. I'm aware of all the costs related to touring, venue operations, insurance, and marketing. I'm grateful for the sponsorships, because sales of recorded music are going down due to the advent of the internet and sharing. One tragedy is that, in the large venues, due to sound distortion, you're not hearing us at our best, but the economics don't permit smaller venues. If the industry doesn't get a handle on this, there will be very few people who will be able to experience live performances. That's sad, really, because hearing music performed live, and seeing the musicians play is not as passive an experience as listening to recordings. I think live music is more inspirational."

"Oh, that's certainly true. Seeing the musicians is a wonderful experience."

"I believe it is, too, but it's gotten complicated. I've seen films of the Beatles and other rock groups from the 1960s, and they just played their instruments and sang. No stage set, really. Now, I think concert goers expect a show like KISS does, and that's expensive to put on. And, truthfully, it rather, um, I want to say *obfuscates* sound quality. We'll make a decision after this next tour. Touring is rough. I can't do much else on tour even if I bring a bunch of computers with me."

It was 2003, and I was tired. We'd do the western hemisphere only, then decide if we'd go to the Far East. We had an opening act with us that were purely rock, and decided we'd audition string and horn players and another keyboardist when we got to L.A., where we'd start.

For this tour, I brought the children, and arranged with Alison, the music teacher, to be with us as a governess. Levine got us a suite of rooms wherever we were, and arranged to either have a piano in the suite or to make sure she and Simran could get to the venue early to practice before our sound check.

I liked Alison. She was mature, handled stress well, and spoke French to the children, which was important to me. Simran asked why I didn't sleep with Alison, and why Peter slept with so many women. You think kids don't notice these things, but they do. I told him, "I conducted my social life differently than Peter, and it works for me."

After thinking about Simran's question, I decided that it was as good a time as any to discuss sex and what I believed, with the children. If only I had planned what I wanted to say.

We went down to breakfast one morning, around 7:00a.m. Adam and Michelle joined us. There were no other diners, which was a good thing. I had the same discussion with the children every morning. They had to have juice or fruit, and decide what they wanted. I always suggested eggs and they could split an order of bacon or sausage, but we could not waste food.

While we were waiting for our food, I dived in. I said to the children, "I want to explain a few things to you because I know you wonder about them. You guys know I was a child in Africa, right? Where Babu and Bibi still live." They nodded their heads.

"OK. So, when I was younger than you are now, I saw a lot of animals mating, having sex. Have you seen animals having sex?"

Michelle gasped and gave me a look.

Mena piped up, "So, Baba, when people have sex, do they turn around and not face each other like dogs do?"

Simran, Michelle, and Adam burst out laughing.

I knew Mena was serious and I stifled a laugh: "That's a very good question, Mena. No, they don't. But people can have sex in all sorts of positions. You'll understand when you get older. Also, I want to tell you, so you are prepared. What happens to girls, when they are physically old enough to have babies, they bleed for a few days once a month."

Mena's eyes suddenly got very large. She inhaled, screamed and started to cry. Simran looked horrified and asked, "Through the nose?"

Everything happened so quickly. Adam burst out laughing again. For a few seconds I didn't know what to do but comfort Mena, and also set Simran right. "Now, now, it won't hurt, it's just messy," I said, knowing I wasn't making this any better.

Michelle shot me a look that let me know I was an idiot. She got up to put an arm around Mena and said, "It won't hurt. Girls aren't as lucky as boys. It won't be so bad."

Turning to Simran, trying not to laugh, I responded, "No! Not through the nose."

"When will it happen? Do you know?" Mena asked, calming down but still traumatized. She was shaking.

"You'll start getting breasts, and hair in your armpits, and groin, when you're becoming a teenager. There's no exact age," I answered. "Your friends will start talking about it. It's at least six more years. But I want to talk to you about something that I think is more important. Nobody talked to me about any of this, but I think it's important for you to know. How I learned about sex." I hesitated. I really wasn't sure what I wanted to say.

"There was this young woman I knew. She was the daughter of Babu's business partner. I always liked her. She was very kind to me, and she and her sisters wanted me to teach them to speak Swahili, and juggle. She was older than I was. We had a lot of fun together when she and her sisters came to visit. They were from America. They brought us all sorts of things we could not get in Africa, like books, board games, and a record player and records. When I turned sixteen years old, and her family returned to visit us, I started liking her in a different way. I was a teenager, getting to be an adult, and I wanted to touch her. Now this is very important. You can't go around touching people without their permission, and you shouldn't allow people to touch you, either. Do you understand?"

They nodded their heads as they chewed. I noticed Adam and Michelle had stopped eating and were listening to me. Simran asked, "What do you mean, you wanted to touch her?"

"I wanted to hug her. I wanted to hold her hand. I wanted to kiss her."

"Why?" Simran asked. I certainly didn't remember that one day I was normal and the next sex crazed. I had to think for a few seconds.

"Hormones. When you start to become an adult, there are chemicals in your body called hormones that make you feel different. I liked her a lot, and my hormones made me want to touch her."

Simran looked worried and asked, "Will this happen to me?"

Both Michelle and Adam giggled. "Yes," I said. "When it happened to me, my beard started growing and my voice started changing, and I started growing bigger. It was a lot to deal with, but you'll survive."

I took a breath. I didn't know if he was getting what I was saying, but I kept on. "So, what happened was, she wanted to go to Kenya, the next country over, and her parents didn't want her to go alone. It's dangerous for women to be alone in much of the world. Some men don't respect women and hurt them. So, I offered to escort her, to keep her company, sort of to protect her from strange men."

Adam burst out laughing again. I shot him a sidelong glance.

"And, uh, I asked her to teach me about sex. She was divorced, so I knew she had had sex." I didn't know what to say next, but I had to plod on.

"Why did she want to go to Kenya?" Mena asked.

"The train trip from Nairobi to Mombasa is very beautiful, and the train went slowly enough that we saw a lot. There were a lot of wild animals back then."

"What does being divorced have to do with it?" Simran asked, tilting his head. "Did she teach you about sex?"

Adam and Michelle were giggling again.

"Married people have sex. She was wonderful, and I fell in love with her. But she had to go back to live in the United States, and I was just a teenager. I had to go to school."

"You mean she's in the United States? Here?" Simran asked, surprised.

"Well, I'm not sure she's in the United States now. This was a long time ago, way before I met your mother. I intend to find out. But that's not my point. This woman, she didn't want to hurt my feelings, and she knew I loved her. She knew because I kept telling her I loved her. She told me, 'Don't confuse love and sex. We are having a good time, but we can't be together. Our parents won't allow it. You must finish your studies. For your own mental health, you must have perspective.' Do you understand?"

Both Simran and Mena shook their heads "no." They were still eating.

Michelle pointed at me with her fork and said, "Dayal, this is a bit complicated for them, I think. How old are you, Mena?"

Mena looked at Michelle and seemed to be thinking. "I'm five and a half."

"I'm nine and a half," Simran offered.

"What I learned from this woman who taught me about sex was that when you have a partner who cares about you, whom you trust, it really is an act of love. It brings you closer. Do you understand?"

They both looked up at me and nodded.

"Not everybody feels that way. I don't want to have sex with people I barely know. Peter doesn't want to be emotionally close to anyone. So, he has many partners. There are some very terrible diseases you can get from sex when you are not careful and don't know your partner."

"Why did she say your parents wouldn't allow you to be together?" Simran asked.

I hesitated, because I remembered how it was. Just the memory brought back all the disappointment and reality of the situation. "There were several reasons. One was she was much older than I was—eight years—and when I was so young, the age difference was a big deal. Also, it was true. I had to go to school. She even said to me she would not be with me if I didn't finish my schooling. We were different religions, and Babu and Bibi wanted me to be with a Sikh woman."

"So, what did you and Ama have in common?"

"Oh, Simran, that's a great question. We were both Sikhi. Babu wanted me to marry a Sikh woman and give him and Bibi grandchildren. So, Babu met Ama's father, and her father wanted her to get married. They are also Sikh. But, as you probably know, Ama was educated in a Catholic school, and her beliefs changed from Sikh to Christian. Also, Babu Makkar is very wealthy. You know he has another wife besides Bibi Fatima, right?"

They nodded their heads, and Mena said, "Farid and Bala are our cousins."

"Yes, that's right. Actually, they're your uncles, but that's a small point. When I met Ama, I was so young. I wasn't sure I wanted to be married, but I wanted to share my life with one woman. Not just sex, but other interests. I did not want to be alone. I wanted a woman who believed what I believed, so we would not argue. I wanted us to build a life together. I was also still in school, and just starting to earn money from music. She didn't know what it was to be Sikh, and she believed a lot of Catholic nonsense."

At this, Adam guffawed. "I was raised Catholic. It *is* a lot of nonsense," he said, addressing the kids. "I am now lapsed, as they say."

"Ama has taken us to church a few times," Simran said.

I stopped eating. "She has? When?"

"When we went to Dubai and when you went to Germany," Simran revealed.

"And when you went skiing sometimes," Mena added.

I had suspected. "What did you learn in church?"

"That we're sinners and if we ask Jesus to forgive us, we can go to heaven," Mena answered.

"I don't think you're sinners. What are your sins and where is heaven?"

Mena looked at Simran, and he responded, "I don't know what sins are, but heaven is in the sky."

Adam chortled. I asked, "Is it? Have you looked up and seen heaven?"

They shook their heads.

"Sins are bad things you do that hurt other people. Just because people ask Jesus to forgive them, do you think their characters have changed? That people who do bad things are now good and honest just because they've asked Jesus to forgive them? Do you want to be in heaven with people who can't be trusted?"

They both stopped eating and looked at me. Simran looked down as though he was thinking, then asked, "Don't you believe in heaven?"

"No. We Sikhi believe once we die, that's the end of us. Heaven is a fairy tale place."

"Ama said it was beautiful," Mena responded.

"Someone she trusted told her that, but she's never been. You can't go there if you're alive. At least that's what Christians tell each other. So, how would she know? She's mistaken."

We ate in silence for a few minutes.

"Let me ask you this: Ama and the Christians believe that Jesus is both the son of God, and God. They all say they believe in one God, but they pray to Jesus, don't they?" I asked.

"Ama says God and Jesus are the same," Simran responded.

"Is it? How can you be your own father? What kind of sense does that make?"

They looked at each other.

Mena asked, "Don't you like Alison? She's nice. She could be your girlfriend. She told us she doesn't have a boyfriend."

Adam and Michelle giggled.

"Well, yes, she is nice, but first of all, I employ Alison to take care of you. I don't think it would be right of me to have an affair with her just for sex. When you get older, you'll understand. She's Christian, too. I'm hoping as you two get older, you'll understand the important differences of how we choose to live. I have no savior but God. I believe it's up to each of us to make ethical and moral choices, be generous, and give back to the world. This is why I teach and perform. I believe that our souls get reincarnated. That means our souls get recycled.

You make choices that you can live with here on Earth. I hope you will come to think the way I think. But to get back to my original reason for bringing this up, the woman who taught me about sex was honest with me. I know she cared about me. The feeling I got from just being with her, just cuddling, made me feel safe and good. I hope you both find partners who make you feel the way this woman made me feel. That's what I want for myself. Peter wants something different, but I don't know that he's thought too deeply about how he lives his life."

I thought the children understood what I had said, but as we were going back up to the room, in the elevator, Simran asked me, "Baba, this woman you loved—how did you convince her to let you touch her?"

Wow. I really had to think about how to answer this. Simran was only nine-years-old. *Was this too much information?* "I seduced her. Do you know what that means?"

They were both looking at me. Simran said, "Sort of. Not really. You enticed her?"

"Yes. That is what I did. I enticed her."

"How?"

*Oh my lord, what do I do? They were way too young.* I didn't want to lie. "I said some things to her to let her know how much I liked her," I said, stalling. "We have to discuss this later. I have to go for the sound check. Alison will take you out this morning." I let them into the suite, kissed them both, and left in a rush.

When I got to the venue, Adam started laughing as soon as I came in, and said, "Dayal, I think you made things more complicated than they had to be. Did it ever occur to you that Simran is curious because he wants someone to cuddle, and he thinks that's what Peter's doing with his girlfriends? And poor Mena!"

"No, and I'll tell you why. When I was just a year older than he is now, I was thinking of more than cuddling when I thought of Mara. Don't you remember how it was for you?"

"If I was thinking of more than cuddling, I was thinking of a girl jerking me off," Adam responded.

"As for Mena, in Africa, children see a lot more sex. They see their sisters go into seclusion and sit on mounds of sand when they get their periods. She'll be fine. You're never too young to know about your own body."

As I sat down at the piano, Michelle came up to me, shaking her head. "Dayal, don't you ever think before you speak? My parents never talked to me about sex, even when I got my first period."

I sighed and responded, "I wanted to tell them that they should not have intercourse unless their partners could make them feel good with their fingers and tongues, but decided to save it until it was relevant."

Michelle rolled her eyes and shook her head as she mumbled, "Smart." ✪

# CHAPTER 17

After rehearsal, I called Shayla. I thought I'd have to leave a message, but she answered the phone, greeting, "Bedlam central. Shayla speaking…"

"Habari gani, mpenzi wangu! (*How's it going, my dear).*"

"Habari yako! Where are you?"

"I'm touring again. I'm in Chicago. We're zigzagging around. I've tried calling Mara's phone number, and it goes to an answering machine. How can I get in touch with her?"

"She's in California, helping some guy train his dogs. Her roommate doesn't answer the phone because it's not for him."

"She lives with a guy?"

"A Japanese guy, a roommate. He barely speaks English."

"Can you get downtown for dinner?"

I had been in touch with Northwestern, so I called my contact in the engineering department. He told me that they really hadn't had an opening, but was sure, because of the music, and radio/TV/film departments, and also because I could speak kiSwahili, he would email me a draft contract in the next two weeks. I didn't expect it to be as easy as it was, but I'd have to teach calculus the first two years.

Jimmy Paxon and I had stayed in touch, first via postcards, then through email. This was before anyone had a Facebook account. He'd send jokes or ask if I'd heard a performer. He happened to be working on a benefit for AIDS charities, so he asked if we could perform. After we agreed on what ticket costs were and how much would go to the charities, I had Levine sign a formal agreement for us. There were several American performers and us, and it was a nice event in New York. Jimmy had me give a short speech because I had told him how AIDS had devastated my home community, losing school friends and their parents. He asked me to be on his TV show. We had to be on another show the next morning, so I told him it would have to be another time. We were going to California. He said he'd also be out there in a few weeks.

I played "How Can I Go On?" on the piano, as an instrumental. When complimented on my performance, I explained that the song was written by Mike Moran and Freddie Mercury just before Mercury died of AIDS, and what a musical genius our culture had lost. We then went on to talk about how AIDS had devastated the performance community. To close the show, after a discussion about the tour, we did "I Can't Quit Her," and I did the vocals.

Being involved in this made me think. Were we doing enough? I talked to the guys about this and asked them to allow me to put donation links to Amnesty International, Human Right Watch, and UNAIDS on our web page.

I got to have dinner with Shayla in Chicago. I sent Alison and the children on a dinner cruise on Lake Michigan. We went to the restaurant at the top of the Hancock Center and were able to watch the sunset over the area as we ate. It was great catching up with her, and she spent the evening with me. We always had a wonderful time, and she told me how to contact Mara.

I called Mara within hours of arriving in LA and getting everyone settled in. I was so nervous, I was actually shaking. The cal went through, and when she answered, I said, "Mpendwa, mimi ni Dayal. Tutaweza kukuona lini? *(Dearest, it's Dayal. When will we be able to see each other?)*

"Oh wow!" she responded. Then I heard her crying. "Mpendwa! Nini tatizo? *(Dearest! What's the problem?)* "I'm so happy to hear your voice! I've been waiting so long!"

"I'm just outside of Los Angeles in a suburb called Pasadena. I'm working a job. I'll be here at least another month." "Kweli kabisa? (*Truthfully?*) I'm in Los Angeles! I'll come to see you!"

"You're in LA? Really?"

Coincidence? We Sihki don't believe in coincidence. We believe everything is preordained.

"Kweli Kabisa! I have wanted to be with you for so long. You know I've been with Shayla. I've always asked about you."

"I know."

"Mpendwa, tunaweza kuwa na furaha. *(We can be happy.)* I can't wait to see you." She gave me her address and told me what landmarks there would be on the way.

I was so excited, I could barely contain myself. The next day I arranged to rent a car. I hadn't seen Mara in eighteen years. How could it be that she was within twenty miles of me? She was standing by the front door when I came up the drive. Her hair was in braids and she was wearing a T-shirt and jeans. She had hardly aged at all. She just looked mature, and beautiful.

She greeted me, "Sat shri akal waheguru jee ka khalsa…" As she did, she curtsied.

I returned the greeting. I was surprised that she remembered it. "I'm so excited!" I told her as I hugged her.

I was overwhelmed with emotion. I wanted her, but we were different people now, and I thought we should warm up to each other. The truth, I was shaking myself. I couldn't believe we were face to face.

She took my hand and brought me in. I could feel that she was trembling. Just to the right of the door, which opened onto a big marble-floored foyer, was a big room with photographs on the walls, and a white grand piano. I looked around the room and then went to the piano and played a few notes of *"Shauri yako."*

"Who plays?" I asked her.

"I have no idea. I think it's here for decoration. Like the MaKonde sculptures. They had a decorator. I see you've trimmed your beard." She was standing a few feet apart from me, looking at me as though she was trying to see if I was the same. I knew I wasn't.

"I'm sahajdhari. Do you understand? A believer, but not, you know... both my brothers have cut their hair."

She nodded. We walked to the back of the house, through a nice-sized kitchen, then around several rooms, and out to a patio by an in-ground pool. Dogs barked by a fence to the left.

"Greet the dogs. Let them smell your hands or they won't stop barking. The large ones are Beaucerons, and I've been helping their owner train them. The smaller ones are my dogs. They're Whippets."

"I think my kids will love your dogs. They've been begging for a dog. Sita didn't want a dog and I just don't have the time."

"Would you like something to drink?"

"Just water. I can't believe we're finally together." We sat down on heavy iron chairs by a glass table. I took her hand and reached over to kiss her again. She went inside and came out with a pitcher of water and two tumblers.

"Why did your marriage break up? I thought Sikhi married forever."

"Sita wanted us to move to Dubai and have another child. I should have told her years ago that I could never live in Dubai, and we argued about money constantly. She was doing really well selling jewelry, so when I found out how much she really made, it baffled me. Then there was the religious issue. I think she just liked to argue."

"How are your folks doing?"

"They're fine. Things are very different in Arusha now. AIDS is still a huge problem. With the changes in government, things have not gotten better. Or, I should say, things are better for elites, not regular folks."

"AIDS is just as bad in Malawi and Zimbabwe. Really devastating."

"My father is retired and mostly watches birds and hangs out with the wazee *(old men)* at the hotel. My mum is also a lady of leisure. We bought her a washing machine. They make money brokering carvings that my school chums make, and Maasai jewelry, and they also bake and sell to the hotels. My father even makes ice cream."

"Hassan couldn't possibly still be there."

"His son now, Moktar. He helps with cleaning and cooking, and driving my father around. He learned to fix kitchen appliances, so he does that, too. Ama insisted Hassan bring at least one wife if he wanted to stay on, and he had two, you know. They gang up on him, but they do take care of him. He's always been a hustler, but Moktar does most of the work."

Mara laughed at that. We sat silent for a few moments. "So, what is Arusha like now? A friend told me it got really built up for the tribunal."

I sighed. "Right. It has actually become a big city. There are a couple of microloan banks, FINCA, and KIVA, I think. The infrastructure is better, but there's construction all the time. My parents still use a generator. I got them a more energy-efficient one because city electricity is, well, you know. They get a lot more Chinese and Korean tourists in town, and Russians. It's a lot noisier at night, I think."

Mara nodded. She was looking at me intensely, and she reached over and kissed me again, and lingered. She was feeling my beard. I put my hand on hers.

A large black man came out of the house, saying, "Whose car is that in the driveway?" Mara turned to him, and I stood up to shake his hand.

"Billy, this is Dayal Singh, the guy we saw on TV last week."

"Huh. You look different," Billy said, eyeing me.

"He wasn't wearing the turban on TV because he was performing," Mara explained.

We shook hands.

"I'm off to Orlando. See you in about a week," he said to Mara, and left.

"Good luck!" Mara called after him.

"Why Orlando? Why did you wish him good luck?" I asked.

"His team is in the play-offs. He's a basketball player for the Warriors."

"Who are the Warriors?"

Mara raised her eyebrows. "They're a basketball team, very famous."

Then it struck me. "You saw me on TV?"

"Yes. We saw you on a morning show. The View. We heard you sing and saw you juggling. I usually don't watch TV in the morning, but we had an incident with a dog and partly to distract myself and calm down, I turned on the TV. I heard your voice before I saw you, and I almost fainted, I was so overcome.

They, I mean Billy and his mother, started asking about you. They both remarked about your voice, how lovely it is."

"Do you really think so?"

"Oh, yes."

I let that flattery sink in for a moment. Then I asked her, "How is it you're out here?"

"I wrote an article for a dog magazine about why dogs don't get trained even after people pay to have their dogs trained. Someone saw the article and told Billy. His mother was nagging him. They had three dogs, and nobody had any control. The dogs ruled the house. I didn't like where I was working…. "

"This was a business where you were cutting dog hair, right?" Now that I lived in Europe, I understood that this was what a lot of people did. There were even a couple of pet shops in the malls in Dubai that offered this service.

"Right. The manager was abusive. So disrespectful. I was making money for his company and one day I got a registered letter, which I had to sign for, so I had to go to the post office, a big pain-in-the-neck. I worked on commission, and the letter said they were cutting my benefits because I wasn't working an average of 30 hours a week. I was working 28.2 hours…"

I had to laugh.

"Seriously. So I called HR and I asked, 'Didn't you tell me I raised your dog grooming net by over ten percent in less than a year? You're penalizing me for managing my time well!'"

"Not really!" I responded, still chuckling.

"Yes, and she said to me, 'I know, but that's our policy.' So, when this guy called me, I was really skeptical, but I agreed to an interview because he said he'd pay me a thousand dollars a week, for six months, and I could bring my dogs. So quit the job."

"You follow basketball?" I asked her.

"Not really, but I pay attention to the news. I knew he could afford to pay me. But the other thing was he told me he wanted to breed dogs. Billy has just enough money to get himself into real trouble, and I felt that if I could influence him, he could really help the fancy."

"The fancy? What's that?"

Mara chuckled again and rolled he eyes. She explained that people who love dogs learn all they can about them and cooperate with others, and breed and show dogs, and they call themselves dog fanciers.

"When I go back to Chicago, I'll be able to pay off my mortgage and be picky about where I work."

I was paying more attention to her than to what she was saying. "Mpendwa, I have waited so long to be with you. Is there somewhere we can go?"

She took my hand, and I just felt a warm shock of connection. "Come with me," she murmured.

She guided me back through the house, upstairs to her room. We sat on the side of the bed, and I took her face in my hands and I kissed her, deeply. She returned the kiss and sighed, but I could still feel her trembling.

"Let me undress you," I whispered.

"Oh no! We can't. I don't have condoms!"

"We don't need them. I had myself fixed," I said.

"What?"

"I'll explain later."

I straddled her, pulled her T-shirt off, embraced her and unhooked her bra. Her breasts spilled out before me, and she giggled.

"Your expression! Such bliss!"

"Mpendwa, you have no idea," I said as I put a hand on each breast. "Ah!" I unwound my turban and she pulled my tunic over my head and then she put her hand on my chest and said, "Mmmm."

I was overjoyed and laughed and said, "Mmmm? Is this real life, or is this fantasy?"

She smiled. "You're a man now."

"Kweli kabisa."

"Ndiyo *(Indeed)*. I never thought I'd touch you again." She inhaled deeply, and I saw there were tears in her eyes.

"What is it? Tell me."

She untied my pants and took my erection in both her hands and started stroking me. She looked into my eyes and reached to kiss me again. I pulled her pants off and I just had to look at her for a few seconds. She was just as enchanting to me as the first time I saw her naked, on the train.

I was euphoric. "I feel like I've landed on another planet!" She was so wet and she guided me in. I barely moved and whispered, to myself, 'Zed, y...'"

She moaned and then said, "Dayal, still?"

"I'm so excited. In fact, the last time I had sex was with…."

We both said her name at the same time: "Shayla." She started laughing.

"Please don't laugh."

She was shaking with laughter. "The last person you had intercourse with was my sister?"

"Yes, and I used a condom with her because only God knows who she's been with. I have to stop. You're vibrating."

She was still vibrating with laughter, and I laughed with the pleasure.

"You are so hot! So hot! You're wonderful, Ndugu! Oh!"

I couldn't last. I wanted the feeling to go on forever, and I kissed her passionately. I could not hold back. I came and almost pushed us both off the bed. I said what I felt: "Mpendwa, I love you. Don't tell me I'm confused. I'm not."

I had my arms around her and rolled her to my side. We were lying there, breathing hard. I was feeling her breasts, and she said, "I need to tell you something."

"What is it, Mpendwa?"

"I've never had a connection to any man like I did with you."

"Is it?"

"Kweli Kabisa. I swear, and when you vocalize, and you do when you're ready to come, I feel frisson. It's magic."

I knew what she was saying, because that's how I felt. She was the pleasure I sought. "I want to tell *you* something," I said to her. I took a deep breath, "I have wanted you all these years, for so long. Do you have any idea how many times I asked Shayla where you were?"

"Yes. Shayla told me. But you were married."

I suddenly felt a pang of sadness, and tried to explain. "I so wanted to be with a woman. I didn't want to be screwing around. I wanted a partner."

"I know. I understood. I told you when we were together in Mombasa. It was how it was. Things might have been different for me, but they weren't."

"I felt like you were avoiding me all these years. Why?"

"Because I didn't want to screw up your marriage. It was a matter of integrity. You know, I could have just gone with my heart, but I wouldn't have been able to live with myself. Nobody would have been happy."

The feeling I got when she said that was overwhelming. I didn't have to think about how we would work. "Mara, I want to marry you."

She gave a bitter laugh, turned away from me slightly and responded, "Don't toy with me, Mhindi." She started to get up, but I took her wrist.

"Sicheza. I am not. I want us to be together forever."

"Ndugu…"

"Please, Mpendwa, call me by my name."

"Dayal! We don't really know each other. We've grown up!"

"Yes, and now that I'm grown, my feeling haven't changed."

"You know, we can be lovers without being married, without making too many compromises."

"No. I want us to be committed to each other as partners."

"It's a bit more complicated. You know I live with a man, right?"

"Shayla told me he's a roommate, not a lover."

"Well, that's true. There's another complication."

"What's that?"

"I sleep with dogs."

I looked at her and started laughing.

"Why are you laughing?"

"My father wrote me a letter telling me why I couldn't marry you, and he said, 'she sleeps with dogs in her house!'"

Mara made an amused face.

"Actually, I also have a complication. I have my children with me."

"You see? Let's get to know each other as we really are. Where are your children?"

"With their governess, at the hotel. Or maybe they went out for the day."

We were now standing naked, facing each other.

"Governess, huh? I have to feed the dogs in about an hour. I can try to cook you something or we can go out, unless you have to get back."

"You can cook?" I asked, surprised.

"Not really, no. I've discovered that I was born without a cooking gene."

It took me a few seconds and I burst out laughing.

We went back downstairs, and I said, "I want to play you something on the piano." I played '*Exercise in Free Love,*' the Freddie Mercury song.

"That's beautiful," she said.

"Yes. Freddie Mercury wrote it. Interesting story. He liked all sorts of music. He went to hear Pavarotti sing, and he was singing with a soprano, Montserrat Caballé. Freddie was enchanted. He felt she had the most beautiful voice he had ever heard. He was working on other music, but quit. He became obsessed with her, and asked his agent to arrange a meeting. He had mentioned her in several interviews he had given, and it got back to her brother, who told her it would be interesting to meet him. Did you ever see him?"

She shook her head, and respond, "I think I've only been to two rock concerts in my life."

"I'd never seen him, either. When they were popular, we were starting to tour, and I had school. No time, but anyway, at their very first meeting, he played this for her, and they got on so well they were together for six hours. She wanted to perform it at her very next engagement and asked if they could collaborate. She asked him to write an album of songs for her. She was very specific that she wanted one song for her hometown, "*Barcelona*." They used it for the Olympics in 1992. It was sensationally popular in Europe, and my university asked my bandmate, Adam, to arrange it for orchestra. Adam said it would be great if I could invent a program where we could play music and a computer could notate it. He was just joking, but I knew I could do it. It took me forever. I'll make some money off of it, but the university owns part of it. I'll be on TV again in a few weeks, and you'll get to see it."

"Is it?" Mara responded.

"Yes! I got a technical Grammy for it last year. I wanted you to attend the ceremony with me. I wrote you a letter."

"I never got it. So sorry." She looked like she was thinking, then said, "I wonder how many of our letters got lost in the mail."

We went out for dinner and really started talking.

"Did you ever love Sita?" she asked.

"In a way. I was in such denial when I met Sita. It never occurred to me that a thinking person could be influenced by people just because they were nice. I didn't really know until she put Simran in the Catholic crèche how she really felt. That made me so angry. I didn't want my children to think I accepted her way. In retrospect, of course, I shouldn't have married her, but I was attracted to her, and wanted to give her the benefit of the doubt and make my parents happy. I kept telling myself that we would work out issues, but she was really spoiled, and so jealous of her sisters having servants. A friend told me she thought Sita manipulated me during our entire time together. That's how she was. She was like that with her father. But also, she just didn't want to share ideas with me. Just before the divorce, I told her I was considering moving here, to the US, because I wanted the children raised in an integrated envi-onment. In neither Switzerland nor Dubai do they ever see lack people. Any dark people they see are usually refugees and

servants. When you don't live among different people, you automatically develop a superior attitude, and you know Christianity encourages that. If you're saved and believe in Jesus, it's like
you're enlightened, and the rest of us are stupid pagans. They
seem to believe the lighter your skin, the more 'enlightened'
you are. I couldn't have that. In fact, I wonder what happened
with Shayla. She seems to have embraced Christianity."

Mara shrugged. "I have no idea, really. The stuff—you
know—decorations, music, candy, and a big part is being forgiven for your sins, I'm sure. We don't talk about it."

"So, when was the last time you had sex?" I asked.

She chuckled, "Let me think…."

"But you have this male roommate, a Japanese guy?"

"We respect each other's boundaries. I'm not his cup of tea."

"I had a Japanese lover for a while, Yuki. She was great."

"What happened?"

"She moved back to Asia. Just before I met Sita."

"So, you've been celibate?"

"Except for Shayla, yes. You know, prostitution is legal in
Switzerland, and when I returned after the summer I seduced
you, my mates took me, and I tried it. I didn't like having sex
with strangers. And I have kids. I knew it would lead to problems. As soon as I got the divorce process going, my plan was
to find you. I didn't know how you'd feel about me, but it didn't
matter. I wanted to be with you."

"Ndugu, I was sure at some time in our lives, we'd get together. This is a lot to process."

We sat silent for a few moments.

"I almost forgot, I got a draft contract from Northwestern."

"Northwestern? You're joking. That's just three miles from
me. I'm up there all the time."

"Kweli kabisa? Why?"

"There's a program of African studies, and they have a lunchtime lecture once a week. It's always something interesting. When I'm in town, I go. They have movies and music, too."

"This is perfect!" I exclaimed.

"What about you being fixed?" she asked.

"Oh, well…When Sita was in labor with Mena, she was really having a hard time. I didn't know if she'd make it. I vaguely thought that if we wanted more children, if I made enough money, we could adopt. I decided I'd have a vasectomy. She really didn't want to think about birth control. I took care of it. I wondered if she was of the mind to just have as many children as God gave you, as so many people do. The discussion was part of what really led to the divorce. It sounds funny now, but she wanted to have another child and wanted me to reverse it. She didn't want to adopt someone else's children. "

"That's how they are. I don't get it, either."

I had to ask her: "How is it you never had kids?"

Mara smiled. "First of all, being eldest of three and having babysat, I knew the work. We're taught that Prince Charming will come along and we'll live happily ever after, but he never came. Or, rather, my ex-husband came, and he wasn't so charming. I also know so many women who've had a child so they had someone to love them, and they live in poverty. I never thought it was fair to have a child knowing we'd be poor, or to take care of me when I got old. Also," she hesitated, "My father would have been horrified. His mantra was always. *"Don't make more work for your mother!"*

"Your father said that?"

"All the time. I was seeing this guy I was so attracted to him, but the sex was nothing worth putting myself out for. It was hard to resolve in my mind. When Jiro came to live with me, he was so reliable, it struck me that the guy I was seeing didn't respect me. I decided it was easier to do without sex. So, anyways, what happened with Sita?"

"I told her I was tired of diapers and our children were becoming independent, and if she wanted another baby, we could adopt. She didn't want to adopt. She wanted her own genes. Yet I'd end up taking care of the baby when she wasn't breastfeeding. Surrogacy is becoming a thing in Europe, where they pay women to have your babies. Christians. They don't want someone else's children, and certainly not dark ones. I wasn't going to do that. She was furious and took off for Dubai, and I decided I'd had enough."

Mara was quiet for a moment, then asked "Tell me," she said, "do you like performing? Is it what you imagined?"

"Believe me, my life is not what I thought it would be. I do love performing. When I first started playing in our school orchestra and at our local club, it really helped me meet more people and make friends. I love that it's something my mates and I can do without just hanging around a bar. I'm not much of a drinker. I love the connection we get with our audience. It's an ego rush to have fans, and know they enjoy my music. It's gotten to be too complicated and expensive. I did not set out to perform. I set out to get my education."

We talked more about music. She told me where she worked was always noisy, but she sometimes went out to hear jazz at area clubs, and particularly liked Woody Herman's Thundering Herd and Gary Burton.

"Gary Burton on the vibes! That's a religious experience. Hearing music in a small room, you feel it," she reminisced, smiling.

I knew exactly what she was talking about. I guess I got a thoughtful expression and she laughed, "Ndugu, have you ever actually been in a rock concert audience? Not backstage, but in the hall? The sound is so distorted!"

"I know! I actually invented something to address this. What I never got used to is touring. Sita didn't like it, either. She liked to shop, though."

Mara laughed and said, "I'm not a shopper. Except for underwear, most of my clothes come from resale stores. Working with dogs, everything gets ruined. I'm more into experiences than stuff. Jewelry is a bit of a liability."

"You don't want jewelry?"

"No. I'm pretty casual. You have to insure it. It's too easy to lose."

"Huh. I thought all women loved jewelry."

Mara chuckled and responded, "I do! I love looking at it. But really, when you wear earrings or necklaces, you don't see them."

We sat for a few moments, then she asked, "So why are you why here in L.A.?"

"I'm here because we're working with musicians who are joining us. It's relaxed now, but in a couple of weeks it's going to be crazy again. Then I go back to Switzerland. I start at Northwestern next January."

She nodded.

"I always felt you and I were on the same wavelength. It didn't matter that you were a Jew and not Sikh. I know you conducted your life very much like I conducted mine. I hope you'll get along with my children, but I know that since you have dogs, they will immediately do whatever you want." ✪

# CHAPTER 18

S he laughed, then asked, "Did you ever think about returning to Arusha to live?"

"Sita asked me, clearly fearing I'd put us down amongst black people. It's not the place I grew up in anymore, and it's so far from the rest of the world. I couldn't make a living there. But, I'm thinking of some projects I can work on, because it's home to me."

"Can you stay with me tonight?" Mara asked, taking my hand.

"I wish I could, but I don't want the kids to think I've abandoned them. What I'd like to do is bring the kids up here tomorrow after we're finished rehearsing."

When I brought the children the next day, I told them we were going to meet Mara, Shaylas's sister. The woman I told them about. "She's staying in a very big house, and there's going to be an extra surprise there. Mena, I am telling you now that I don't want you to scream when you see the surprise."

"What's the surprise?" she asked.

"It won't be a surprise if Baba tells you, Mena," Simran admonished her.

When we got there, Mara was waiting at the door. We all got out and I kissed her on the cheek, and she turned to kiss me on the lips quickly, but turned to the kids and said, as she reached and curtsied, "I'm Mara. Your father and I have known each other since he was a little boy. A mtoto."

Simran shook Mara's hand and said, "I'm Simran."

Mena curtsied and went to shake Mara's hand and said, "I'm Mena and Baba said there was a surprise."

"Is there? Well, let's go in and see what it is!"

As we walked in, I said to Mena, "Remember, no screaming…"

We walked to the back of the house, and the Whippets were on the patio. Of course, Mena screamed and kneeled down and started crying. The dogs were looking at her and wagging their tails, and the smaller one came up to her and licked her face.

"Mena, what did I tell you about screaming? You could scare the dogs!" I reprimanded her.

Mena continued to cry, but she was hugging the dog.

"These are your dogs?" Simran asked.

"Yes. The small ones. That one with Mena is Paisley, and the other one here, being a little cautious, is Finesse. Those big ones on the other side of the fence belong to the man I work for. They're Hugo and Adele."

"I've wanted a dog for a long time, but Baba said we didn't have time," Simran said.

"He told me. I train dogs. These dogs are like my family."

"Can they do tricks?" Simran asked.

"Some of the things I've taught them to do may seem like tricks. I'll show you later. Do you guys want to go in the pool?"

"I think they do. Can I go in, too?" I asked.

Mara laughed. "If you have a bathing suit."

"Will you go in with us?" Mena asked.

"Um, sure. I have to change, too," Mara told them.

We spent a fun afternoon in the pool. The kids threw a ball for the dogs, and Mara told the children how to talk to the dogs so they behaved properly. By late afternoon, we were hungry, and I asked them all, "Shall we go out to eat?"

"I've made egg salad if you want sandwiches," Mara said.

The children looked at me.

"Just egg salad?" I asked.

Mara chuckled. "No, of course not. I can make a green salad, and we have chips. Snack food, and Twinkies for dessert."

Mena asked, "What's a Twinkie?"

"It's a little cake. Hasn't your father introduced you to American junk food?"

I smiled and shook my head. "Adam and Michelle took them to McDonald's."

"How did you like it?" Mara asked the kids.

"Um, it was ok," Simran responded.

"I didn't like it, but the pomme frites were good," Mena added.

"Yeah, it's not real food, but a lot of Americans like it. But I can't really cook."

So that's how we started getting to know each other. Mara asked the children what they liked to eat and what they didn't like, and I told them about all the American junk I ate when I was on my first tour. She asked the children a lot of questions, and I was sort of amazed at how much I was learning about my own kids.

When Billy returned home about a week later, he decided to have a party and had Mara invite me and my mates and crew. I asked her who would be there, and she said, "Expect a lot of very tall people."

There had to be at least a hundred at this party. It was a big affair, with valet parking, catered food, a DJ, and flowers.

Someone asked me how I knew Billy, and I told him that I didn't, that I knew Mara. I told them I had met her in Africa. It's always funny when I meet Black Americans and tell them I'm African. It requires a lot of explanation. The children tried to start every conversation in French, so everyone remarked to me how charming they were.

I took Mara to introduce her to my bandmates, Michelle, Alison, and crew. As she shook hands, she curtsied to everyone. I was surprised.

I asked her, "Do you always curtsy?"

She responded, without irony, "A habit most people find charming. I noticed that in Africa, people do a lot in terms of respect for fellow humans that we don't do in the USA. People are a lot more formal there," she added.

"I know. I'm not informal with people I don't know." We both felt the same way, and it was a bonding moment.

A few people recognized us and asked for photos together. Then, Billy's mum asked me to play the piano, so a bunch of people trooped through the house to the front. I had to think of what to play, and chose "Shauri Yako," and explained that it was a Swahili song about a man who isn't rich enough for his lover. The children knew the words, so they sang, and everyone thought they were wonderful. We also did "Poetry Man," and I had Peter sing it to Billy's mum. He sang it with such expression. It was a great tune to leave on.

We were going to start this tour about the time Mara's contract with Billy ended. I wanted her to go with me on tour. She wanted to go back to her home with the dogs. "Dayal, I want to sleep in my own bed. If you want, I'll join you for a few days at a time here and there, and you'll be in Chicago for a few days, but what would I do on tour? I'm not a shopper. I don't stay up late.

You'll be busy for the most part. Pick two or three cities, I'll fly and meet you."

That made me feel anxious. I had not won her heart yet. I didn't want to argue with her. She was right, but I knew I'd miss her. I didn't feel like myself anymore. She was constantly on my mind.

Since Jimmy had asked, and we were both in L.A. I was on his TV show. He had told me that he was going to ask about Mara, but we hadn't really had time to rehearse. I told him how she was the granddaughter of the man who bought my father, and, well, it's on the internet, now.

I was getting too old for this rock star life. This time, about half of the American venues were state fairs or festivals. That's where the kids got to eat more American junk. A few times they got sick, but they recognized they were sick from the food.

I didn't set up "MagicScore" because many of the venues were outdoors and if it wasn't dark enough, it was just a waste of effort. I kept up my routine as best as I could, but I so looked forward to having Mara with me. After the end of tour in Los Angeles, we all flew back to Chicago.

Mara's house was about an hour from the airport. It was quiet when we arrived. "Where are the dogs?" the kids asked.

"I bet Jiro took them to work with him."

"He can do that?" I asked. Who ever heard of taking dogs to work? It was apparently an American thing.

"Sometimes. My dogs are very well behaved."

We walked through the house, which seemed very large. I passed one room, and noticed clothes, clutter, and open boxes were all over. "What happened here?" I asked.

"C'est une catastrophe!" Simran remarked.

Mara looked up and saw where we were, chuckled, and said,

"That's Jiro's room."

"Where does he sleep?"

"He's probably been sleeping in my room."

"Your room?"

"Ndugu, I wasn't here. He usually sleeps in the living room. You can see there's no room in there! The bed is covered by clothes, right?"

Both kids were staring into the room. Mena said, "Est-il un plouc ? Un adulte?"

"Y a-t-il quelque chose qui ne va pas avec lui?" Simran asked me.

"But why is it such a mess? Why do you allow this?" I asked.

"He thinks he's going to move any day, and it's not about me allowing. I pick my battles. He's a great guy. He just has a high tolerance for clutter."

"I couldn't have this."

Mara sighed, then added, "You know, Ndugu, in the general scheme of things, it's not important. It doesn't stink. He doesn't have food in there. I used to be like you, very rigid in my thinking, trying to control what I couldn't. You have to accept the good with the bad. I'm sure you have some annoying habits I don't know about yet."

"Me?" I responded. The children were looking at me.

She laughed and shook her head. "You don't think we both have irritating habits? Kids, what does Baba do that's irritating?"

"Rien. Baba est parfait. Très organisé." Mena said authoritatively.

"What did she say?" Mara asked.

"That I'm perfect." I proceeded into the living room. I noticed all the carpets were askew. "Why are the carpets like this?"

"The dogs run in from the back door and slide."

There seemed to be a lot of furniture. The walls were painted dark blue, and the curtains were blue. I walked into another room, and there were a bunch of what looked like framed diplomas on the walls, but when I looked closer, they were something else, and I called to Mara, "What are these?"

She came into the room and laughed and told me they were certificates for her dogs' performance titles. She said they demonstrated that she had off leash control of her dogs and helped her get dog training work.

"Do you still want to show dogs?" I asked.

She shook her head and sighed. She said she got the Whippets she had for free after their show careers were over, and that breeders gave away good dogs all the time to make room in their homes for younger dogs. "If I had that kind of money, I'd try to make the schools in Africa better, or support groups that address human rights."

When she said that, I knew I had made a good choice to be with her.

She said to the kids, "I want to show you my library."

"You have a library?" Simran asked.

Mara smiled as she opened a door to another room. "Not really a library. Bookshelves. Lots of dog books, books about Africa, reference books. I have a set of encyclopedias from the 1940s that belonged to my father."

I had followed the kids, and I noticed a whole shelf of books about sex. Mara saw the expression on my face, and said to Simran, "These are interesting books, but maybe your father will want you to wait until you're older to read them."

"No," I said. "If they're factual, the kids can look at them now. If they find something confusing, they can ask us."

Mara noticed that the children were looking carefully at the books. "Don't your parents have books at home?" Mara asked Simran.

"Most of my books are in my office at school," I said.

"Mostly about dinosaurs and geography. Places we've visited," Simran responded.

"How about your mother? Does she have books?"

I chuckled.

"Livres sur la mode et les bijoux. Pas beaucoup. Her job is selling beauty," Mena offered.

"I have a shelf of art books you guys might like," Mara said.

The children turned on the TV. I dozed off and was awoken by the stampede of dogs running in. I heard Mara talking to Jiro, so I got up. He was about my height and rail thin. I reached to shake his hand, saying, "Hello. I'm Dayal. I hope I don't inconvenience you too much. I've come to be with Mara, and she has talked about what a wonderful roommate you are."

Jiro smiled. "Thanks," he said, adding, "I hope you haven't come for her cooking, because she's terrible."

Mara laughed and retorted, "I haven't poisoned you yet!"

Jiro turned to leave the room, muttering, "There's still time!"

"Yes, there is! Shall I have a go at you tonight?" Mara shouted back.

"No, I brought pizza home. That's what's in the bags, and salad. We had a thing at work. So we live another day!" Then he saw the kids as they were giggling over the dogs.

"Who do we have here?" Jiro asked.

The children got up and introduced themselves, and Mena asked Jiro, "Parles-tu français?"

"Un peu. quelques. Est-ce que tu parles japonais?"

"Non. You have to teach us."

"Do you want me to set a place for you in the dining room?" Mara shouted.

"No, I have work to do," Jiro shouted back. He retreated to his room. I was happy their banter was much like brother and sister. He seemed very easy-going.

"His English is very good!" I said to Mara.

Jiro heard me and responded, "So's yours!"

I started laughing.

"You want to know how I learned?" he shouted. "She and her sisters talk so fast, I really had to pay attention. I had to ask about all the idioms."

The first morning I woke up in Mara's bed was magical. I just felt, immediately, such a glowing, physical sensation. Mara was facing away from me. I put my arm around her and woke her and kissed her, and we just kissed sensuously for a few minutes. Then, she put her face and her hand on my chest and said, "Mmmm."

I hugged her to me, and she said, "I love smelling you."

That's how I felt, too. I loved smelling her. It was reassuring. I felt so wanted.

"Is this OK?" she asked, as she reached down to caress my penis.

"Mpendwa, oh…" I whispered.

"You feel so good," she whispered back.

"Stop," I said. "I'll come too soon, and I'm not ready yet." She just lightly caressed my dick as I ate her, and I could feel how excited she was getting.

Then she said, "You really know me, More. It feels so good." When she came, she shouted, "Oh! You're incredible!" I turned around and entered her and she clung tightly to me. She continued to vocalize, "Mmmm," and it really turned me on, and I came fast. I just felt that I belonged to her.

As we lay there, I said to her, "I wish we could stay in bed all day."

"I'm surprised the children haven't woken us."

"I have a rule that when the bedroom door is closed, they dare not bother me."

"And that works?"

"Yes, but it started working better when I showed them how to fix their own breakfast."

After breakfast, we took the dogs for a long walk, to Lake Michigan, which was very close to Mara's house. Jiro left early in the morning and I never heard him. I realized what might have been enough room for two people was not enough for three, certainly not enough room for five. I wanted a grand piano and a place to set up the vibes. I could exist with the portable keyboard for a while, but I did not want my life to be tentative. I wanted to be settled.

After lunch, Mara said, "I have to go for a mammogram. Preventative medicine."

"You're ok?" I asked.

"It's free."

I followed her into the kitchen. "We have to talk to an estate agent. This place is obviously not large enough."

"You're talking like we're already married. You want to disrupt my life and move me to a larger home."

"No! Well, I mean… ."

"I understand, but I don't want you to have sticker shock."

"What's that mean?" I asked.

"It means that you see a place you like and are surprised at what it costs. Do you have any idea how much this house is worth?"

I shook my head.

"I bought this house five years ago for $119,000. It is now worth $350,000."

"Wow! Almost triple!"

"Yes: inflation, and being so close to the L and the lake. What's your budget?"

"Mara, you will never have to worry about money ever again. I've done very well. Thanks to you, I'm rich."

She raised her eyebrows and smirked.

I couldn't believe I said that and realized how arrogant I sounded. Frankly, I had never said those words out loud.

"So, you're a rich rock star, is it?" she asked, mocking me.

"Don't be cheeky," I responded. "Our music gets played a lot. In fact, when we were in the grocery store the other day, I heard one of our songs playing. My point is that you don't have to worry about what I can afford."

"Well, your money is yours. I won't tell you how to spend it."

"When you marry me, it will also be yours," I replied.

She started laughing. "Excuse me? You have our lives all planned out. Slow down, give me a chance to ruminate. Did it ever occur to you that I might be as annoying as Sita?"

I laughed in response, "I think we'll work everything out because you talk. By the way, where's your stereo?"

"I don't have one," she said, emptying the dishwasher.

I gasped. "Your lover's a musician. How can you not have a stereo?"

She stood and said, "In defense of myself, when I left here, had no lover. I left a boom box in Malawi, where the people I worked with thought this cheap thing from China was a real luxury. I left them a lot of cassette tapes, too. Aren't things on CDs now?"

"I'll buy us one," I said.

"Because you're a rich rock star," she mocked.

"Don't be cheeky."

"You didn't expect me to be cheeky? I love it when you use those cute British expressions. So sexy. Do you want to set me right in the bedroom?"

"I thought I just did. Where's your toaster?"

"Uh, another thing you can buy, rich rock star… or do you want me to call you 'doctor rich rock star'? I don't have one. I don't eat toast. In the morning, it's yogurt and granola, or oatmeal."

"I want you to make a list of what you want in a house. We let the dogs in from the yard and they skidded on the carpet and pushed it into the couch there and almost knocked that over. I need a place to put keyboards and the vibes. We'll find ourselves a good-size place, and if Jiro wants to join us, that will be fine. We can get new furniture, if you want. Your style is… interesting."

"Yes, 1980s thrift store accented with alley finds, except the carpets are from my grandparents. I'll give you the name of an estate agent who knows this area. I want at least two bath-rooms, and if possible, a laundry room on the main floor. It has to have a fenced yard, or at least a yard we can fence. Jiro will want a garage, and you'll appreciate that in the winter. I want to stay close to the lake and L if possible."

While Mara was out, I started sorting out my life. I hadn't checked email or my phone in three days, which was unlike me. I got emails from Oscar, Peter, and Adam asking where I

THE PLEASURE SEEKER ROBYN MICHAELS • CHAPTER 18

was. One was from Sodhi, asking if I had found a solicitor to help Baba. It turned out Philips really wanted the house.

When Mara returned, she seemed perplexed, and said, after kissing me, "Is there something you want to tell me?"

"Well, yes, actually," I said, but she started talking immediately.

"Dayal! You didn't see it?"

"Mpendwa, see what? I have no idea what you're talking about."

"The magazine: *People*. They had a photo of you with something you said."

"It's a magazine called *People*. This is what you're telling me?"

She sighed and rolled her eyes. I seemed to confuse her a lot, but this time she was definitely confusing me.

"Yes! Someone asked you how you felt when you saw that your invention worked, and you responded, *'Like the first time my wife and I made love. Exhilarated!'* There was a great photo of you laughing and juggling."

"I remember. I was actually referring to you. Do you have a copy?"

"No! I left it at the hospital."

"Maybe I can see it online."

Her phone rang and she fished it out of her purse. "Oh, hi, oy." She was listening, then said, "Well, how about here Saturday afternoon? My boyfriend…"

I yelled, "Fiance!" I heard laughter on the other end of the call.

"He has two kids. Yeah, about noon, if that's OK. I'll call Karla and Gala." Pause again, then she said, "No, I emailed them. You can all meet Dayal." Pause again. "Old friend from Africa. I'll marry him if he can keep me in the style to which

I would like to become accustomed." I could hear laughing again. I moved to embrace her as she ended the call.

"Don't say if, say when. We will marry. I want my parents to see I've been serious."

"So, are you going to draw up a prenup?" she asked me.

I laughed and replied, "No, I trust you. You wouldn't rip me off."

"Well, I wouldn't, unless you cheated on me and then I'd take you for every penny you have."

"I'm not going to cheat on you. You've been my fantasy woman since I've been a teenager. You really don't know me."

"That's what I keep telling you. We have to get to know each other. By the way, I plan to have some friends over Saturday. We usually play Scrabble, but we'll do Jumble. It's similar."

We managed to look at several very large houses close by the next afternoon. Mara kept reminding me about heating bills and property taxes. I was surprised that property taxes were so high. When I compared monthly land rent costs in Chicago and my canton, they were about the same. We just paid for things differently. It reminded me that I had to deal with what was happening to my parents' house.

"When I was in Blantyre, in Malawi, would you believe their land rents per square meter were higher than they are in Chicago?" she told me, making conversation in the car.

"In Africa? How can that be?"

"Yeah. inland Africa, too, because of a shortage of improved land with water infrastructure."

"You're joking."

"No, I'm not. I was shocked, myself."

"How did you learn this?"

"One thing the government there wanted me to work on was convincing people they'd have to pay property taxes, and I learned that people were paying for, essentially, sleeping space. In fact, the very poor pay more per square meter than the middle class. I told you about the housing estate with the burned brick houses and no water infrastructure. Stupid, just stupid."

This got me thinking about my parent's situation. "Mpendwa, we have to go see your father. I thought my parents' plot was freehold, but it's leasehold, and I need to know if he signed the lease over to my father, because the city wants his plot."

"What do you mean?"

"I mean they want to buy out Baba's lease, and if your father never signed it over, it will make things more complicated. For the past couple of years, the Local Authority has been hinting to Baba to sell the land. Arusha has really grown. When I was there in June, some guy saw us digging a trench for water pipes and told us we needed a permit, so we went to the planning office, and he doesn't own the land. It's on a 99 year lease. It's apparently up in 2033. He'll be dead by then, but they want to buy out the lease and make him move. My brothers and I were so frazzled, we didn't look to see if the contract was even transferred by your father to Baba. Also, it would be rude of me to not see him. If he finds out I was here, and didn't greet him, I think he'll feel disrespected. I have to head back next week. I'm going to charter a plane if you know anyone who wants a one way to Zurich. I own part of the company. I'm doing it so you can bring the dogs. I want you with me. It's going to be a mess for a few weeks. I have to teach and get the kids back in school, but I swear I will make it up to you."

"Have they discussed money?" Mara asked.

"Yes. They're talking about offering the equivalent of $30,000."

"What?" she yelled. "Oh, no! It's worth at least $100,000! Have you talked to a real estate lawyer?"

"You're joking," I replied, amazed.

Mara opened her eyes very wide and had an incredulous expression on her face. "This is serious," she said. "We have to ask my father. But don't you have someone in Arusha who can look at the contract and see if it was signed over? You have to be pro-active. They can take the land, even if the lease is in his name, because they do it for economic development. I can show you some buildings right down the street that were taken. I don't know if the original owners were compensated fairly. You need to get him represented by a solicitor." Then, she added, "I'll have to call my mother to see if it's OK to go up there," she said.

"You have to ask permission to visit?" I asked.

"We don't want to schlep out there to surprise them and not find them home. But I want to warn you, his sense of humor is unusual. He thinks he's funny."

The next day at noon, the doorbell rang. The dogs got up and went to the door, but they didn't bark, which I thought odd. I answered the door because Mara was working in the kitchen. First in was Mara's friend Gala. As we shook hands, she said, "You are a handsome dude."

"Thank you," I mumbled.

Almost immediately, Joy came in, saying, "I brought wine because I know you probably don't have any. So, you're the guy! You really are good looking. Mara didn't exaggerate."

I blushed.

They sat down at the table and took the Jumble cubes out. "Where's the hour glass?" Joy yelled.

My children materialized from the bedroom that had the TV. Joy looked up and asked, "Who are you?"

"These are my children, Simran and Mena," I said making introductions.

Mena immediately asked, "Parles-tu français?"

Joy lit up and immediately responded, "Oui! Parles-tu anglais?"

"We do, "Simran responded, "but we're learning the strange expressions."

"I've lost most of my French, but I can help with the American idioms. Who wants to be my partner?" Gala asked.

We started playing, and about twenty minutes in, Karla rang the bell. I stood up to shake her hand, and she said, straight out, "I saw you in *People*!"

"Mara said something. I haven't seen it."

"You're in *People?*" Joy asked. "You're famous?"

This was nice… to be with someone who didn't recognize me. "Infamous," I responded, and Gala and Karla started laughing.

I called, "Jiro, are you joining us?"

"No. they cheat. Watch them."

"We had another friend who made up words," Mara explained.

Then Joy asked, "Really, why were you in *People?*"

I sighed. "I invented something and a reporter wanted to know my reaction when it worked."

"Both Karla and Joy own buildings," Mara said. "You might want to talk to them about contractors."

"You want to buy a building?" Joy asked.

"Yes. This house isn't large enough for a piano… and all of us."

"Where are you living?" Joy enquired.

"We live in Switzerland, but we'll be moving here late this year."

"You're famous for being an inventor?" Joy asked.

"More for being a musician. I'll set up the electronic piano after we're finished playing. Who's keeping score?"

"I am," Simran said.

We played three games and I set up the portable keyboards and played the Mitchel Forman song he did with Gary Burton, "Reunion."

Mara arranged to go up to her parents the next day. She said her mother had invited us for dinner. Shayla would be there with her kids and Anya as well. Jiro came in, heard us and said, "Oh, this should be good! I'll come, too."

"Why do you say that?" I asked.

"Family drama!"

We, meaning Mara, Jiro, the kids and I, drove to Mara's parents which took over an hour.

I had decided to wear my silk shalwar khameez with my blue turban. Mara thought I was overdressed, and I thought she was underdressed wearing a plain t-shirt and jeans. I wanted the kids to dress up, but Mara said, "As long as they're clean, believe me, they'll be better dressed than Shayla's boys."

When we got to the house, Mara looked at me, smiled, shook her head, raised her eyebrows… and said nothing. We got out of the car, and she rang the doorbell. Anya answered the door. "Nice threads," she said to me. Then she greeted the kids and Jiro by dramatically saying, "Bonjour! Come in, you don't have to take your shoes off."

"Where's your mother? I have to greet her," I said, looking around.

Anya pointed to the kitchen. I walked in as she was taking something out of the oven. She took my hand in greeting. "We'll be eating in about half an hour."

"Where's your father?" I asked the girls, who were standing and chatting in the front hall. My kids looked bewildered.

"He's out on the patio," Anya said, and pointed to the sliding door at the other end of the room.

"OK, here goes," I said, walking toward the door. The children followed me.

"This should be interesting," I heard Jiro mutter as he followed behind us.

Ira Glazer was sitting on a lawn chair, smoking a cigar, looking out into the yard. I walked in front of him, held out my hand for him to shake, and said, "Habari gani!"

He looked shocked, and said, "Nzuri. Which one are you?" He motioned for me to sit down, so I grabbed another chair and sat opposite him, and told the children they could sit on the stoop if they wanted, or go back in.

"Dayal."

"Oh yes, the musician. Shayla's told me you've been singing. How's your family?"

"Everyone's fine. My brothers live in Kuala Lumpur with their families. I got my PhD last year."

"Mazel tov! So what brings you here? Are you singing?"

"No. I've come to be with Mara."

"Mara? She's quite a bit older than you. You mean Anya."

I took a deep breath. I could see the girls and Jiro watching from the doorway.

"No," I said, "Mara."

"Why would you want such an old woman?" he asked.

I gasped. "In the dark, you can't tell." I heard them laugh at that. I added, "I plan to marry her if I can convince her that I can keep her in the style to which she would like to become accustomed."

He laughed, and took a puff on his cigar, but he didn't say anything. It was awkward

So I said, "I have a question. Do you know, when you signed over the assets of the business to my father, if you also signed over the lease on the land?"

He looked up and seemed to be thinking. Then he took a puff on the cigar and said, "You know, I don't remember. It's a 99 year lease, right? It isn't freehold, is it?"

"Right. But Mara says they can take the land if it is underutilized, and we want to make sure he gets what he's entitled to. If your name is still on the deed…"

"I think it would be my father's name on the deed. You'll have to go to the Local Authority and check. I really don't remember."

I sighed and got up to go back into the house.

"I told you, and you didn't believe me," Mara said to me.

"Your father is… ." I replied, searching for a polite term.

"You know, he was joking. Don't take it personally," Anya said to me.

"I have to think about what to do," I remarked to nobody in particular.

"This is what I think," Mara offered. "We get a power of attorney form that he'll sign giving me power to represent him in Tanzania, and we'll have it notarized. You might want to call the Tanzanian Embassy to find out if that would be ok."

I looked at her and replied, "You're brilliant."

The dinner Mara's mother cooked was simple and fine: she made a salad, baked chicken breasts, and some sort of rice dish that had vegetables. She served cookies from a bakery for dessert. The kids ate it all.

Simran said, "Mrs. Glazer, this is the best food I've had in months."

Mrs. Glazer laughed and replied, "Really? I'm so happy you like it. I'm not known for my cooking."

"None of us are known for our cooking, "Shayla mumbled. We all laughed.

"Where have you been eating?" Mrs. Glazer asked.

"The hotels we stay in," Mena said.

"Do your parents cook?" Mrs. Glazer asked Mena.

I moaned. I didn't mean to, but Mara heard me and started giggling.

"My father can keep us from starving, but I don't think my mother knows how to turn on a stove," Simran answered.

"C'est vrai," Mena whispered.

Everyone started laughing.

I knew I had upended Mara's life, and our lives would now change drastically. That evening, when we returned to her house, I said to her, "This is what I have to do. I have to go back to Zurich and get the children back in school. I, *we*, have to go to Arusha. Not immediately. We have a few weeks. I need you to help me. We won't be there long, at least not this trip."

She sighed, and said, "I'm trusting that we can work this out."

Mara knew a lot more about how to handle this real estate issue than I did. She had me email Levine to see if his lawyer knew of any real estate solicitors working in East Africa. She also had me email the Curtis's and ask if they knew of a solici-tor, and if he could to take a photo of the deed and make sure he got the signatures, and to ask him about estate agents. She suggested we might want to see if there were any economic geographers at the university in Dar who might help if it got contentious. We needed to know the going price of land per meter, and she said experienced estate agents should have an idea. I knew there had to be some scientific way to determine the value, I just didn't know where to start. I also emailed my brothers and told them what we were doing, and suggested that they meet us in Arusha. I knew we would have figured out what to do, but she saved us a lot of time. Mara told us it wasn't just the land, but they had to find another plot for my parents and help us get an architect and construction firm to build a new house. That was another reason she thought we should ask for more than just the land value.

So, this is how it went: We got the charter at O'Hare a few days later, and only Jiro, Adam, Peter, and Michelle came with us. None of Mara's friend wanted to spend the money on a re-turn ticket. Mara and I got to join the *mile high* club, in style. When we got to Zurich, I hired a van to get us all back to the house. We fell into bed.

I got the children enrolled in school and Adam and Michelle agreed to stay with them and the dogs. Jiro headed back to the USA after taking a few train trips. Mara and I flew to Arusha.

While we were in Arusha, as long as we were at the Local Authority, I looked into getting a marriage license. The rules were that because Mara was white, and I was Asian, there was a waiting period. Also, we hadn't been married in Tanzania, and were both divorced, so we had to show divorce decrees (actual-ly, a certificate of "no impediment") and wait 21 days.

I said to Mara, "This is more complicated than I thought it would be."

Mara took a deep breath and replied, "You know some-thing? If you want to get married, I want the whole shebang."

"What's that mean?"

"I want the red sari and churri, the introduction of families, *you* reading at least a page from the Guru Granth Sahib, the exchange of garlands, and the mehndi."

She surprised me. "How do you know about all that?" I asked.

"With the internet, you can learn a lot about Sikh customs. You want your parents to understand that you take this seriously, us seriously. That's why it's important to me, too. We can get married when we go back to the US, and invite your parents and family. There's a gurdwara close to Chicago."

It took us about a year, but that's what we did. You might say that marrying the granddaughter of my father's owner is the best revenge, but that's not what this relationship is about. It never was. It was about having a partner I could trust. Someone who also felt strongly about human rights, and giving back.

Being with Mara is all I hoped for and more. I love her being the first face I see in the morning and the last I see when I go to sleep. The conversation never ends. ✪

# GLOSSARY

**Ama** . . . . . . . . . . . . . Mother (from Hindi)

**Baba** . . . . . . . . . . . . . Father (from Hindi)

**Chezi** . . . . . . . . . . . . Funny

**Choo** . . . . . . . . . . . . Outhouse

**Duka** . . . . . . . . . . . . Small Grocery Stand

**Habari Yako?** . . . . . How are you?

**Habibi** . . . . . . . . . . . Arabic for "My Love"

**Haraka Fanya** . . . . Hurry Up!

**Jiko** . . . . . . . . . . . . . . A Little Cook Stove, like a Barbeque

**Kachera** . . . . . . . . . . Sikh Underwear

**Khanga** . . . . . . . . . . This is a two meter piece of cotton cloth with a border, usually a medallion in the middle, and a Kiswahili phrase under the medallion. It was originally conceived as "forgiveness cloth."

**Kweli Kabisa** . . . . . Truthfully

**Lini** . . . . . . . . . . . . . . When

**Matatu** . . . . . . . . . . Usually a Truck or Minivan, Originally with Three Bench Seats, Used as a Bus / Taxi in East Africa

**Mhindi** . . . . . . . . . . Kiswahili for Asian

**Mishegas** . . . . . . . . Yiddish for Craziness

**Mtoto** . . . . . . . . . . . Child

**Mzungu** . . . . . . . . . White Person

**Ndugu** . . . . . . . . . . . Brother

**Ngono Ya
Kupendeza**. . . . . . . Have furtive sex

**Satsang** . . . . . . . . . . A Gathering of Sikhs Who Don't Have a Gurd-wara to Worship in

**Shalwarz
Khameez** . . . . . . . . Loose Tunic Outfit Worn by Both Men and Women in Africa and India

**Sikhi**. . . . . . . . . . . . . . How the Sikhs Identify Themselves

**Sicheza**. . . . . . . . . . I'm not joking.

**Swahili** . . . . . . . . . . . People in Africa Who Live along the Coast of the Indian Ocean

**Swami**. . . . . . . . . . . Hindu Religious Leader—Used as a Slur

**Tutaonana** . . . . . . . We will see each other.

**Unanifahamu** . . . . "Do you understand me?"

**Wapi**. . . . . . . . . . . . . Where

**Watoto** . . . . . . . . . . Children

**Wazungu**. . . . . . . . White People

**Yoni** . . . . . . . . . . . . . Hindu for Vulva

# AFTERWORD

Several people have asked me how I came up with this story, which is based on history, but not totally factual.

In the USA, most of us learn nothing about Africa except that "the slaves came from…" there. I was in high school (1970) killing time in my school library when I picked up an *American Heritage* magazine and read a story about the Yoruba of Nigeria. It was the first time I had ever read any real African history. My life changed then. I realized that we had been lied to. We had been taught that Africans were savages, with no culture, no language… no real history… and of course, that made it easy for us to accept slavery. We were even taught that white people/Europeans did the Africans a "good deed" by enslaving and civilizing them. Because of our biased educational system in the USA, a majority of white people still (as of 2023) believe that.

> In the USA, most of us learn
> nothing about Africa…

I wanted to go to college and learn about African history, and my parents would never permit that. I really didn't know what I wanted to do, but I didn't go to college until after my first trip to Africa, in 1985. By then, I was 30. I then took CLEP exams and majored in anthropology with a concentration (my own doing) in Africa area studies, including learning KiSwahili (which I've mostly lost).

I returned to Africa for the summer of 1987, to see if I wanted to join Peace Corps as well as to improve my KiSwahili. With a group sponsored by a nonprofit (Operation Crossroads Africa, Inc), I spent about five weeks at the African Inland Church Girls Primary Boarding School, in Kajiado, Kenya. In a nutshell, not only were we the first white people the town had ever seen do physical labor (we made bricks… long story…), but we were the first *Wazungu* (whites) who weren't missionaries. That was eye-opening.

At that time, I met Asians and Wazungu who had been born in Africa. During a side trip to Malindi, on the coast, we met several Sikh and Moslem men who were very kind and charming.

I didn't think about writing until I saw the movie, *Bohemian Rhapsody.* Although extremely fictionalized, I started learning about Freddie Mercury and Brian May.

Freddie, a Parsi by birth, was a classically-trained musician who had spent his early years in India because there was no way for him to get an education in Africa. Brian May was teaching and working towards a Ph.D. in astrophysics—which he ultimately attained. I learned that many rock musicians were classically trained musicians, and many performers also teach.

By chance, I stumbled across Gaiutra Bahadur's book, *Coolie Woman,* which is a biography/history of her relatives, brought from India to work in South America. This slave trade went on for several decades. Business owners wanted these people, who were indentured, because the "natives" would run off when they'd had enough disrespect. The imported Asians could not. This was also true in East Africa, for the same reason.

I made Dayal Sikh because I had experienced what it was to be a minority, being a Jew. Not so much in my enclave of the northern suburbs of Chicago, where we were a very large minority, but in rural parts of the USA. Of course, we are tolerated because we are mostly white, and "Jesus was a Jew," but as I write this, Christian nationalism has taken hold of our political system. I could imagine easily what it would be like to be a visible minority, not just how he'd physically stand out, but hold beliefs that, while most whites, particularly Christians, would consider sensible and fair, would be threatened by. Sikhi believe in reincarnation, not heaven or hell. They believe women are equal to men. They don't believe in caste structure or racism. Of course, you will find some more conservative and more tied to cultural norms, but this is the gist.

I knew there were Jews in East Africa, though, much like the Jews in India, most had migrated to either Israel or the USA. There is an enclave of South African Jews in the northern suburbs of Chicago.

We also have a dispersed Sikh/Punjabi community in the Chicago area, but they are somewhat self-segregating, because they are often confused with Moslems, and… well—if you're an American—you know the prejudices. ✸

# SONG LIST

*Following is a list of songs mentioned in the story. All URLs are data as accessed in 2023:*

**Sabre Dance (Khachaturian) performed by Victoria Fatu:**
 https://www.youtube.com/watch?v=CY9Jz7GONEk

**Gregor Nesterov:**
https://www.youtube.com/watch?v=MHFacHGqeOU and list=RD-MM&start_radio=1&rv=g3Fd0LHbXgA

**Let Me Into Your Heart Again (Queen/ Mercury and May):**
https://www.youtube.com/watch?v=eCbxTTW_B0A

**Rondo Alla Turca (Mozart) Ronald Brautigam:**
https://www.youtube.com/watch?v=HMjQygwPI1c

**Flight of the Bumblebee (Rimsky-Korsakov), performed by Rousseau**
https://www.youtube.com/watch?v=aeEmGvm7kDk

**Splashin' (Maceo Parker) (Will Boulware, Hammond Organ)**
https://www.youtube.com/watch?v=yJnwwSASWnA

**I'm A Loser (Lennon and McCartney:**
https://www.youtube.com/watch?v=f70Z3cvrQd0

**The Good Bye Look(Don Fagen) performed by Mel Torme featuring John Campbell on piano):**
https://www.youtube.com/watch?v=VIAZdoE1fCA

**Empty Pages (Winwood/Capaldi) performed by Traffic:**
https://www.youtube.com/watch?v=dRH0CGVK7ic

**Easy Evil (John Kay):**
https://www.youtube.com/watch?v=05jhZt1CaZ8&list=RDM-M&index=3

**She's a Vixen:** *Doesn't exist. I made it up.*

**Don't Hustle Me:** *Doesn't exist. I made it up.*

**Sugar and Spice (Cryan Shames, 1966)**
https://www.youtube.com/watch?v=Fe7RlzkVS3U

**I Wanna Meet You (Cryan Shames)**
https://www.youtube.com/watch?v=dY7fJv4nMy4

**Poetry Man /Phoebe Snow:**
https://www.youtube.com/watch?v=CPaNdTAC_ZE

**Vehicle: Ides of March/Jim Peterik:**
https://www.youtube.com/watch?v=TXvegzWNIps

**Journey to the Center of the Mind (Ted Nugent /
The Amboy Dukes):**
https://www.youtube.com/watch?v=mrUH9pGk90w

**Malaika (Adam Salik), sung by Miriam Makeba:**
https://www.youtube.com/watch?v=Q1UID0vEeqI

**Shauri Yako;Mbila bel:**
https://www.youtube.com/watch?v=1FxsdylRSGM
*accredited to:* Nguashi N'Timbo and L'Orchestre Festival du Zaire

**New Frontier (Donald Fagen):**
https://www.youtube.com/watch?v=FtovFI8etOg

**Ruby (Jerry Leiber and Mike Stoller) arranged and
performed by Don Fagen:**
https://www.youtube.com/watch?v=kbVdRGev6r8

**Glad (Steve Winwood):**
https://www.youtube.com/watch?v=4v8YQ6sU6I4

**I'm a Believer (Neil Diamond) performed by the Monkees:**
https://www.youtube.com/watch?v=wB9YIsKIEbA

**Take the Long Way Home ( Roger Hodgson /Supertramp):**
https://www.youtube.com/watch?v=qmWC5dGVvH4

**Goodbye Stranger (Roger Hodgson /Rick Davies) Supertramp:**
https://www.youtube.com/watch?v=wB9YIsKIEb

**Hot Fun in the Summer Time (Sylvester Stewart)
Sly and the Family Stone:**
https://www.youtube.com/watch?v=Bg0tFRea0wA

**A Little Less Conversation (Mac Davis /Billy Strange)
Elvis Presley:**
https://www.youtube.com/watch?v=9fVF-FAaZDM

**Is This Ok?** *Doesn't exist. I made it up.*

**Barcelona (Freddie Mercury and Mike Moran);
performed with Monserrat Caballe):**
https://www.youtube.com/watch?v=Y1fiOJDXA-E

**How Can I Go On (Freddie Mercury, Mike Moran;
performed with Monserrat Caballe):**
https://www.youtube.com/watch?v=ksNoe8W2jTc

**Exercise in Free Love; Freddie Mercury:**
https://www.youtube.com/watch?v=EJo6YoAMeF0

**Toy Soldiers (Liz Story):**
https://www.youtube.com/watch?v=WjP_0mTK_Z8

**Dreamin' (Mulgrew Miller):**
https://www.youtube.com/watch?v=fxo16SBkweI

**Can't Quit Her (Al Kooper and Irwin Levine):**
https://www.youtube.com/watch?v=i292TuHcnec

**Reunion (Composer, Mitchel Forman, with Gary Burton vibes,
Mitchel Forman keyboards, Pat Metheny guitar, Will Lee bass,
Peter Erskin drums):**
https://www.youtube.com/watch?v=4YRN3CwuU4U

# ACKNOWLEDGEMENTS

**Prince Charles Alexander**, MS Professor, Berklee College of Music. Music Production and Engineering/Commercial Record Production Berklee OnlineCo-Author of Vocal Production, for answering my questions about digital sound recording.

**Dr. Devinder Pal Singh** (especially for Sikh concepts).

**Kathy ver Eeke**, who runs "Get a Book Deal" on Facebook. Although I didn't find an agent, she helped me hone a query and through her feed, I met most of my beta readers.

**Fran Lebowitz**, for early development editing.

**Many beta readers (*who read all or part of the story*):**
Stephanie Albright, Dana Boyer, Victoria Dahill,
Janet Davidson, Harriet Garfinkle. Anne Pavlik Greer,
Craig Hastings, Mags Hearnden, Vicky Kelly, Sandy Lawrence,
Basha McCrumb. Mona Vorhees Mehas, Sundar Kanta Walker.

# ANNOTATED
# BIBLIOGRAPHY

You can find the Guru Granth Sahib at:
http://www.khalsadarbar.com/PDFs/SriGuruGranthSahibJiDar-panEnglish.pdf
This is Sikh scripture, a 1400 page poem. It's worth checking out.

Chinua Achebe, *Things Fall Apart.* This is available on multiple platforms.

John Backus, *The Acoustical Foundations of Music.* 1977 W.W. Norton and Company

Gaiutra Bahadur, *Coolie Woman*: *The Odyssey of the Indenture*, 2014 University of Chicago Press

Catherine Fitterman Radbill, *The Music Industry: An Entrepreneurial Approach,* 2013 Routledge press

Abdulrazak Gurnah, *Paradise.* (*Nobel Prize 2021*) Penguin/Random House. Also available as a pdf online.

Balli Kaur Jaswal, *Erotic Stories for Punjabi Women*. Morrow/ Harper Collins

Landeg White *Magomero, Portrait of an African Village.* University of York

Isabel Wilkerson, *Caste: The Origins of Our Discontents.* 2020 Penguin Random House

# MORE INFORMATION

Here are some resources for the interested reader:

**Coalition to Abolish Slavery and Trafficking:**
https://www.castla.org

**Human Rights Watch:** https://www.hrw.org/

**Population Services International:** https://www.psi.org/

**Charity Water:** https://www.charitywater.org/

**National Peace Corps Association:**
https://www.peacecorpsconnect.org

**Sikhnet:** https://www.sikhnet.com/

**The Sikh Coalition:** https://www.sikhcoalition.org/

# BOOK CLUB QUESTIONS

**1** Do you think Dayal is a moral person?

**2** Do you think Dayal was unfair to Sita?

**3** Do you consider yourself religious? If so, how? Do you feel more connected to God or your religion?

**4** Do you have any good friends who are of a different religious group or race?

**5** Have you ever traveled in Africa? If so, what impressions do you have of how people live?

**6** Do you think the ideas Dayal has addressed about human rights and U.S. foreign policy are valid?

**7** Have you ever had a strong friendship with someone of the opposite sex?

**8** Do you remember a time in school when a teacher taught a fact you knew wasn't true? If so, what did you do?

**9** Have you carefully read both the Hebrew Scriptures ("Old Testament") and New Testament?

**10** Do you think you were taught real history in school? Were you disturbed by what you learned?

# ABOUT
# THE AUTHOR

**R**obyn Michael's writing has been published in University of Chicago Press / *Memory House* magazine, *Pink Disco*, *Choeofplainin* (Anthology), the *Down in the Dirt* anthology, *Sighthound Review*, and *Groomer to Groomer*.

She learned to groom dogs as a teenager, winning awards in dog grooming contests, and she has titled dogs in obedience, rally, lure coursing and conformation. A couple of her dogs have been nationally ranked in their breeds. She has also helped others pick dogs to show and taught people to train their dogs. She is now retired.

Robyn didn't go to college until she was 30, taking CLEP exams to avoid prerequisites. She has an undergraduate degree in anthropology with concentrations in African and Indian studies, and a master's in urban planning.

She was a Peace Corps Volunteer in Malawi, A U.N. election supervisor in Bosnia, and has also volunteered in Kenya and India. ✪

For bookings and more on Robyn, go to:

rpcvmalawi@yahoo.com

disparateinterests.wordpress.com

https://www.facebook.com/Myehudi1

Milton Keynes UK
Ingram Content Group UK Ltd.
UKHW022242050124
435526UK00016B/700

9 798218 241698